LIZZIE THOMAS

A LOVE REMEMBERED

Can a teenage romance survive the turmoil
of the Swinging Sixties?

LIZZIE
THOMAS

A
LOVE
REMEMBERED

Can a teenage romance survive the turmoil
of the Swinging Sixties?

MEREO
Cirencester

Mereo Books

1A The Wool Market Dyer Street Cirencester Gloucestershire GL7 2PR
An imprint of Memoirs Publishing www.mereobooks.com

A Love Remembered: 978-1-86151-724-1

First published in Great Britain in 2017
by Mereo Books, an imprint of Memoirs Publishing

The address for Memoirs Publishing Group Limited can be found at www.memoirspublishing.com

Cover design and artwork - Ray Lipscombe

The Memoirs Publishing Group Ltd Reg. No. 7834348

The Memoirs Publishing Group supports both The Forest Stewardship Council® (FSC®) and the PEFC® leading international forest-certification organisations. Our books carrying both the FSC label and the PEFC® and are printed on FSC®-certified paper. FSC® is the only forest-certification scheme supported by the leading environmental organisations including Greenpeace. Our paper procurement policy can be found at www.memoirspublishing.com/environment

Typeset in 12/18pt Century Schoolbook
by Wiltshire Associates Publisher Services Ltd. Printed and bound in Great Britain by Printondemand-Worldwide, Peterborough PE2 6XD

CHAPTER 1

Life on an island

It was the summer of '67, and the sixties were in full swing. The whole of Britain was crackling with an air of excitement; new possibilities were opening for the youth of the country on an almost daily basis and a new lifestyle was rapidly emerging. It was a lifestyle that was totally different from anything that had gone before, and one that was in so many ways alien to an older generation that had endured a harder, more disciplined and principled upbringing in the years following the war. The rules for living had changed dramatically for modern teenagers and, in their minds, there was to be no going back to the old ways. Life was for living, with a sense of freedom and excitement, and it was definitely meant to be lived in the fast lane.

All over the mainland, from Glasgow to London, teenagers were waking almost daily to the sounds of the new bands, new music, ever-changing fashions and new dance crazes that were sweeping the country. Liverpool prided itself on being at the epicentre of the new pop culture, with new bands seemingly forming on every street, performing in local clubs before being spotted by hungry talent scouts and launching their songs on an excited and eager audience through radio and television. Channels were rapidly gearing their programming to the wishes and demands of their growing band of avid young listeners. Top of the Pops and Radio 1 ruled, OK? Schools across the land were filled with the buzz of teenagers competing daily to be the first to have heard the latest releases from the bands of the day, show off their new hairstyles or be the first to discover and announce the latest fashion trends. GCEs? Who needed them when you had The Beatles or The Stones to feast on?

Boutiques were springing up on almost every street corner. You wanted fashion? Head for London, where the bowler-hat brigade had been rapidly consumed and outnumbered by the jeans and mini skirt contingent. Carnaby Street was the envy of every city throughout the land and beyond, with trendsetters flocking from far and wide to savour its groovy new world dedicated to wild, wonderful and frequently outlandish fashion.

A mood of optimism engulfed the country, aided and abetted by a glorious combination of bright lights, heaving pubs and clubs in every town and city offering a heady combination of loud music and alcohol-fuelled dancing for young men and women with money in their pockets, energy to burn and a seemingly endless range of freely-available talent to die for.

Against such a backdrop it would be easy for the casual observer to think how dull life must have seemed for young people growing up in such exciting times yet seemingly stranded on a small island bang in the middle of the Irish Sea. For that island was a four-hour boat trip on a good day from Liverpool; their Mecca, the city where they knew it was all happening, so near and yet so far away.

But how wrong the casual observer would be, for in so many ways life on that rock was just as exciting as it would have been in mainland Britain at that time, if not more so. In fact, life on that relatively small island, far from being boring, offered many opportunities for teenagers to grow and develop their personalities and to satisfy their eagerness to take on all things new and modern in what, in reality, was a wonderfully free and easy-going environment.

Strange as it may seem, the Island lifestyle enjoyed by the teenagers of the day was in almost every respect freer and more relaxed than that on offer to their counterparts on the mainland, yet so different and just as new and exciting. Perhaps without conscious effort on their part, the relaxed attitude of the islanders themselves afforded the ideal environment for young people and young minds to flourish. It was a natural environment where life was more free and open, where the locals were easy-going and so much more accepting of the need for the youth of the day to find their feet in the adult world in which they were living.

Since Victorian times the island had been a vital and thriving holiday destination for thousands upon thousands of visitors. Eager holidaymakers were drawn to its shores by its well-deserved reputation for all the varied holiday pursuits it had on offer for those seeking the chance to soak up its wonderful, bustling atmosphere and benefit from a hard-earned and welcome release from the boredom of their everyday lives.

Indeed, throughout the sixties the Island maintained its reputation as a destination of choice for many thousands of fun seekers just bursting to spend their hard-earned savings on their annual two-week summer break from the tedium of their working lives. Many of the visitors were teenagers who were yet to experience the wonder and excitement of continental travel, charter flights and low-cost package holidays, which were still in their infancy. Spain and all it had to offer with its guaranteed sunshine, sand, sea, sangria and excitement was still a pipedream for the majority of working people on mainland Britain, but there was always that little island off the coast, ready and waiting to welcome visitors to its beautiful shores, relaxing way of life and entertainment aplenty.

In the long summer months, the island would teem with visitors, filling the pubs, clubs, dance halls, theatres, promenades, and walkways with bustling activity. Week by week the two splendid ballrooms in the island's capital would heave and rock to the sounds of groups such as The Stones, The Who, The Kinks, The Animals, The Bee Gees, Manfred Mann, Pink Floyd, all the great bands of the day, almost without exception, queuing up to take the opportunity of showcasing their latest wares in ballrooms which then provided big paydays in large venues thronged with young admirers only too eager to soak up the music generated by their heroes and to revel in the heady atmosphere. It was the precursor to music festivals and stadium concerts, and young locals and visitors alike seized greedily upon the opportunity to become part of the scene, to experience the excitement and sheer joy of feeling alive. It was a feeling of belonging in an almost tribal way with all those around you; of revelling in a loss of inhibitions and a freedom to express yourself, fuelled by alcohol and the adrenaline buzz created by the throbbing music and the excitement generated by the horde of enthusiastic fans, swaying in time as one with the pounding, rhythmical beat of that music.

Often described affectionately as 70,000 alcoholics clinging to a rock in the Irish Sea, the Isle of Man's inhabitants undoubtedly benefited from living in an environment and culture which was both tolerant and easy-going. The pace of life was slower and more relaxed than that on mainland Britain. 'Never do today what can be put off until tomorrow' was a creed and attitude adopted and accepted to a greater or lesser degree by the vast majority of the locals, and it served well to illustrate their approach to life in general. Life was there to be lived and enjoyed, and other pressing issues, which were often deemed to be an unnecessary interruption to this laid-back lifestyle, could quite readily be put on the back burner, or mentally filed under pending further attention when the need arose; after all, the problem would still be there tomorrow.

But in the summer months all this changed, as the Island burst into life with the huge influx of visitors, young and old, who turned it into a bustling community, and at the same time brought a welcome injection of cash into the local economy. This was the time when the locals emerged from their winter hibernation and entered fully into the annual burst of activity required to take advantage of the chance to swell their coffers. During these months, the normally sleepy Island awoke and the creed the people normally lived by swiftly reverted to one of 'never put off until tomorrow what you can do today'. In the overall scheme of things, it was only for five or six months of the year, wasn't it? To the locals benefiting from the tourist trade, this was clearly deemed to be bearable, even in Island terms, for the winter was long and the rewards of those glorious summers were considerable.

For the Island's younger generation, and teenagers in particular, the long summer months afforded an almost never-ending production line of talent to satiate their teenage lust, passion and sense of excitement. Teenage boys especially were renowned for having winter girlfriends who suddenly became jilted as the winter months drew to a close and the summer months loomed into view, signalling the opportunity to seek out new and exciting holiday relationships on a seemingly rolling two-week rota throughout the season. Fickle? Thoughtless? Most definitely. Understandable and justifiable? In male teenage terms and minds? No question whatsoever. What self-respecting, red-blooded teenage boy could possibly turn his nose up at the opportunity of seeking out new and exciting relationships and possible conquests when they were dangled in front of him with such regularity?

In truth, the same opportunities were on offer to the girls too, but they were frequently either less inclined to seek out such relationships or possibly sought more permanency in their lives. However, when the opportunity arose, who were they to turn their backs and walk away from new experiences and the undoubted thrill of a holiday romance?

Though the crowds diminished and life inevitably slowed down again for the locals during the winter months, there were still plenty of activities to occupy the minds and free time for local youths, with local bands taking over where the rock and pop stars left off. The venues may have been smaller, but they offered the same heady mix of booze, music and young thrill seekers, dedicated followers of fashion, eager to taste the excitement of those thrills and emotional highs. They wanted to experience romance, even love occasionally, and they were only too ready and willing to take advantage of all that was on offer to them.

The Island comprised a mix of large towns, smaller towns and villages, all of which were fairly close-knit communities where the local police had very few major issues to deal with. Local bobbies generally had a close relationship with the general public, with whom they were fairly familiar, often having grown up in those communities themselves. For minor misdemeanours, young children and teenagers would be sent on their way with a good ticking off; people found drunk driving, unless paralytic, would also be sent on their way with a warning to take it easy on their way home, or advised to get a taxi for the rest of their journey. On the odd occasion, they might even benefit from a lift home from their friendly local bobby, especially if they were well known to each other, or possibly grew up in the same neighbourhood.

In truth, the Island afforded a truly idyllic lifestyle for all of its proud and contented inhabitants, and young children and the youth of the day in particular, offering as it did a genuinely carefree and safe haven in which children could develop their instincts, personalities and independence to the full. From a very early age, children benefited from the safety and freedom to grow up in an environment which allowed them to develop in a relatively uninhibited manner. Untroubled by the need to be pampered and cosseted by their parents, they could roam freely, enjoy themselves and develop an innate sense of adventure through taking advantage of the many and varied opportunities for fun and pastimes on offer, from numerous safe beaches and beautiful seaside ports and harbours all around the Island's coast through to glorious country pursuits inland.

And the same freedoms existed for teenagers. Whilst licensing laws were fairly strict and appeared on the surface at least to be well policed, a good but unspoken understanding existed between the local bobbies and the landlords. In many cases those same bobbies would even be present during after-hours lock ins, just so they could keep a watchful eye on things whilst enjoying a pint or two of the local brew themselves. Nowadays, such dedication would no doubt be classed as community policing, so in that respect the Island's police force was years ahead of its time. It's true that the police carried out regular formal visits to the local pubs in their area, but invariably the landlords either knew where they were on the visiting list or were tipped a quiet nod beforehand. Strangely enough, on those nights the licensing laws were always seen to be strictly adhered to.

In such circumstances, landlords were happy to turn a blind eye to under-age drinking, happy in the knowledge that the police would probably take the same even-handed, if somewhat blinkered, approach during their visits, even if the odd teen, or group of teenagers, happened to appear in the wrong place at the wrong time. After all, what self-respecting, dedicated and hard-working copper could possibly justify all that unnecessary paperwork and unwarranted hassle for all concerned, especially when they were on night duty?

One thing the police adopted a firm stance on, however, was violence of any kind, though they did so in an extremely civilised manner, being careful to adopt a fair and even policy of standing outside pubs and waiting patiently, and with remarkable reserve, for any fights which had erupted to peter out before calmly taking control of the situation and considerately mopping up the bodies without adding to the violence themselves.

Police cars were few and far between at the time, as indeed were cars and other traffic generally. The Island roads had no need for traffic lights or dual carriageways, and there was not so much as a traffic roundabout in sight, as halt signs and the odd give-way sign at junctions seemed to do the job of controlling traffic quite nicely. The driving age for youngsters was officially sixteen, but many teenagers, with the total disregard of youth, simply ignored the laws of the land and took advantage of the relevant freedom of movement afforded to them to ride motorbikes or scooters and drive cars unlicensed and uninsured from a much younger age.

Against such a backdrop, and in such a free and easy-going environment, it's little wonder that the youth of that seemingly isolated backwater of a rock in the Irish Sea actually enjoyed a lifestyle that would have been the envy of their peers on the mainland –or at least it would have been if only they'd known how thrilling and expansive life could be away from the restrictions of large town and city living. And what an environment it truly was to grow up in for those privileged enough to live through those wonderfully exciting and carefree teenage years, and to fully embrace the joy of living, laughing and loving, in equally unrestrained measures.

For two teenagers in particular, Mitch and Melanie, that summer of 1967 would turn out to be the most eventful and wonderful summer of their young lives to date. Both were fun-loving individuals, rebellious by nature, full of life and enthusiasm, blessed with the excitement of youth and the newness of everything unfolding before them and ready to embrace all that was on offer to them in that carefree environment that the lifestyle of the times had engendered.

Although alike in so many ways, their lives and upbringing were almost complete opposites. Mitch was born and brought up on the lower, tougher side of town and came from humble beginnings, whereas Melanie had led a somewhat sheltered life, living in the more sophisticated upper end of town and attending public school.

In many ways both were products of their environment; Mitch ebullient and outgoing by nature, coarse at times even, whereas Melanie was refined, shy, sensitive, more reserved. To the outside observer theirs would not, at first sight maybe, appear to be a relationship made in heaven, but love has a mysterious habit of casting its magic spell in wondrous ways, often in the strangest and unlikeliest of circumstances.

CHAPTER 2

The Group of Four's big night out

One evening early in the summer season of 1967, still in term time, young Mitch and his sidekick, Tony, set off for the local pub they'd been frequenting for the last year or more. As was their normal routine on such nights, they were off to down a couple of swift pints of the local brew at the Woody before heading off to sink a few more bevvies and check out the talent on view at that night's dance at the Palace, at the time the biggest dance hall in Europe.

Age was no deterrent for teenagers wishing to gain access to the heady delights of the Palace, since the bar was upstairs and across the large foyer from the ballroom itself, which was, at face value, an alcohol-free zone. As it happened, both the management and the local constabulary were extremely lax in their own interpretation and application of the Island's licensing laws, so thankfully for teenagers of the day, age was no barrier to their gaining access to the bar. As can be imagined, they were only too happy to take advantage of this.

Having traded light-hearted banter with some of the locals over a couple of pints and a game of darts at the Woodbourne pub, Mitch and Tony set off on their quest to end the evening in style, fuelled with the confidence gained from the early flush of alcohol and armed with the sense of bravado that comes with it. Not lacking in either looks or charm, and their pockets filled with cash they'd earned from their weekend jobs, the two young chancers set off on their evening talent-spotting mission filled with expectancy.

Earlier that evening, in a more upmarket part of town, a group of four excited young girls had gathered in the Jackson household to make themselves ready for their big night out of the week. The group had congregated early in Melanie's bedroom, where Sammy, Shirley and Anna had joined her in the frenzied bustle of getting ready. Sammy and Melanie, the wild cards of the pack, shared a cigarette held out of the bedroom window and started the process of demolishing a half-bottle of vodka which one of Melanie's older male friends, Mark, had bought on their behalf.

Sammy, being the most daring, was the first to savour the delights of the neat vodka. "Here, Anna!" she shouted across the room. "Weren't you supposed to bring a bottle of lemonade or something to go with this?"

"Oops, sorry Sam, so I was," came the reply. "It just completely slipped my mind with all the other things I had to organise, shoes, makeup, clothes. I've brought three skirts and three tops. You know how it is, all the important stuff a girl needs if she wants to make a good impression. Frankly, lemonade was the last thing on my mind."

Anna posed, twirled, and pouted in front of the full-length mirror on which her full attention was focused. "Just hold your nose and swallow quickly, you'll be fine, I'm sure. Do you think I look better in this purple skirt, or should I go for the yellow one, maybe?"

The other three looked at each other, rolled their eyes, and almost without thinking chorused as one: "Oh no, that purple one looks gorgeous on you."

"Mmm, I thought so too, but I just wasn't sure," Anna murmured to nobody in particular, which was a good job, because the other three weren't listening anyway.

Back at the window, Sammy took a deep breath, raised the bottle to her unsuspecting lips and savoured her first taste of neat vodka. Perhaps 'savoured' would not have been her description of the experience as it turned out, since the fiery liquid seared her mouth and engulfed her unsuspecting throat like a lava burst, leaving her gasping for breath, coughing and spluttering uncontrollably and in need of a serious mascara revamp. Melanie and Shirley dissolved into fits of laughter at their friend's predicament, whilst Anna remained blissfully unaware of what was going on around her as she continued to admire herself in that beloved mirror.

Melanie was undeterred by Sammy's experience and, determined to show the others she was made of sterner stuff, she leaned elegantly across to where the bottle was resting so innocently, raised it gracefully in the air and, with a hearty "Cheers everyone!" tilted her head backwards and took a healthy swig from the bottle.

Less than fifteen seconds later she began to realise the error of her ways. As the full impact of the liquor struck her airways, she clung desperately to her senses and used what little breath seemed to be left in her body to blurt out "Us Jacksons always take our spirits neat" before turning back to the open window, sticking her head out and furiously gasping in lungfuls of the night air. She did manage to cling on to her dignity, just, and she had managed to uphold the family tradition, something her dad would have been proud of, if only he'd known.

Throughout this process Shirley, ever mindful of her sense of responsibility, had stood behind the two girls, dutifully wafting a bath towel to and fro at full tilt to ensure that the last vestiges of smoke were forced through the open window and out into the night air. Just as Sammy and Melanie were about to turn their heads back into the room, having regained their composure, they were met with Shirley's plaintiff voice.

"Can I stop waving this flipping towel now? My arms are killing me."

On hearing this, the two girls turned back towards her, saw the look on her face, and all three collapsed into a fit of the giggles, following which Anna conceded "Of course you can Shirley, it's your turn for the vodka now anyway."

Upon hearing those words a little shiver ran down Shirley's spine, for this was the moment she'd been secretly dreading. Drinking neat vodka was something which didn't appeal in the slightest to her sense of decorum, and yet at the same time she was conscious of not wanting to be the odd one out.

As she grasped the bottle gingerly in her hand, however, she hit on a great idea. She put on a good front, raised the bottle to her lips and, when she tilted her head back, swiftly forced her tongue into the neck of the bottle so as not to have to swallow any of the nasty stuff. She lowered the bottle to the accompaniment of appreciative nods from her friends. True, she did have a disgusting taste on her tongue, but she smiled happily, basking in the knowledge that she'd not only saved face but gained the respect of her chums, albeit with just a hint of deception. Mission accomplished, and the subsequent warm glow that spread over her had nothing whatsoever to do with the vodka.

Shirley beamed with pride as she passed the bottle to Anna, whose eyes never left the mirror as she downed an unseemly quantity of the contents without so much as batting an eyelid, for she was still fascinated by her own image beaming back at her. The others waited, and looked quizzically from one to the other, until Sammy's impatience finally got the better of her.

"Well, what was the vodka like then Anna?" she barked across the room.

Anna somewhat reluctantly removed her gaze from the mirror and casually replied over her shoulder "The vodka? Oh, it was OK I suppose. Do you really think I should wear this purple one?"

"Oh, shut up!" came the joint response.

Upon hearing their disapproving chorus, Anna turned briefly towards them, a slightly chastened look on her face, which quickly faded as she saw the laughter on their faces.

"Oh, you lot!" she said. "It's just that I quite like the yellow one, it goes so well with my other top."

She had to duck quickly to avoid the cushion that whistled past her ear and thudded softly against the wall behind her. This did the trick, as she couldn't help but join in the laughter ringing around the room. With a shrug, she finally gave in.

"OK, you win, the purple one it is," she conceded as she moved to join in with the others, but not before taking one quick look back, just to be sure.

With Anna's outfit finally having been resolved, the other girls were able to concentrate on their own preparations for the evening. Accompanied by the Beatles' latest album, Sergeant Pepper's Lonely Hearts Club Band, the activities and preparations commenced in earnest. They all busied themselves parading around the room in their latest gear before concentrating on the serious business of making sure the chosen makeup, mascara, lipstick, and nail varnish were all applied and colour co-ordinated, not only to their satisfaction but also to that of their friends, the ultimate arbiters of fashion and taste in their young minds.

Sammy was first up on the catwalk. She sashayed up and down the room in her brand-new bell-bottoms.

"Oh Sammy, they're simply gorgeous and you look so good in them," cried Melanie. "Don't you just love the way they float around as you walk? I wish I had a pair like them. Can I borrow them next week? I won't look as good as you in them but they're just simply fab. Where's your top, hurry up, which top are you going to wear with them?"

Sammy soaked up the compliments with obvious

delight, and a big smile spread over her face, which was by now glowing with the effects of the alcohol.

"Aha" she said. "That's the best bit. I've got a little turquoise top to go with them. But guess what? I've got turquoise eye shadow to go with my top. You just add water to it and literally paint it on!"

There were squeals of delight from the others. "Wow, I didn't even know you could get turquoise eye shadow. How simply fab is that!" said Anna, with just a hint of jealousy in her voice. "I really must be reading the wrong magazines" she added, a touch dejectedly.

Shirley had already arrived in her clothes for the night, a sleeveless, ribbed beige jumper with a black skirt, short, but not as short as Melanie's, as she was soon to discover. She looked comfortable with what she was wearing, but she did have a couple of surprises up her sleeve.

"Come on Shirley, what have you got in that bag?" the cry went out.

Shirley, blushing slightly, made her way to her bag in the corner and delved inside, hastily shouting over her shoulder as she did so, "Don't look, don't look you lot, not until I tell you I'm ready. Promise?"

"Yes, we promise" came the reply as they all shut their eyes and waited in expectation.

As Shirley donned the rest of her outfit there came good-hearted encouragement. "Come on Shirley, hurry up, the suspense is killing us. How long are you going to be, for heaven's sake? We're meant to be going out tonight you know, not tomorrow."

Shirley was not to be rushed, but when she was satisfied everything was hunky dory, she had a quick look in the mirror, shook her hair back into place, turned to the girls, took up her best model pose and put them out of their misery. "OK you lot, you can open your eyes now, I'm ready" she announced. She felt some trepidation, which proved to be totally unwarranted as it turned out, as she was met with a communal "Wow!" from all three of her pals. For Shirley, their quiet, reserved, and normally conservatively-dressed chum, had teamed her outfit with a vivid red necklace down to her waist, a matching red shoulder bag and bright red platform shoes. No, they weren't seeing things. Shirley was indeed wearing bright red platforms.

Silence reigned for a brief moment before mild pandemonium broke out. All three of her pals clamoured to heap compliments on her.

"Gosh, you look fabulous!"

"What a stunning outfit!"

"Where did you get those shoes? They're just so trendy!"

"Have you got a hot date lined up tonight? You'll slay him in that outfit."

Poor Shirley was overcome with joy as the questions piled in from her chums, and she blushed profusely. She quickly diverted their attention in the direction of Melanie. "Come on Melanie, you're up next, hurry up and show them how hot you look, and I just love what you've done to your hair."

Melanie, having experimented earlier with putting tiny plaits either side of her hair and adding a flower, had liked the look and decided to keep it that way. She was quietly confident that the brand-new orange mini-skirt she'd persuaded her mother to buy for her would have the desired effect on her friends. She'd fallen in love with it herself the minute she'd tried it on in the shop, and her taste in clothes had never been called into question by anyone in the group, not even by Anna, the self-appointed queen of fashion. This confidence wasn't derived from arrogance or any hint of self-esteem; she was simply comfortable in her own skin, and blessed with a natural instinct for sensing what looked good on her and what didn't.

She slipped across the room, opened her wardrobe and turned back to reveal a trendy new orange mini-skirt, to further giggles of delight from her fellow fashion devotees. "Wow and wow again!" yelped Sammy.

"How bright is that? Nobody's going to miss you in that, and it's just so you," chirruped Shirley, shaking her head. "Only you could get away with that Melanie, only you. Quick, put it on, let's see it on."

Even Anna was impressed. "It's gorgeous Melanie, really gorgeous. I just love it, and orange is so in now."

Anna did indeed love it, and her compliments were genuine, but even whilst she was saying it she was thinking to herself, "I wonder if I should wear that yellow skirt after all?"

Encouraged by the others, Melanie slipped off her jeans and wriggled deftly into the tight-fitting skirt to reveal it in all its glory, which once again brought squeals of delight from her friends.

"It looks fabulous Melanie, it just looks so good on you and it's so short as well, it's nearly up to your bum for heaven's sake!"

"And you've got such lovely legs, you can really carry it off," said Sammy as she ran across the room and gave her pal a big hug, then stepped back to admire the skirt again.

"Shirley's right" she said. "It is ever so short. It's simply stunning and the colour really suits you. Where did you get it, and when? Tell me, tell me, I need to know."

"Oh, my mother bought it for me. She was in a good mood, so after we'd finished playing tennis at the club the other day she took me down to that new boutique in town and she treated me. If I want a treat I always let her win, it never fails. I just hope she doesn't twig. We should all go there, they've got loads of fab new gear, but this one just caught my eye, and I simply couldn't resist it."

This information brought a gasp of astonishment from Sammy. "Your mother bought it for you? It's so short, I'm surprised she would approve of that, though she's much more relaxed about these things than mine is. I'm surprised she even let you look at it, let alone buy it for you."

At this a grin lit up Melanie's face. "Ah well" she said, "it isn't exactly the same skirt that she bought me."

A quizzical look crossed Sammy's face. "I don't understand. What do you mean it isn't the same skirt?"

"Well, it was quite a bit longer than this when she bought it, but I took the hem up last night by a good three inches. All I've got to do now is to sneak past her somehow on the way out without her noticing or I'll be grounded again. And I don't fancy having to climb out of that window in this mini-skirt!"

At this point all four of them descended into laughter again. When it eventually subsided, and the fun was over, Melanie quietly crossed to the wardrobe and slipped on the rest of her ensemble, which consisted of a simple black sleeveless top with cutaway shoulders, which not only complimented her new skirt but also served to show off her recently-acquired early summer tan, and some black patent leather sandals which she knew she would be taking off at the first opportunity. She hated dancing in shoes. Her whole outfit was quickly put together, and after putting her small collection of beads and bells over her head and taking a quick glance in the mirror, she rejoined the others, for the serious business of applying their makeup was about to commence.

Sammy and Melanie painted the turquoise shadow onto and under their eyelids, but it was too bold for Shirley, and Anna had already spent most of the afternoon getting her make-up right, so she wasn't going to change it now, however much she fancied a go with the new product.

"Do you think this eye shadow looks OK, or is it a bit much? I just can't make my mind up" Melanie asked Anna. "You've always had a natural flair for these things."

"I know, some of us have it, and some don't," Anna laughed. After a brief inspection she reassured her, "No, I think you've got it spot on. It's just the right shade and depth and it highlights those eyes of yours perfectly. I've always said your eyes are your best feature, haven't I? And they're simply sparkling tonight."

As a final touch, they all applied dark eyeliner and the palest of lipstick, which were the ultimate fashion statements of the day. Then they were ready.

All the while this was going on there was a constant stream of excited chatter about anything and everything that entered their minds, mainly boys, the pop scene, the latest fashion trends and all the latest gossip that Anna had picked up in passing.

"Did you see Top of The Pops this week?" Sammy asked.

"Oh yes," said Anna. "The Hollies are my favourite band, and isn't their latest single just fab? And that Allan Clarke is to die for, isn't he? What I wouldn't give to go out with him."

Sammy thought for a moment, then responded, "Oh, I don't know. I don't think they're anything special really. But The Who? Now that's my kind of band. Their music's just so alive and original. I just love them."

"Me too" said Melanie. "And that Roger Daltrey's got to be some kind of sex god."

Sammy and Melanie had different tastes when it came to the opposite sex so, forceful as ever, Sammy jumped in. "Daltrey? A sex god? Really Melanie, what's happened to your taste in men? Moony's much better looking, and he's so cute. Don't you just want to hug him?"

"Is that Keith Moon you're talking about, the drummer?" Shirley piped up.

"Yes, that's him, why?"

"Well he's like some kind of wild man apparently. I read somewhere he takes drugs and smashes up hotel rooms wherever he goes. I hardly think you could call that cute, or cuddly even come to think of it."

"Oh, they all take drugs and smash things up Shirley. It doesn't stop Moony from being cute though, and I'd cuddle him any time given half the chance. And you never know your luck, do you? They're playing at the Palace later on this summer. We've just got to get tickets for that one. I've heard they're fabulous live. And Moony had better look out if I chance upon him, that's all I can say. Who's playing tonight anyway girls?"

"Nobody special I don't think," said Anna. "But Sounds

Incorporated are the resident band this summer. They're supposed to be really good, and I hear they start with a fab version of Sergeant Pepper, so it should be a great night."

Suddenly, they heard Melanie's mother's unmistakable voice drifting up from below. "Come on you girls. Stop messing around up there and get yourselves down here. Your father's ready to give you a lift and you don't want to keep him waiting Melanie."

"Shit!" Melanie said. "Come on, sort yourselves out you lot. And splash some more perfume on before we go down. We don't want mother smelling smoke or booze on us or we'll never get out. And whatever you do, crowd around me and keep her occupied. I don't want her seeing this skirt."

They all made their way quietly down the stairs, but when they reached the bottom of the staircase, Melanie's mother Julia was looming there waiting to check on the girls before saying goodbye and wishing them a great evening. The girls did their very best to hide Melanie from the closest of inspections as she flew past her mother as swiftly as she deemed acceptable in an attempt to avoid too close a scrutiny.

Melanie initially thought she had succeeded in avoiding her mother's attention, but she failed to spot her mother's raised eyebrow as she passed her by. In fact, Julia had been well aware of Melanie's alterations, but she discreetly chose to say nothing on this occasion. As Melanie disappeared through the front door though she heard her mother's voice shouting instructions to her father James, who was the chauffeur for the evening and already on his way to his car. "Jim, she's wearing far too much eye makeup. Tell her to tone it down a bit."

Paying little heed to her mother's comments and dismissing her with a backward wave, Melanie continued blithely on her way and piled into the car alongside her dad, who simply turned towards her, smiled and said, "Just ignore your mother, you look gorgeous". A beaming smile lit up her young face. Julia knew just how pretty her daughter looked and she knew short skirts and lots of make-up were in fashion, but she felt she had to at least outwardly make signs of disapproval, so she merely smiled inwardly to herself as she watched them go.

As they drove down to the Palace, James sat back and closed his mind to all the excited small talk from the four girls. He was happy with his own thoughts and content to let the girls relax and be themselves in the knowledge that he wasn't keeping an eye on them or interfering. But he couldn't help thinking to himself how different and exciting life was for young people nowadays, and how dull and innocent his own formative years seemed now in comparison.

As James drove, his mind wandered to his own thoughts about his wonderful young daughter, who he loved and adored, and the special relationship they had with each other, one which he cherished and never wanted to lose. He thought about how much she'd changed over the last twelve months, and how proud he was to see her becoming more independent in her thinking and actions as she started her journey towards her adult life. Teenage years were difficult to come to terms with, that he knew, and he was happy for his daughter to enjoy some lifting of the parental restraints of childhood and enjoy the time ahead of her.

James had always been aware of how intelligent,

sensitive, and thoughtful his young daughter was, but now she had grown in confidence. She had her own views and opinions, and she wasn't afraid of expressing them, forthrightly and constructively. She was even developing an interest in politics, and he enjoyed sitting in the house of an evening discussing the events of the day with her if her mother had retired to bed early. He couldn't explain how, or why, there'd been such a change in her, but he welcomed, embraced and encouraged it, for he got so much pleasure from watching his only daughter blossom and grow into both her body and her mind.

Yes, his lovable daughter had become a bit rebellious, a bit of a tomboy, a daredevil even; but he knew that was only to be expected when children entered their teenage years. And he still remembered how he'd experienced those feelings himself, not all that many years ago, it seemed to him. But at heart she was still the same old Melanie when it came to her dad, and he loved the fact that they were so close.

He also knew that her mother was struggling to come to terms with the new Melanie. He was only too well aware how their relationship was changing; she was striving for freedom whilst her mother remained somewhat protective, which Melanie just saw as a constraint on her wilder instincts. James knew this to be difficult for each of them, as they were both strong-willed individuals, and he had to play the role of diplomat from time to time to ensure a happy household was maintained. A wry smile crossed his face as he thought what a good job it was that Julia didn't know the half of what her daughter got up to when she was let loose with her friends... or did she?

In his heart, James somehow knew that wherever life took her, Melanie would always need him, and he was determined that he would always be there for her, her rock, the one she knew she could always rely on if the going got tough.

On reaching the Palace, James emerged from his reverie, eased to a halt on the promenade and kept the engine running while the four girls disembarked.

"Have a good time, you lot. And are you sure you'll be all right getting home afterwards? Because I'd be happy to give you a lift. And don't forget to be home by eleven, Melanie. We wouldn't want to go upsetting your mother again, would we?"

Having received the necessary reassurances, he sat back with a smile on his face. Being a relatively young man still himself, and fairly open-minded, he knew that you had to give your children some slack at times, afford them a degree of trust and freedom and just hope that trust was justified. He watched Melanie and the girls tottering their way up the slipway, and Melanie especially, in that ridiculously short mini-skirt she was wearing, and felt a sense of pride in his girl. She was beautiful, headstrong, and everything he could have wished for in a daughter. The last thing in his mind as he slipped the car into gear and eased his way into the evening traffic was 'She'll be fine. I know she will. Hopefully.'

It wasn't long until he relaxed comfortably back into his seat again, confidence restored, and a smile back on his proud face as he whistled quietly to himself on his journey back home. Yes, he did know his girl, and he also knew she would indeed be fine.

CHAPTER 3

Mitch and Tony's Palace evening

As it happened, as James made his way homeward along the prom he passed young Mitch and Tony, heading in the opposite direction towards the Palace, where their night on the town was about to begin in earnest.

They were decent lads at heart, both well-mannered and well brought up, as indeed were the rest of their bunch. But, as with most young lads of their age, when they were alone together, be it in a group of boys, socialising with other men in bars, or wherever for that matter, they tended to be uncouth, coarse, often foul-mouthed, and always disrespectful to their mates, ribbing each other unmercifully. For that was simply the way it was, what it took to be seen as one of the boys; to be accepted and respected in the circles in which they moved, where they felt at home, where they wanted to be. But when they were on their own, or alone in the company of girlfriends, freed from the pressures and the need to conform to the stereotypical male image, they could be so different: charming, attentive, receptive to those around them and totally accepting the need to show some respect and, occasionally, even love and affection.

And so it was that during the course of their journey, for no other reason than to pass the time of day, they slipped easily into their normal, joking and mickey-taking mode, fondly hurling abuse, oaths and insults to and fro en route to the Palace, all in good fun.

"How'd you get on with that Jennifer bird the other night, To? Did you get anywhere then?" was Mitch's opening gambit in the verbal jousting.

With his usual air of resignation Tony responded "Nah! Tight as a duck's arse she was, wasn't she? Easier to break into Fort Knox than her knickers mate, I'll tell you."

Mitch raised his eyebrows at this as he looked scathingly at his pal. "She's a lucky girl then matey" he said, leaving the statement hanging teasingly in the air for Tony to stew on, which he duly did.

"Lucky? What the hell are you on about, dipshit?"

"Well, you'd have been a big disappointment to her wouldn't you mate?" Mitch replied before lapsing into silence once more.

Tony, by this time looking more than a touch bemused,

took the bait once again. "How come?" he queried.

This was it, thought Mitch. He'd only gone and walked straight into it.

"Well, you couldn't screw a Polo mint with what you've got between your legs, could you mate? Be honest" he grinned mischievously, at which point Tony exploded with a combination of derision and laughter.

"That's rich you twat. Coming from you anyway," was his swift response, followed by an afterthought: "Especially as you were right at the end of the queue when they dished the old todgers out matey."

"Yep, spot on Tony. There you were, right up at the front of that queue with a big smile on your ugly mush and me and the rest of the boys were stuck way down at the end of it. Bet you were well pissed off when you found out they were handing out all the tiny ones first though!" he pronounced with glee, a big grin all over his face, at which point they both dissolved into laughter, gave each other a friendly barge across the pavement and continued jauntily on their way, banter flowing easily between the two as they went.

Before long, feeling that he might just have come out on the wrong side of their last engagement, Tony felt the need to enter the fray again. "Anyway, sunshine, I don't recall seeing you out with any raving beauties lately. Lost your touch, have you?"

"Me? Lost my touch? You're having a laugh, aren't you? You just haven't been looking, that's all. There's a string of them dying to get to grips with me. It's my own fault, I suppose, I'm just too picky."

"Picky? You? The only thing you're good at picking is

your fucking nose mate. And that's only because it's so big you couldn't miss it."

It was Mitch's turn to laugh at this one, "Fair dos" he conceded, winking at his mate. "We'll call it a draw then, shall we? Fat arse" he added, jumping agilely out of the way to avoid a playful kick up his own backside from Tony.

As they meandered along the prom, happy in each other's company, the banter and friendly rivalry continued in similar vein, occasionally drifting into England's chances in the next World Cup, or the upcoming Test Match series, but always reverting back to their favourite subject, sex and girls. Sport and women, women and sport. Whoever said that was all men and boys ever talked about? But then, in reality, these two were no different from the rest of the males of the species. "Simple subjects for simple minds," as Mitch's mother was fond of saying.

As they wandered along, the boys couldn't fail to note the array of female talent heading in the direction of the Palace. Soon they were consumed by the sight of all those lovely young girls, laughing, giggling, and parading themselves in all their finery on their evening out, most of them wearing the flimsiest of mini-skirts and figure-hugging tops. They revelled in the sight of all those long legs disappearing so mysteriously and tantalisingly into those swaying hipped mini-skirts as the bevy of girls ahead of them meandered sensually on their way.

"I don't know who invented the bloody mini-skirt Mitch, but they had to be a genius," Tony drooled.

"Yep, a pure, unadulterated bleeding genius, mate," Mitch concurred, nodding appreciatively.

In truth, although the pair of them felt the need to

compete for bragging rights and loved nothing more than boasting about their alleged sexual conquests and achievements, neither had gained any real sexual experience of note. But amongst boys it was an accepted and unspoken rule that you couldn't admit to that. Of course, you'd been there and done it. Yes, you'd gone all the way, who hadn't? But neither of them had actually experienced anything more than a fleeting fondle of a breast, or a hasty, often rejected, grope, and somehow, that wouldn't have been deemed impressive in anyone's eyes. Both boys, being decent individuals, realised this, but it didn't stop them from playing the game, or making all the right noises. To their credit though, and unlike most, they were careful never to name names and sully some poor unsuspecting girl's name or reputation. Nor did it stop them from yearning for the real thing, and trying their utmost to overcome that hurdle at each and every opportunity that presented itself, for hope sprang eternal in their young hearts and minds.

Their appetites and enthusiasm were well and truly whetted as they neared their destination, for these indeed were the best days of their lives, and they longed to enjoy them. It was still relatively early when they eventually arrived at the Palace, but the evening was already showing promise as they dutifully headed straight up to the main bar to down a couple more pints before the main event of the evening kicked off in the ballroom. Plenty of time then for the pair to mix and mingle with the locals, enjoy the crack and settle down to wait in anticipation of the real fun and games they hoped were about to unfold.

When Melanie and the girls had entered the foyer of the ballroom some time earlier, it was already crammed with people mingling and chatting expectantly as the time neared when the resident band would emerge onto the stage to start proceedings. From inside the ballroom itself, they could hear a blend of soft background music mixed with the unmistakeable buzz of conversation generated by the ever-growing crowd of young revellers gathering in animated groups, either clustered around on the main dance floor itself, or seated around tables surrounding the dance floor and in the various balcony alcoves strategically located around the full-length walkway which encircled the upper floor of the ballroom, all chattering away twenty to the dozen and eagerly awaiting the forthcoming music and dancing.

As the girls knew that there was still some time left before everything kicked into gear and got under way, they drifted up to the upstairs bar, but not before popping into the nearest ladies' powder room, just to check that everything was just so, and nothing was left to chance with their appearance. As usual, Anna was first in and last to leave, still licking her fingers and smoothing her eyebrows artfully as the other three stood impatiently in the doorway.

"Anna, come on!" rang out from the doorway.

"OK, OK. What's your problem?" intoned Anna as she indulged herself with one final preen in front of the mirror before reluctantly dragging herself away to join them. Having been fortunate enough to bag themselves a table near the bar's entrance, which would give them full view of all the comings and goings, the girls delved in their handbags, set up a kitty for the evening and dispatched Sammy to buy a round of drinks; as she looked the most mature amongst them, and certainly wasn't lacking in confidence.

As it turned out, the four of them were so intent on chattering and avidly taking on board all that was going on around them that they only had time for the one drink before realising that time was pressing and they really should make their way down to the ballroom so as not to miss out on all the excitement to come.

And what a decision that turned out to be. No sooner had they made their way into the ballroom amidst the throng of people jostling for position on and around the dance-floor than the lights dimmed dramatically. Tension and anticipation rose, and the spotlight boy based on the balcony opposite the stage jumped into action, thrusting beams of piercing white light arcing and surging across the mass of young people packed below. As if from nowhere a thundering drum roll boomed out, shattering the silence, before the curtain rose slowly moments later to reveal the stage swathed in total darkness as all eyes focused on the scene in eager expectation. Without warning, the stage was suddenly engulfed with searing lights, flashing images and a cacophony of sound, as Sounds Incorporated launched into an ear-blasting, nerve-tingling rendition of 'Sergeant Pepper's Lonely Hearts Club Band', at which point the place erupted, with cheers ringing round the vast ballroom. The atmosphere was electric. The girls were immediately caught up in the sheer emotion that surged through them and were hardly able to contain themselves as they soaked up the thumping beat and hypnotic effect of the music, the prancing lights, the enthusiasm of the crowd, the joy of simply being there, being part of it all, experiencing the thrill of that moment, and the release of their pent-up teenage energy.

At first, they simply couldn't tear their eyes away from the scene unfolding in front of them, their minds entranced by the atmosphere generated by the music, the lights, the mass of heaving bodies on the dance floor and the sense of elation surging through them. Sammy, the excitable one of the bunch, was the first to react; she just couldn't contain her enthusiasm. Caught up in the moment, she turned to her friends, her face wide-eyed and beaming, and excitedly implored them, "Come on you lot! Let's go! What are we waiting for?"

Needing no further encouragement, the four of them swiftly eased themselves into the bustling melee in front of them. Having found the nearest available piece of floor they effortlessly engaged with the pulsing beat of the music, their bodies swaying enthusiastically to the rhythm and their senses heightened dramatically by the sense of joy and freedom released from within them.

Meanwhile, oblivious to all the frenzied activity taking place in the ballroom below, Tony and Mitch were still ensconced in the bar, deep in conversation with their mates and enjoying the convivial atmosphere. The beer was good and the atmosphere was great. They were in good company and, as usual, they were at the centre of things, dishing out and taking all the stick that was going, and revelling in it.

Almost inevitably, when they got together with the lads, the two of them were in two minds as to whether to remain there or seek a different kind of enjoyment where the main action was taking place. The answer, however, was never in any real doubt; there would be only one winner, for Mitch anyway that is. Perhaps more than the others, and for reasons he would never deem to try and explain to his mates, the pull of being alone with a girl was strong in him, and he would often opt to go on a date rather than spend an evening supping beer and mixing it with the boys on a wild night out. Much as he loved being with the boys, he knew they struggled to comprehend it. "How could anyone prefer taking a girl out rather than going on a booze-up with the lads for heaven's sake?" was a question he frequently had to dismiss with some quick-witted aside and shrug of the shoulders, for he knew that they would simply rib him and take the piss unmercifully if he tried to explain his true emotions and feelings to the dozy bunch of oafs he so enjoyed knocking round with.

Eventually, therefore, it was Mitch who broke the deadlock that was forming in their minds. "Come on then To, let's get downstairs and see if we can't do the business, eh matey?" he said.

"Aye, let's go son. I've had enough of this lot of dozy buggers anyway," pronounced Tony, swiftly downing what remained of his pint. The pair rose from the table and headed off in the direction of the ballroom, their ears ringing from the friendly abuse hurled their way by their pals. Before making their final exit however, the pair glanced knowingly at each other, nodded, turned in unison and threw a brace of two-fingered salutes in the direction of their mates. Then they turned jauntily on their heels and continued on their way to the ballroom, from where the strains of a thumping rhythm and beat indicated that proceedings were well and truly under way.

On entering the ballroom, the boys couldn't fail to be caught up in the atmosphere, the pounding beat of the music and the sight of so many young people enjoying themselves and dancing in enthusiastic couples and groups on the crowded dance floor. Not much for dancing themselves, the pair wandered around the fringe of the activity before settling in a spot on the side of the floor which gave them an uninterrupted view of proceedings. They struggled to hold a conversation against the background noise of the band and the excited chatter surrounding them and instead focused on the action taking place in front of them, both on the lookout for any likely-looking girls who might take their fancy.

Mitch was casually surveying the scene around him, casting his eyes contentedly at the bevy of girls dancing happily away as far as his eyes could see, when suddenly he lit upon one girl who immediately gripped his attention. He was stunned into silence at the sight of her. She was quite simply the most beautiful girl he had ever laid his young eyes on. She was such a beautiful creature, her hips swaying so tantalisingly and seductively in time to the music, her features so perfectly framed by her hair, with two tiny plaits floating gently from side to side so gracefully, in perfect harmony with the beads and bells that hung from around her neck, swaying gently as she moved. He loved the particular way she gently, almost shyly, tilted her chin downwards, whilst smiling so warmly towards her partner. She looked so relaxed and carefree, her face alight with a beaming smile, her whole demeanour full of enjoyment. She wore a flower in her hair and a stunning orange mini skirt. She was a beautiful, graceful mover, and those legs were out of this world. Mitch could feel a smile lighting up his own face as it dawned on him that she was actually dancing with no shoes on as well, a true free spirit if ever there was one.

This was the girl for him. He knew it straight away. He couldn't take his eyes off her; it felt almost hypnotic; just watching her move enthralled him. Feelings of want and desire such as he'd never experienced before surged and pulsed through his young body and mind. His whole being yearned to be out on that dance floor, savouring the experience of dancing with her. He knew deep within that he simply had to be with this girl.

He stood there for quite some time, his mind in turmoil, his stare never wavering. Dance after dance slipped by as he struggled with his own emotions, his own inactivity so uncharacteristic of him. He desperately wanted to seize the moment, take the opportunity to ease himself on to the floor and ask for a dance but, daft as it seemed to him, he'd never ventured onto to a dance floor in earnest before. Everything in life so far had come so easily to him. He'd never experienced the shame and embarrassment of being made to look inadequate, so he stood by, a frustrated onlooker. He was strangely hesitant and uncertain about how he would cope on the dance floor, yet deep in his heart he so badly wanted to impress this girl of his dreams, moving so gracefully and silkily across the floor, her body in tune to the rhythm of the music.

Convinced that she hadn't noticed him staring at her, he decided that his only option was to wait until she and her friends tired of dancing and vacated the floor. Then suddenly, without warning, her head tilted in his direction. She had noticed him, at last, and she held his stare. He smiled at her and, almost involuntarily, a smile spread warmly across her face too. That smile was for him. He was in with a chance, and she fancied him too! His heart leapt.

He knew that he just had to get to know this girl; he just had to manage to dance with her. His resolve stiffened, and his courage returned. He had to overcome his embarrassment and fear of failure and launch himself on to that dance floor at the very next opportunity.

As Melanie was dancing, she had sensed that someone was watching her. Finally, she chanced to look towards the edge of the dance floor, and caught sight of a tall, handsome boy staring at her intensely. Somewhat thrown, and a little bemused and embarrassed by his attention, she immediately looked away, unsure whether or not he'd seen her glancing over at him.

During the next few dances she surreptitiously sneaked a few more swift glances in his direction and he was still there, rooted to the same spot and still gazing intently at her with that fixed stare of his. Intrigued, Melanie eventually decided to face up to his attention, raised her head and returned his gaze directly, only to be somewhat disarmed by the instant smile he threw in her direction, which she somehow couldn't fail to return. Clearly, he fancied her. And that smile was so cute. It transformed him, and her, and she saw him in a new light.

The girls had just decided to take a break when Melanie felt a presence behind her. Turning around, she saw it was him, and close up he was the cutest boy she'd ever seen. She felt drawn to him instantly, in a way she couldn't quite understand. Without speaking, they danced. She was a good dancer and usually quite comfortable on the dance floor, but she felt awkward in his presence. He seemed uneasy too, just shuffling on the spot looking at the floor, as if he was embarrassed, or uncomfortable even. He certainly was no dancer, of that much she was certain.

When she eventually gave in to the urge to look up at him he was staring at her in a very unnerving way. His eyes were deep and burning into her, but she couldn't work out their expression: desire, yearning, embarrassment? Something else? Whatever it was, he made her feel hot and fuzzy. She hoped the next song would be a slow one and he would take her in his arms and they would dance closely together.

When the music stopped, she waited for what seemed like forever, rooted to the spot. He hesitated momentarily, half-smiled, turned away, walked off and disappeared into the crowd at the edge of the dance floor. Melanie was completely flummoxed. 'He didn't like me!' was the immediate thought that flashed through her mind. What had just happened? By the time a boy made up his mind he wanted to dance with you, it was because he'd decided he fancied you, so he always hung around for a second dance. More often than not, the girls had to politely decline these requests. This was a tricky situation. The girls had discussed it and made a pact that one would come to the rescue of another if it was obvious that she needed an escape route.

'He's just walked off and abandoned me!' was the only thought in her head. Not having experienced the feeling of rejection before, Melanie was mortified. Her mind was racing and her heart pounding. 'He doesn't like me. He doesn't want to be with me!' she thought uncomprehendingly, and she found it deeply upsetting. Inexplicably to her at the time, she became all choked up, and could feel herself blush. She was left looking over hopelessly at her friend Shirley, who sensed her distress and joined her on the dance floor as the music started again.

Melanie felt humiliated, but she laughed, a false laugh, held her head up and flicked her hair back. If by any chance he was watching her, she wanted to make sure he thought she was enjoying herself and that he hadn't made such an impact on her. She acted as if she didn't care and, outwardly at least, she appeared to be in high spirits in her friends' company. 'That's OK, there are plenty of other boys here' was the thought she consoled herself with. But it wasn't OK, and she couldn't even begin to understand, or explain, the emotions that overwhelmed her at that moment.

The rest of the evening felt flat, and she subtly looked for her tall, handsome boy in the various groups of young people about the place, but she knew nothing about him or who he hung out with. No matter what, she just couldn't get him out of her mind.

But as the evening progressed, Melanie started to feel better about herself. Soothed to some extent by the great music, she enjoyed several more dances. Some were with boys, none of whom appealed, and all of whom she politely declined when they sought a second dance. Others were with her friends, and as the night wore on she began to wonder if it had actually happened. Had she really danced with him and felt such a strong emotion? 'Just forget it,' she told herself. She'd had fun in the end, hadn't she?

At half-past ten, she retrieved her shoes, which she had kicked underneath one of the tables earlier, and prepared to leave with her friends. They had to be home for eleven. Once outside, she hugged and said goodbye to Sammy and Shirley, who lived in the opposite direction, and set off homewards along the prom with Anna. It was a beautiful early summer's evening, and Anna as usual was just chatting away and making Melanie laugh, the first genuine laughter she'd experienced since that moment when she'd been so unceremoniously abandoned on the dance floor that evening.

Unknown to Melanie, she was far from abandoned and unwanted. Confused and bewildered, it was Mitch who had experienced the real angst on the dance floor, squirming with embarrassment and suffering from delusions that he must have been the subject of amusement and derision as he struggled so in her presence. Try as he might to concentrate on trying to follow her footsteps, to find some kind of rhythm and movement, he had failed miserably, and suffered torment. His actions and thought processes had been inexplicably strangled by his own ineptitude and sheer embarrassment. In the panic that had engulfed him he'd been unable to act naturally, let alone speak to the girl he wanted so much to impress. Instead, his embarrassment was such that the only thing in his mind he could think of when the music ended was to make a hasty retreat. He was blissfully unaware that he had left his dream girl a mystified onlooker, suffering her own bewilderment, struggling to come to terms with her own disappointment and attempting to deal with rejection for the first time in her life.

Unaccustomed as he was to failure, all Mitch wanted was to disappear rapidly from the scene to seek some comfort in a few more pints of the local brew. Once he and Tony were ensconced at the bar, Tony, being the sensitive type, quickly realised how distraught Mitch was and, as only best mates can, he stepped valiantly into the breach in a brave attempt to soothe his pal's feelings of ineptitude, or at least make the rest of the night bearable.

"You call that dancing?" he began. "You looked like a bloody constipated gorilla out there mate. You haven't got a bleeding snowball's of copping for her after that little performance, you tosser. Even I was embarrassed for you. God knows what she must have thought. I don't know how the poor girl stopped herself from laughing. I was dancing with her mate and we were both pissing ourselves. We couldn't even dance for laughing, could we?"

By this point, Mitch was somewhat mystified. He couldn't quite believe what he was hearing. When Tony paused for breath, with as much restraint as he could muster, he managed to blurt out "Shut the fuck up why don't you, shit for brains? That's just what I want to hear from you isn't it? Thanks for your support mate. Is that it, you finished now?"

But Tony wasn't finished, far from it in fact. It seemed to him that things were going quite well, all things considered. So he took Mitch's response as a form of encouragement to finish his piece and carried on undeterred in similar vein.

"Just get a few more down you and forget her. She's history as far as you're concerned, fucking history mate. Face it, you blew it. Best-looking bird in the place and you only went and blew it. There's plenty more where she came from anyway. Drink up, and get them in, it's your round."

Having delivered his verdict, and feeling quite pleased with himself for being so supportive, Tony sank back into his chair, basking in a warm glow of satisfaction from knowing he'd done his very best to lift his pal's spirits and get him back into the fray again, confidence fully restored. The voice of experience, that's what he needed, Tony thought. After all, what were best mates for if they couldn't be there for you, help you see the bigger picture, encourage you to move on when you've fucked up and you're feeling a bit down? Yes, a job well done, most definitely.

He studied his young friend's face, which, in his considered opinion, seemed a little calmer, more resigned to the situation, more at ease somehow. No doubt about it, a little light-hearted banter always did the trick where Mitch was concerned.

Wrong. Seriously wrong. Mitch stood up slowly, gathered himself, glared angrily into his best mate's eyes, and exploded with rage. "You're a fucking knob To, a fucking first-class knob. Why don't you just go and fuck yourself arsehole, 'cos nobody else would. What would you know about anything, you bloody great moron?" With that, young Mitch threw a look of downright disgust in his so-called mate's direction, shook his head in disbelief, and stormed off in the general direction of the bar.

To be fair to Tony, he took this little outburst unflinchingly on the chin. 'Hmm' he murmured, that look of satisfaction spreading over his face again. 'Seems to have done the trick then, he's back to his old self. The old caring touch never fails.' Being the oldest member of their group, Tony had an almost unshakeable belief in his own ability to set an example to the younger, less experienced members of the crew, and was always more than willing to give them the benefit of his wisdom. It wasn't always heeded, admittedly, but freely given all the same, such was his generosity of spirit.

As it turned out however, Tony's intervention had, albeit unwittingly, served a useful purpose, for it had allowed Mitch the chance to let off steam. Tony had set himself up as a focal point, a target on which Mitch could vent his anger and the frustration that had been boiling up within him. This boy just wasn't used to failing, or being found wanting. His pride was hurt, he needed to take it out on someone, and Tony had kindly offered himself up like a lamb to the slaughter.

As psychologists go, Tony clearly didn't have a clue but, somehow, he'd managed to press all the right buttons and release the tension building up in Mitch. And Mitch really wasn't one for holding anger for long, nor in fact bearing grudges. Get it said, get it out there, then move on was more his style.

"Here's your pint, bollocks, hope it chokes you. But with a mouth that big there's no chance is there?" Mitch said when he returned from the bar a few minutes later. He slammed Tony's glass down on the table, a slight smile flickering across his face. "All right, I did screw up. It was my own fault, I know it was, but I just don't need a dickhead like you taking the piss. Sup your pint and we'll head off, I've had enough of this place tonight."

"OK. Apology accepted," said Tony, and they both broke into the first hint of gentle laughter since Mitch had sloped off the dance floor some time earlier with his tail fairly and squarely lodged between his legs. Now they were best mates again. It didn't take much, and it didn't take long. It never does where best mates are concerned.

But Mitch Mitchell, charmer extraordinaire, knew in his heart that he had failed for once, and he was still finding it difficult to come to terms with his own ineptitude. One thing for sure though, he knew quite clearly that this was never going to be allowed to happen again, and he was going to learn to dance if it killed him.

CHAPTER 4

A chance encounter

The night wore on and still neither Mitch nor Tony had 'copped for' a female, so eventually, having quaffed sufficient beer, they meandered out of the building and down on to the promenade, which was heaving with people. It was a beautiful evening. Mitch's mood was lifting and the two lads were indulging in their usual pastime of eyeing up the talent as they wandered their way homewards.

Suddenly, and without warning, Mitch became very animated. "It's her To, it's her!" he exclaimed.

"It's who, dickhead? What am I? A fucking mind reader, or what?" was Tony's considered response.

"The girl from the Palace, the one I danced with. It's her. I can see her up ahead."

"Oh no. Fuck me gently. Don't even go there Mitch.

You've got no chance with her, mate. Face it. You screwed up and that's it. Don't make it any worse than it is. Look, there's loads of talent around. Pick on someone who doesn't know you yet."

"No Tony, it's her, seriously, I know it is. I can't let her go. I might never see her again."

"That'll probably make her happy then mate," said Tony, hoping to avert any further embarrassment for either himself or his pal and at the same time not wanting the evening to sink back into doom and gloom if Mitch failed miserably, as he suspected he just might.

But Mitch just wouldn't let it go. Grabbing Tony's arm, he looked him in the eye and said, "I'm serious Tony. I really fancy her, she's gorgeous, and I won't screw up this time. Besides, I don't care what you say, I think she fancies me too. Really, I do, seriously. Anyway, what would you know about women, you ugly sod? Come on, you can have her friend, she's a looker too."

But Tony just sneered dismissively, so Mitch tried a different tack. "Not up to it then, mate? Or did she give you the elbow on the dance floor and you're not cracking on?"

That did it. Never one to shirk a challenge to his pulling ability, Tony took the bait, threw Mitch a withering look and set off alongside his pal without further ado, the pair of them now determined to seek out the two unsuspecting young girls ahead of them.

Mitch had a purpose in his stride now. He was outside in the open with not a dance floor in sight and he could feel the confidence flooding back through his veins. This was his environment. He knew he could walk, talk and charm all at the same time.

Quickening his stride, it wasn't long before he drew alongside his dream girl, matched his stride with hers, and leaned carefully in towards her, slipping his arm around her shoulder as he did so, before launching into his patter.

"Hi. My name's Mitch, you're beautiful and I'm here to walk you home, wherever that is."

Startled by this approach, Melanie was silent for a moment. Yet as she took in Mitch's effortless charm and confident air and the warmth of his softly spoken voice, she felt a tingle of excitement. It was him, the boy from the dance. Suddenly there he was beside her, and a surge of excitement pulsed through her as she realised that he did fancy her after all. She sensed that her heart had started racing. Her face had flushed noticeably.

She looked over questioningly at her friend Anna, who just shrugged her shoulders, a look of resignation on her face.

Although a little unnerved by the shock of the moment, Melanie really couldn't resist this boy. As she returned his gaze and looked back up into those intense eyes of his, she felt both mystified and elated at the same time at the realisation that she was helplessly drawn to him. He wasn't a dream after all; he was real and he was there by her side, his arm resting protectively around her shoulder, an adoring look on his face, his eyes peering intensively and invitingly into hers. By way of response, that amazing smile of hers gradually lit up her face. She nodded slightly and slid her arm in turn nervously around his waist, resting her head gently against his shoulder.

An enchanted silence settled over them as they meandered on their way. Romance was in the air and they were caught up in their emotions, immediately so comfortable in each other's presence that they seemed to drift effortlessly along together, recognising that words weren't necessary and oblivious to anything and everything going on around them. Neither felt the need to break the magic spell of that feeling of togetherness, and the joy of that almost instant pull of mutual attraction and desire that each of them sensed.

The pair continued on their way for a little while before Mitch broke the spell. He paused, gazed at her quizzically, laughed gently, and shook his head.

"What's your name anyway? I've been so taken up with you I forgot to ask."

"Hmm, it's about time" replied Melanie, laughing along with him. "I thought you'd never ask. It's Melanie."

Mitch gave a brief nod of approval. "Melanie's a lovely name. It suits you, and I've never been out with a Melanie before," he said.

"Oh good" Melanie giggled, "I wouldn't like to be just another one on your long list of Melanies."

They laughed and cuddled closer together, chatting happily away.

"I couldn't take my eyes off you when I saw you on that dance floor tonight," said Mitch.

"Oh really?" replied Melanie "And there was me hardly able to escape that stare of yours for three, or was it four, maybe, dances? I can't say I noticed at all really!"

"That obvious, was it?"

Melanie grinned. "What on earth makes you think that? Do you do that with all the girls, by the way?"

"No, of course I don't. I only do it with gorgeous ones, the ones I really fancy. That's why I've never done it before, probably." He laughed, looking longingly into her eyes, before breaking the spell once again as he continued. "Only I felt a bit sorry for you as well," he said in a serious tone.

"Sorry for me? Why would you feel sorry for me?" replied Melanie, a look of disbelief on her face.

"Well, I could see you were struggling a bit with the old dance moves, and I really wanted to help you out, but you looked so lovely and I didn't want to embarrass you in front of your friend. That's why it took me so long to ask you to dance." A cheeky grin spread over his face as he did so. To her credit, Melanie saw the funny side of this immediately and played along with his little game.

"Oh really?" she replied. "That was so kind of you. You're just so thoughtful," she added, stifling a laugh as she did so.

Quick as a flash Mitch came straight back with, "I know. I thought you'd understand. That's why I didn't throw in all my moves and just shuffled about a bit so as not to show you up."

Melanie could contain herself no longer and burst out laughing. "Well, thanks again. I thought it was good of me not to laugh, actually" she said, still giggling.

"No, of course you wouldn't laugh" Mitch responded with raised eyebrows and feigned seriousness, adding after a slight pause "That's because you couldn't see yourself, could you?" He flashed the smile that had first attracted her.

At this point Melanie, catching on quickly, threw her head back and laughed, genuinely taken with his quick-witted response.

"Anyway, once we get to know each other you can maybe show me some of your moves," said Mitch. "One or two of them weren't bad actually, now I think about it."

Mitch's confidence fully restored, he relaxed fully into the company of this wonderful girl he'd stumbled upon. She really was something else. Stunning looks and a sense of humour. What a combination. But at the same time his father's words of wisdom played in his head; "Play it cool with women" he'd always said. "Don't let them see how keen you are. Not too soon anyway son. Keep them guessing where you're coming from, then, when you've got them hooked give them the old 'lovey doveys' and they'll love you for it. But always, whatever you do, show them the respect they deserve."

Melanie in turn was truly fascinated by this boy. He was so different from all the other boys she'd met. He was so disconcerting in his manner. There was no doting, no fawning or trying to impress her; instead there was a certain confidence about him, bordering on arrogance almost, but offset by charm, a ready smile, a quick sense of humour and a warmth in his delivery. At the same time, she sensed an intensity lurking beneath the surface, a subdued tenderness and sensitivity that hadn't fully emerged, but which intrigued her. He knew he was good-looking, that she could tell, but that ready smile and charm somehow softened his character. And when he looked at you, those eyes were so deep, so intense. It was almost as if they were boring straight through to your soul.

Although slightly lacking in confidence herself, Melanie looked directly up into those eyes, raised a quizzical eyebrow and, in her cutest tone, enquired, "Have you always been cocky then? Or is this just for my benefit?"

Mitch managed to look incredulous at the very thought of this and paused for a moment before looking straight back into her eyes, a comical, hurt look on his face.

"Cocky? Me? Hmmm... yep," he responded with a deadpan expression before dissolving into the widest smile imaginable, and they both burst out laughing again.

"Oh, that's all right then. I wouldn't like to think you were putting on an act just for me," she said, with a knowing look on her face as she nestled her head back into the crook of his welcoming shoulder. What was he doing to her? She didn't normally act like this. She was the one who was supposed to be in control.

Tony and Anna were tagging along behind them, but they might as well not have existed as far as Mitch and Melanie were concerned, for they were in a world of their own, totally engrossed in each other. Very little more was said between them on the remainder of the relatively short walk to Melanie's house, and they arrived too soon at the road where Melanie and Anna lived. Melanie said goodbye to Anna, who had been talking non-stop to Mitch's friend, as was her nature, promising to ring her the next day.

Mitch and Melanie were left standing alone together at the front gate to her house, and Melanie looked into Mitch's eyes for the last time that evening. "Thanks for walking me home," she said and, taking a half step back, she looked up at him and smiled with tingling anticipation. She could feel herself blushing.

"Can I kiss you?" he asked. He placed a hand on her cheek and touched her lips gently and tenderly with his own. She responded briefly to his touch before he took a step back himself, looked longingly into her eyes, and said "I've wanted to do that all night." After such an intimate, but brief moment between them Melanie couldn't speak, so she just smiled and squeezed his hand warmly.

"I'd really like it if you came to Tony's party next Saturday," said Mitch. "Bring your friends and I'll see you there?"

"Great, but where does he live?" asked Melanie after a moment's hesitation.

Mitch smiled, leaned in towards her and whispered Tony's address into her ear, lightly touching it with his mouth as he did so and sending an electric shock through her body. Then he turned and walked away, leaving her momentarily dazed.

Entering her house with a beaming smile on her face, she popped her head round the living room door to say hello to her parents. She certainly didn't want a long-drawn-out conversation with them. She just wanted to go straight to her room and explore her feelings.

Her parents had always expressed themselves freely in front of her and had a quite relaxed and tolerant approach to her upbringing; her father adored her, and her mother just wanted her to be happy, but Melanie had always put up a shield when it came to anything personal, a shield that she had used in childhood to stop too much hurt building up inside her, and still she kept her emotional distance, only ever telling them as much as she thought they needed to know. She certainly wasn't sharing tonight's events with them, especially when she hadn't had a chance to examine and analyse them herself.

"Looks like it was a good night," her mother said, taking in the bright smile that lit up her daughter's face.

"Yes, it was great, but I'm off to bed now, I'm really tired Mum," she said, and with that she made her exit and headed off directly to her bedroom, where she threw herself down on her bed and lay staring at the ceiling. Was she in love? Was this what it felt like?

She caught a glimpse of the moon outside, the very same moon that she had just been kissed under, and her body shivered involuntarily. She watched the patterns of swaying trees which the light from the lamppost outside was projecting onto her bedroom wall. They seemed to be moving in time with the beat of the music that was still deep inside her body.

When her mother popped her head round the door on her way to bed a few minutes later, Melanie lay feigning sleep She just kept thinking about that kiss and the way it had made her feel; excited, elated and happy. She desperately wanted to see Mitch again to make sure it was real. But she would have to wait a week before that could happen. How was she going to survive a whole week? At least she would be able to talk about it to her friends tomorrow, she reasoned, but there again she wasn't sure they would understand her feelings. As far as she was aware, nothing like the complex emotions she was going through now had happened to any of them before.

Back in the Mitchell household, the scene was totally different. Mitch's mother had made her way up to bed, as was her practice, so he was able to settle down and share a large whisky over a relaxing smoke and chat with his old man, Mitch senior, with whom he'd always been close. He'd always admired his dad and they'd shared an open relationship from as far back as he could remember.

"Did you have a good night then, son?" Mitch senior enquired, picking up on the contented mood of his boy.

"Great night, thanks mate. Went to the Palace and met a gorgeous bird, absolutely stunning she was. Well, actually I hooked up with her outside on the prom and walked her home."

"I hope you walked on the outside of the pavement son, like I told you? Manners, you know?"

"Yes daddy" Mitch replied mockingly. "As if you'd let me forget. Girls aren't bothered about things like that anyway, these days. You're living in the past, old man." Mitch laughed and pulled a face.

"Bloody know-all. Some things never bloody change do they, you tosser," was Mitch senior's response, albeit good humouredly. "Tell me about her then. Blonde, is she?"

"Huh, it's always blondes with you, isn't it? Have you got a thing about them or what? No. She's got black hair, beautiful eyes, a fabulous smile and terrific legs, as it happens.

"Is that it then son? What about her personality?"

"Oh, she's got bags of that, and a sense of humour. Can't believe my luck. A bird with a sense of humour!" He laughed.

Seeing that his boy was seriously smitten, Mitch senior slipped easily into his fatherly role. "Did you play it cool like I told you then son? You don't want her thinking she's got you where she wants you, you know."

"Relax. I know you don't think so, but I do listen to you sometimes you know, even if you do talk a load of shit most of the time. But I really don't want to lose this one mate."

"Keep your wits about you son. You'll be fine. You're a Mitchell remember, a good catch for any girl."

"Oh yeah. I nearly forgot that mate. Thanks for the tip,"

said Mitch with a smile. "Night anyway, I'm off to my pit. See you in the morning."

"Aye, I'll be off myself son. See you in the morning."

With that, Mitch made his way up to bed, undressed, climbed into bed and dropped straight off to sleep, a big smile on his face.

CHAPTER 5

From a boy to a youth

The Island environment and the lifestyle of the times, with all it had to offer, along with enlightened parental guidance and attitudes to life generally, combined to form the character of the young Tom Mitchell and his inherent carefree and open approach to life throughout his formative years and beyond.

An only child, Mitch had spent his early childhood in a small council house on the poorer side of the Island's main town, Douglas. He was born into a small, hard-working, and close-knit family unit comprising his maternal grandmother Ellie, or Nan as she was affectionately referred to by Mitch, his mother Mary, and his dad Alf, all of whom were respected and upstanding members of the local community and social circles in which they moved and lived.

Mitch's Nan was a five-foot-nothing, bubbly, bouncy, chuckling bundle of fun and laughter who had sadly been widowed at the age of forty-seven, the year before Mitch was born. She was a strong woman who bore her loss with dignity, never complained about her grief and dedicated the rest of her life to her family and their happiness. She never found anyone who came remotely close to matching up to her beloved husband Henry, tales of whom she never tired of recounting to young Mitch, who was always an eager and avid listener. The street where the Mitchell family lived until their son was ten was a somewhat strange mix of a small number of council houses at one end of the street and a larger number of private, rented, larger properties. Times were hard for the Mitchell family, and indeed for most families in the street, in those early years. Although they did without many things for themselves, they always made sure that Mitch never went without, and got the very best of everything they could afford.

One thing he was never short of was love and affection, especially from his Nan and Dad, with whom he formed very close bonds. He inherited the warm, affectionate and loving side of his character from them, together with a quick wit, a somewhat cheeky sense of humour and a certain natural charm, which was to hold him in good stead throughout his life. In many ways, he was blissfully unaware at the time of the hardship, struggles and sacrifices his devoted family made on his behalf, and he benefited greatly from a happy and contented childhood and all the love, support and encouragement his little family unit provided for him.

Indeed, it wasn't until much later in life that Mitch would come to realise, and fully appreciate, just how fortunate and privileged he had been.

From a very early age it was obvious that Mitch was an observant, bright, intelligent and adventurous child, being quick to walk, talk and get up to all sorts of mischief; a natural in that department, as things would turn out. On more than one occasion he would somehow manage to slip out unnoticed through the invitingly open front door and emerge into the big wide world which lay outside, disappearing into the blue yonder with not so much as a word of goodbye, let alone any hint of where he might be bound for.

As it turned out, this was something which would become a recurring theme throughout his teenage years, much to the chagrin of his often-frustrated mother who, quite mystifyingly to Mitch, appeared to think she had an unquestionable right to know where he was going, what he'd be doing, who he'd be with, and when he was thinking of returning home. Naturally she was destined never to find out, as she had never managed to acquire the ability to accurately interpret the series of grunts, groans, and mutterings that such questions inevitably elicited from her normally intelligent teenage son.

Throughout his life, Mitch's relationship with his mother would remain somewhat strained at times, as she was the disciplinarian of the family, the one who set the standards she expected her boy to maintain. Mother, or Ma as he would come to call her in his teenage years to gently annoy her, was much less tactile. Having married so young and with Alf in a somewhat insecure occupation as a joiner,

Mary, like many other women in a similar position, was obliged to go out to work herself to supplement the family's income, whilst Nan lovingly took on the role of mother figure in Mitch's life.

Even with Mary supplementing the family income, times were still hard. When Mitch wasn't much more than four, the family moved to a larger privately-rented house on the opposite side of the street, so that they could take in visitors during the summer months. This move would provide a welcome and much-needed source of income for the Mitchell family from Easter each year through to early autumn.

Having completed his primary education, Mitch morphed effortlessly and seamlessly into life at his new junior secondary school, again an all boys' school, favoured by the powers- that be at the time. Being the only boy from his primary school to attain the exam results necessary to qualify for entry to the school's top academic form, it was inevitable that he would form friendships with his new classmates, all from different island schools and having varying backgrounds and interests, rather than with his former school pals. It was here that his competitive, academic, and sporting appetites would be whetted.

In those days, great emphasis was placed on sport and the part it had to play in school life, thanks to the belief that it helped in building health, character, and a competitive instinct in young minds. With sport playing such a major role in his life, Mitch naturally gravitated to the older boys who comprised his sporting teammates. Sharing the same interests, sense of humour and easy-going attitudes, he formed friendships with three boys in particular, friendships that would last throughout their rebellious teenage years and beyond.

CHAPTER 6

The blossoming of a young girl

From a very young age it was apparent that Melanie Jackson was a bright child and an independent thinker. Born in the respectable upper part of the Island's main town, she had a happy and privileged upbringing. Her parents, James and Julia, were perceived as pillars of the local community. James was a lecturer in sciences at the local College of Further Education, while Julia was the dedicated mother and housewife. It's fair to say that, typical of the period, neither of them was particularly demonstrative or affectionate, but Melanie still always knew she was loved by each of them in their own way.

Perhaps understandably, being an only child, Melanie was somewhat shy by nature, and more inward-looking and prone to examining her own feelings than most of her peers. But as she developed, and possibly at an earlier age than most young girls, this deep-thinking child gradually became aware of the passion and sensitivity she'd also been blessed with. As time went by, she just couldn't help letting this sensitivity and a certain stubbornness get in her way. From an early age, she would sulk at the slightest altercation with her parents, feeling wronged but at the same time resenting her inability to control the depth of those feelings. It was a contradiction in her, which she was aware of in her more reasoned moments, but she was unable to tame it and sometimes it scared her.

Throughout her formative years, Melanie's family remained very traditional in nature, her father, going out to work and her mother staying at home looking after her daughter.

For some reason, which Melanie couldn't quite put her finger on at the time, although she may have intuitively sensed Julia's hidden frustrations, something was stirring in that active young mind of hers and she was already subconsciously questioning these roles in her head. In later years, this uneasiness would grow into understanding as she came to realise that her mother wasn't actually the domestic goddess and role model that she had assumed.

During the 1960s, as she matured and grew into womanhood, Melanie would become aware of, and grow to welcome, subtle changes taking place that were affecting the views and aspirations of women in general as they began to question and challenge their traditional position in society. Indeed, Julia could also feel these changes, for she was an intelligent woman. At times, she did feel undervalued and dissatisfied in her traditional role of homemaker, although she tried not to let it show; she was conscious that she'd made her choice willingly, and her loyalties lay with her husband and the family life they had forged together. But she still felt that somehow her life could have been very different if only she'd been born in more enlightened times.

In truth, Julia was not an average sixties housewife and she shared a very equal and enlightened marriage with Jim. Like most teenagers, it wasn't until her late teens and early twenties that Melanie would come to realise this and form a close bond and relationship with both of them, which would endure throughout their lives. She would gradually come to appreciate their values and how they had enhanced her life by affording her the opportunity to develop and become her own person whilst they remained in the background, quietly offering support and encouragement along the way. Julia herself had grown up in a very relaxed way, with no fixed rules: she was independent of spirit, and possessed an open-minded attitude to life, often suppressed to the outsider as she had a strong sense of values and was deeply committed to her husband and family. She herself had been considered a bit wild and risqué in her youth, which was why she understood Melanie and her behaviour so well as she advanced through her teens. She frequently avoided confrontation or interference as her beloved daughter ploughed her own way relentlessly, fearlessly, and often dangerously, through those difficult and challenging years that all teenagers experience.

By the time Melanie took up her place at the island's premier private school for girls and came into contact for the first time with other girls from varying backgrounds, she had realised that she was not quite like most of the other girls. Although their core values and backgrounds appeared similar, and she could relate easily to them, many of them appeared somewhat naïve by comparison.

As Melanie moved through her first couple of years in this new school environment, her choice of friends became more selective. Whereas her friendships had previously been formed among those she shared sports and activities with, the children of friends of her parents or neighbours, she now had sufficient insight and awareness to realise that she was capable of moving on, of being more selective in the friendships she formed, and of making her own choices. Gregarious by nature, despite her natural shyness, Melanie gravitated, almost imperceptibly at first, and seemingly effortlessly, towards three girls with whom she formed a close bond. Sammy, Shirley, and Anna.

Around the time when these friendships were fully cemented, at the tender age of just thirteen, Melanie's life would come to be governed by a revelation, which struck her like a bolt from the blue one day as she sat as usual daydreaming her life away with that awful Miss Latimer's tedious monotone droning away in the background during another one of those gruesome Latin lessons which the school timetable forced the pupils of Lower Five to endure with painful regularity.

As she sat doodling aimlessly on her new pencil case and gazing longingly out of the window at a group of fourth formers happily honing their netball skills in the courtyard below, a strange awareness came over her whole being, as if from nowhere. Her brain went into overdrive, her receptors heightened to a level she'd never experienced before; her thought patterns, normally so abstract and carefree, suddenly became totally focused by a revelation that was forming from deep in her subconscious mind. It was the dawning of an understanding of something strong and somehow frightening, and its impact would shape her life from that moment on. As if from nowhere, and without conscious effort on her part, the previously somewhat naive, happy-go-lucky teenager had suddenly been struck by a revelation of her existence; what set her apart from her peers.

She sat for a while in a daze. Could this really be happening to her? Of course it could, she reasoned. The vision was so real and felt so relevant in her young mind. The concept of Melanie! There she was, sitting amongst her friends and peers, but she suddenly saw herself as an individual, separate from the situation she was in and the other people in it. She became aware that she had her own identity and that she, and she alone, was responsible for her own emotions and how to control them.

She had obviously been aware of certain emotions as a child, those of joy, pain, hurt, and laughter, but she was suddenly becoming conscious that what she felt emotionally now would affect her life and her future choices. From this point on she would be responsible for her own actions. Beforehand she'd had her own beliefs and thoughts on things which, until now, she had not thought of as having any value; she hadn't until that moment really looked inside herself to see who she was.

The concept was scary, because what was emerging made her think she was different; she was separating herself from being a child and becoming her own person, and all during the course of one boring Latin lesson. This thought was all-consuming and confusing at the same time. The young, innocent, fun-loving Melanie she'd been comfortable with up until then was swiftly becoming conscious of her own body and mind.

She realised that she could question things; she no longer had to accept the way things were. She had thoughts, attitudes and feelings that belonged to her and to her only. With extraordinary clarity for one so young, she knew that she was setting out the personality traits that would lead her through her teens and beyond. She knew she would be rebellious, questioning and stubborn, amongst other things. With the certainty of youth, she knew instantly that she was going to have to take this new self on board, with all its emotions, because it was inside her and unique to her.

She looked around the class; everyone else, including her friends, seemed as unconcerned as they had been minutes before. How could they be? And would her parents not sense a change in her when she got home? Would they and their roles in her life not now seem different to her?

With this thought lodged in her mind, she was seriously taken by surprise when she got home that evening to find that nothing had changed; her tea was on the table and the evening progressed in its usual fashion. The world had just turned upside down on her, yet everyone else was carrying on as if all was normal.

She realised that from here on in, her life was going to become more complicated. Top of the Pops, teen magazines, and loving George Harrison would be replaced by events she would initiate and participate in, real events and real relationships. But once she got over the initial shock, she was well and truly ready for this change.

With the dawning of this realisation, almost imperceptibly at first, Melanie began moving into an independent, more adult world, and her closest three friends shifted effortlessly with her as she did so. The group of four was strengthened, sensing the change in her, recognising her newly-formed sense of identity and keen and eager to follow her lead. Her priorities changed, her close friends were all important to her, her family life less so. And then there were boys, and all the emotional highs and lows that went with liking a boy for real, rather than one on a poster or in a band.

From that moment on the young Melanie left her childhood behind her, but she was not yet an adult. She was young and wanted to live, explore, be adventurous, feel passion and intensity but feel scared at the same time. She wanted things to happen, but she wasn't sure what. She knew that she would fall headlong into relationships without holding back. And more than anything, she wanted to be a rebel.

Although this revelation had not fully crystallised in her mind, and she could not have explained any of it at the time, Melanie knew that she was going to be a free spirit, one that was not beholden to anyone.

CHAPTER 7

A gang of young mates

Almost from the beginning of junior school Mitch had struck up a friendship with Tony, from the very first games lesson they had as it happens, where they both played good football, scoring goals and emerging triumphant on the winning team. During the excited chatter in the changing rooms after the game they found that they shared an enthusiasm for the game, and their friendship was cemented upon discovering they also shared a passion for their beloved Red Devils, Manchester United. In their teenage years they would share another passion, for Dusty Springfield, the unattainable blonde pop goddess with the deeply mascaraed eyes, bleach blonde hair, sensually swaying hips and sultry voice.

Tony, like Mitch, was a happy-go-lucky, easy-going lad with a good sense of humour. Untouched and untroubled by the cares of the world, he took everything in his stride and would never go out of his way to upset anyone. Possessing as he did a frank and open attitude to life in general, he had a knack of opening his mouth and sharing his worldly-wise thoughts and opinions with anyone who would listen without first fully engaging his brain. Never renowned for his intelligence and understanding, apart from in his own mind possibly, 'To', as he was known to his chums, was normally blissfully oblivious to the effects his utterings might have on others.

Tony's outpourings, often presented in a serious manner and with an air of great awareness, were usually viewed as blunt by others. However, his friendly demeanour ensured that he seldom, if ever, caused offence. Tony was Tony, and his laid-back manner and sense of humour meant that his pronouncements were often met with quizzical looks, mystified stares, or hoots of laughter. Tony would invariably interpret such responses as a lack of understanding on their part before continuing to blithely scatter his pearls of wisdom.

Tony and Mitch became best mates. Comfortable in each other's company, they were constant companions from the beginning. When they were not either playing sport, talking about it, or enjoying a shared love of pop music, they would constantly be ribbing each other unmercifully and revelling in the banter that passed between them. During the long summer holidays their pleasures were simple. Their days would be spent at the local recreation ground with their pals, kicking a football around, playing cricket or tennis or, when they had some pocket money left over, doing battle on the little pitch-and-putt golf course all day long to their heart's content.

Tony was one of the older boys in the class and usually took it on himself to share what he believed to be his undoubted extra wisdom and experience with the younger ones. His advice and guidance were often ignored, but this didn't deter him, for he was convinced that eventually the light would dawn on them and they too would come to see the wisdom of his words. Not that it would have mattered a jot to him. He often misread the reactions he got back from them, and believed that he had racked up another mission accomplished.

Mitch was aware of this aspect of Tony's nature, but it in no way diminished his respect for his pal. In fact, he found it to be one of the endearing aspects of his character, as he knew Tony was a loyal friend who did genuinely care about his mates and in his own way he felt that, as the old head in the group, he was there to pass on the benefit of his experience to those less worldly wise than himself. Both lads knew and understood each other. Though it went unspoken, they also knew that their friendship and camaraderie was built on a solid foundation and, should the going ever get tough for either of them they'd be there for each other, come what may.

Their friend Jack was an uncomplicated soul and the real comedian of the pack, breezing through life with an irreverent attitude and a smile on his face and comfortable in his own skin. He was never found wanting of a swift wisecrack, and saw the funny side of any situation. Short and stocky he might have been, but as an athlete he was swift as lightning; not as talented or skilful as the others, but tough as nails on a football pitch and prepared to run through brick walls for his team, and his mates. A bit of a daredevil, Jack was up for anything, and loved a challenge. It never took much egging on from the other lads when they came up with another of their hare-brained schemes or crazy escapades.

The sense of adventure in all the boys was always to the fore and Jack was usually right there at the centre of any action; he was an intelligent lad, but that wouldn't stop him from abandoning all thought of danger and indulging his inherent love of thrills and risk taking, often with little or no thought as to the possible consequences. As it turned out, fortune usually did favour the brave in Jack's case, and invariably he'd end up with a big grin all over his face, urging the others to step up to the plate and follow his lead, and without fail they would. After all, if Jack could survive a ten-foot jump from the promenade railings onto the beach below, or climb a cliff face without falling off, then why the hell couldn't they? It all seemed to make perfect sense; if you abandoned logic, disengaged your brain, and didn't think about it too much, that is. And, true to form, they never did.

Ray was the quiet one of the group and could appear somewhat distant or remote compared to the others until you got to know him or, probably more to the point, until he got to know you and felt comfortable in your company. Once the ice was broken, however, his true personality would emerge. Something of an introvert by nature, he was prone to be moody, sullen even at times to an outsider, and would consider his thoughts and words carefully before delivering them, but in the company of his trusted friends he would relax his poker face and reveal a sharp observational wit and a dry sense of humour, engaging fully with all the lads and everything they got up to.

Ray wasn't a naturally gifted scholar, initially featuring midway down the class order when it came to exams, but he was determined and studious, and once he set his mind to it his endeavours paid off and he would rise to be one of the most successful pupils in his year. The same determination featured in everything he did, including sport. He would rise early each day and go for a training run around town every morning before setting off for school, a practice which would stand him in good stead as he became the school cross-country champion year on year.

Football was an area where Ray effortlessly came into his own, being an extremely talented and natural centre forward who popped goals in for fun and with consummate ease. He was always a great asset, which tended to make him extremely popular with his grateful teammates. Mitch and Ray got on well together, but were never destined to become bosom-buddies. Underneath Ray's friendly exterior, Mitch always sensed an underlying feeling that he harboured a slight disapproval of the way Mitch breezed through life taking everything for granted and apparently with little effort, whereas Ray had to graft for all the success that came his way. Cross country would be a fine example of that. Whereas Ray spent hour upon hour training, Mitch and Tony would set off weekly on the cross-country course and happily watch their pal Ray disappear at full tilt into the distance before sussing out the nearest shortcut and reappearing close on Ray's heels at the finish, subsequently basking in the assumed glory of a race well run. Such escapades and japes served to annoy Ray and, try as he might, he could never hide his frustration as the two jesters would proceed to rib him unmercifully in the full knowledge that they could wind him up with no fear of him ever stitching them up with their sports master. The boys were nothing if not loyal, and taking the piss came naturally to all of them.

The third year at high school was to be eventful in more ways than one for Mitch and his young mates. The third and fourth years at their school were referred to as Middle School and comprised boys from thirteen to fourteen years old. By this age they were all good footballers, capable of mixing it with the men they would encounter as they graduated into playing in the Island's senior amateur football leagues, for at that time there was no such thing as junior football teams. The old adage applied - if you were good enough, you were old enough. You were tossed in at the deep end, and if you survived your initial baptism amongst the big boys you were there to stay and accepted by the men in the team, who became your friends and teammates, regardless of age.

Mitch would never forget his baptism of fire in the men's league, shortly before his fourteenth birthday. A central defender normally, he was selected to play on the right wing on this occasion, as the team's normal winger had failed to make an appearance and, after putting in a strong appearance, he went on to score the winning goal. From that point on he would become a regular in the team, as indeed would his pals, which would influence their development through their teenage years, but not necessarily in the right direction, as it would turn out. In the early days, the boys would be left to their own devices, comfortably ensconced in a car or luxuriously, for away matches, in the coach which would be hired to transport the team to and from matches. Meanwhile, the rest of the team would congregate in the pub for a well-earned pint or five before heading homewards, and one of the team would pop out pints of shandy for the boys to indulge their growing taste for alcohol.

It wasn't long before the boys managed to persuade the others to let them tag along, to enjoy the camaraderie and do a bit of bonding with the rest of the team inside the pub. Licensing laws being as they were on the Island, underage drinking was prohibited, but landlords being what they were, such legal formalities were normally disregarded, and from then on this would become the norm for the four young lads as they enjoyed the convivial company and banter of their teammates, and quickly grew to be treated as equals.

Before long, pubs generally would become the normal habitat for the boys, and drinking in particular, would become a regular social pastime and pleasure. The pub life meant that Tony and Mitch would also be drawn into the dubious pleasures of smoking but, fortunately for them, Jack and Ray were never attracted to this habit, displaying more common sense than usual.

Throughout their third and fourth years Mitch continued to excel in sport, captaining the Middle School football team, vice-captaining the cricket team and gaining his school colours in both sports. He also captained the school rugby team, and in the process became the only third former ever to gain their middle school rugby colours. However, in direct contrast to his success on the sporting field, his light gradually waned on the educational front, thanks to his diminishing interest in his schoolwork and an increase in his rebellious nature and carefree approach to life. During this period he became almost unmanageable at home, so far as his mother was concerned anyway, but still remained close to his nan and dad, who reluctantly was to become the meat in the sandwich between his wife on one side and his son on the other. It was a difficult position to be in for Alf, who was a real family man, but he never gave up trying manfully to retain peace between the two warring parties in his own household, a previously settled, happy and contented family unit.

Nothing his mother tried could dampen or restrain Mitch's wilder instincts and bring him back into line. Ground him and he'd bunk off through his bedroom window in total defiance of his mother's authority and go happily on his merry way wherever the mood took him, usually to the pub, or down to Dixie's house, a friend the boys had reacquainted themselves with during fourth year, where he'd spend many a happy evening helping Dixie deplete his mother's whisky and rum stocks whilst the pair put the world to rights.

Eventually, the relationship between Mitch and his mother deteriorated to the extent where they would hardly communicate and Mitch would go out of his way to avoid her whenever he could. The crunch came as Mitch turned fifteen when, following another row, he waited until his parents were in bed, gathered a few possessions together and simply upped and left home, leaving a brief note to say that he would be fine, before spending a week shacked up in the cellar of one of his best friends. Finally, at his wit's end, his dad traced his whereabouts and managed to persuade him to return home, which Mitch did, but only on the clear understanding that there was no way he would be pushed into backing down and apologising to his mother.

At school, Mitch's antics and attitude gradually became more unacceptable to his persevering teachers, their patience stretched to the limits by his constant challenging of their authority. Easy-going by nature, and still a decent, well-brought-up lad with firm values and a cheery outlook on life, he retained his sense of humour, and his ability to use his charm to ease his way out of the more difficult situations he found himself in from time to time, such as when he was caught hurling javelins in the general direction of the eight hundred metre runners on the school playing field for a bit of fun. And those teachers never gave up on him, for despite an apparent disinterest and lack of effort on his part, he somehow managed to maintain his position amongst the achievers in his class, never quite achieving the top position which he'd formerly occupied, but still right up there amongst the best when exam time came around.

Mitch and his pals remained close throughout their Middle School years, and from the age of fourteen onwards their ever-expanding social activities became the main focus of their lives. Unrestrained as they were, they made sure they took advantage of the easy-going lifestyle on their Island home. As their horizons widened, their tight-knit group gradually expanded to include a more flexible, loose knit group of individuals, who included several older teenagers who they teamed up with along the way. Mitch was possibly the least devoted to simply heading off at every opportunity for another boozy evening with the boys. He had always been comfortable in the presence of girls and as he grew older, he was not slow to take advantage of the easy way he had with girls to launch himself enthusiastically on to the flourishing teenage dating scene. This mystified most of his pals, and he took some considerable stick for it from time to time.

CHAPTER 8

The Group of Four

Melanie, Sammy, Anna, and Shirley – what a diverse group of personalities they were, and yet they gelled together so well. It wasn't long before Melanie's influence and enlightened attitude to life was brought to bear on her close friends; she couldn't resist it, and they were all willing and eager devotees. Whereas they had all formerly accepted advice and information from parents and teachers, their support network was now firmly set amongst themselves. They would freely swap advice, comfort, support, and encouragement based on their own newly-formed and rapidly-developing concepts and philosophies on life. They had their own sense of identity but at the same time they were all, without fail, at their happiest when they were just hanging out with each other.

The four young friends were extremely loyal, shared common interests, and provided fun and excitement for each other. The group spent as much time together as possible at school, after school and especially at weekends, when their lives were transformed and they took every opportunity that presented itself to let their hair down and enjoy life to the full.

They grew more confident, both as a group and as individuals, to the extent that they came to rely on each other more and more. Their reliance on their respective families gradually lost its appeal compared to the company and support of their trusted friends. After all, what did parents know anyway? They were too old and set in their ways to know what it felt like to be young and understand what life was really all about.

Instinctively, they began to question the authority they had previously accepted from the adults in their lives. Rules were there to be broken; authority was there to be challenged; independence was theirs by right and they were more than prepared to stand their ground and argue their case whenever the need arose to support what was, in their minds at least, a justifiable cause.

The four girls flourished in each other's company and swiftly left their previously somewhat childlike behaviour behind them. It was an unspoken but time-honoured rule that their time together, their conversations, their innermost cherished thoughts, their shared secrets and desires were strictly off limits to anyone outside their own private inner sanctum. Life was rich and exciting. They had endless conversations, talking about anything and everything that happened to flit into their active young minds at any given time. It was their world, and for the group of four it just revolved around them.

While Melanie was the instigator in the move towards an understanding of how life could be so different for them all, Sammy was not slow to grasp the nettle and join her as a shining light for the others to follow. They were both impulsive and became natural leaders of the group, making the decisions and the plans and being responsible for most of the troubles they found themselves in, from time to time.

Sammy was not unlike Melanie in many ways, but being less of a thinker and more an action girl, she was less inhibited, more extreme in her thoughts and actions. She was the most rebellious one, always testing the limits her parents imposed on her and becoming such a risk-taker it would leave the others wondering what she would get up to next.

Melanie was an extremely attractive girl, and was comfortable in her own skin. However, she was neither conceited nor arrogant, even though she could not fail to notice the admiring stares she attracted from a seemingly endless supply of lust-filled young male admirers wherever she went. She simply assumed that this was the natural order of things where young boys were concerned, and a compliment that was bestowed on most girls of her age, and certainly where her best friend Sammy was concerned.

In truth, the modest, unassuming Melanie imagined that her own good looks paled somewhat alongside those of Sammy, who she thought, without any shadow of a doubt, was the prettiest girl she had ever known. However, she never felt envy; to Melanie it was merely an observation, for she did not consider herself to be anything special. She was positive, happy, and confident in herself and just not the type to be jealous; she loved and cared about Sammy and it simply wasn't in her nature to make comparisons. In many ways, Sammy felt like the sister she'd always wished for but never had.

Sammy could also be a real flirt, with little intention of forming any meaningful relationship with a member of the opposite sex any time soon; she was just having too much fun. Melanie, on the other hand, whilst certainly keen on meeting boys and having fun, was never interested in flirting and was content to let the boys do all the running.

There was one other striking contrast between the two pals. Melanie often struggled with a deep conflict between wanting to please others and wanting to rebel. She was full of bravado in her relationships with her family and teachers, yet at times, in what she thought of as the big alien world, she could be shy, uncomfortable, and nervous when first encountering new situations. Sammy however did not know the meaning of shyness and nervousness, to the extent that she never picked up the vibes emanating from Melanie when such situations arose. Sammy never sought acceptance and did not give two hoots what other people thought about her or how she should behave; they could take her as they found her. But Melanie genuinely did care about the impressions she left on people, and on many occasions this resulted in her being torn between her natural instincts and those of her friend. Almost invariably Sammy's impulses and instincts would win out though, and Melanie would behave in the same rebellious way as Sammy.

In affairs of the heart, however, Melanie had her own mind firmly set and would never be swayed by Sammy's frivolous attitude to relationships. She did want romantic relationships to fit into her life, to be an important part of it, but not to take it over. Until only a few nights ago, she had been determined to remain an independent thinker and not to allow herself to be dragged down by unrealistic romantic notions. However, after just one evening with Mitch, this mindset was already being sorely tested.

The third member of the group was Anna, the lovely, adorable, wide-eyed, and carefree scatterbrain, who never failed to keep the others in stitches with her madcap schemes and often half-baked antics. Governed almost totally by impulse, and unrestrained by any conscious need to think things through, Anna's whole being was centred on enjoyment, excitement, self-image and fashion. She had a passion for fashion, an insatiable desire for everything that was new and part of the scene, which was the only place she wanted to be.

Anna was also headstrong, irresponsible, disorganised, extroverted, and strong willed. These were ideal qualities, highly acceptable within the group, but not necessarily deemed quite so desirable in her home life, at school or in the outside circles in which they moved. No matter, Anna was oblivious to all influences outside her group of friends and simply ploughed merrily on with her life, oblivious to the views of those whose opinions held so little appeal for her.

To Anna, absolutely nothing was just ordinary. The high princess of melodrama, her life constantly fluctuated from the heights of euphoria to the depths of despair, when even the slightest setback could assume monstrous proportions in her mind. "I've broken my nail!" she'd shriek. "Oh my God. It's a disaster!" The others would share knowing glances between themselves whilst fondly setting about calmly repairing the damage that had assumed such tremendous proportions in Anna's mind, then dispatching her swiftly on her way before any further calamities could raise their ugly heads; an action followed almost immediately by a combined sigh of relief, rolling of eyes, and explosions of laughter from the remaining girls.

Anna was also the group's recognised news gatherer. Absolutely nothing seemed to pass her by as she eagerly soaked up all the gossip and 'skeet' she could lay her young hands on and she was always more than willing to disclose her sources. The other girls loved her dearly and happily tolerated all her highs and lows, because that was just their Anna. She was funny, mad as a hatter, the joker of the group, easy to chat to and just a feelgood person to have around. They trusted her of course, but were all wise enough not to trust her completely with their own deepest thoughts or feelings. After all, she did love her skeet. True, she never dished the dirt within the group, but outside? Melanie for one suspected that you could never quite be sure, so better to be safe than sorry.

And then there was Shirley, at face value the quiet, some would say introverted, member of the group. In some ways, it might have seemed to outsiders that she'd somehow slipped in under the group's radar, for in the early days at least, she certainly did not seem to fit the mould of the other members. What those outsiders wouldn't have realised was that Shirley was the final piece of the jigsaw that was the group of four; the one with common sense; the locking nut that held them all together; the brake-man who knew when it was time to slow the train down before it hurtled out of control. Without her the other three would have ploughed on regardless, taking on the world with no calming influence to occasionally make them stop, think, and consider what they were actually getting themselves into.

Shirley really valued each of their friendships, and they hers. She particularly idolised Melanie, who she thought was independent, self-assured, mature, and fun to be with. In fact, Melanie could do nothing wrong in her eyes and she genuinely would have done anything for her. Melanie was vaguely aware of the attention Shirley paid her, was really fond of her, and was quick to recognise her good qualities. She recognised her value as a trusted friend and her assumed role as peacemaker when frictions arose from time to time, as they inevitably did.

Of the four, Shirley was the one with no great ambitions; she always just wanted an ordinary life and, despite the influence of her close friends, she tended, on the whole, to remain reasonably obedient at school. She was quiet, sensitive, a follower, but a follower who was strong enough to voice her opinion and let her feelings be known when she felt things were getting out of hand. She was a good listener but also the voice of reason when required. And sure enough, from time to time, the others would stop and listen, for they knew when Shirley spoke up that things might very well just be verging on the ridiculous; a step too far, even for them.

Although Shirley would not have seemed an obvious choice as a close friend of any of the girls, she fitted in well; they were aware that she was somewhat reliant on them all and looked up to them, and they in turn, to their credit, were quick to realise that Shirley was indeed a genuinely beautiful soul, unassuming, and unaware of these qualities in herself which were so appealing to them.

So it was that come the lower fifth year at school, the group of four was well and truly up and running, a band of young girls, growing into their minds and bodies, excited by the future and all it had to offer; friendships formed, raring to go, and up for any challenge their early teenage years might thrust upon them.

CHAPTER 9

Tony's party

The four girls met round at Sammy's house the afternoon after that memorable night at the Palace when Mitch had walked Melanie home and she had immediately fallen head over heels. In contemplative mood, Melanie suggested they have a walk along the prom. She wanted to retrace her footsteps from the night before and just daydream, even though she knew she was unlikely to bump into Mitch. There was no harm in secretly hoping, was there?

As the four girls made their way along the prom they laughed and talked about the previous evening, the boys, the music, the crazy dance moves. When Anna spilled the beans over the two boys they'd met on their walk home, they quizzed Melanie incessantly as to how she had got on with Mitch, but when she tried to tell them, for some unknown reason she found herself reluctant to explain the intimate moments she had shared with him and the strength of the feelings he had aroused in her. She tried to keep the jitters she felt to herself and hoped that they didn't notice that the mere mention of his name sent her into a complete state of panic.

She didn't know why she felt unable to share the pure excitement that was deep inside her; it was just an innate sense that they wouldn't understand or even approve. This was the first time she'd held anything back from her friends, but she was scared to share it with anybody in case the bubble burst. She did mention the invitation to the party though, and they were all well up for that, especially Anna, who had taken quite a liking to Tony.

Melanie normally loved school, but the week following the dance at the Palace dragged and she was, unusually for her, unfocused, a fact which didn't go unnoticed at school, or indeed by her understanding chum Shirley, who was much more sensitive to Melanie's mood swings than the other two girls. At school, she was accused of daydreaming and not participating, but however hard she tried she couldn't help wandering off into the realms of fantasy and dreaming of the coming party and meeting up with Mitch again. What should she wear? What would they talk about when they met again?

As the days went on, in her usual fashion she began to analyse the events of Saturday evening, and to worry that he had been quite casual and might not want to meet her again. In her wobblier, less secure moments, and much to her chagrin, the thought flashed through her mind on more than one occasion, "Oh no, what if he's already met someone else?" She knew he had come across as cocky and a bit arrogant, but she had assumed it was a bit of male bravado to cover up his embarrassment. Still, a nagging doubt kept creeping into her subconscious mind. What if that was the way he was and all this didn't mean anything to him? Maybe he was like this with all the girls.

As the days passed by, any excitement she'd been feeling as Saturday approached was rapidly evaporating, to be replaced with self-doubt and panic. Was asking her to a party even a date? He hadn't actually asked her to go to the party with him.

Normally a very positive and confident girl, Melanie struggled to come to terms with the change that had come over her, and all because of a boy that she'd only just met. She tried to keep the negative thoughts at bay by throwing herself into her after-school activities: she was learning to play chess in an after-school club, being determined to eventually beat her very clever, and logical father. She went to guitar class, and went swimming with Sammy. She chatted for hours of an evening on the phone with Shirley, who in turn was very aware that there was a perceptible change in her friend. It was obvious to her that something was troubling Melanie but she didn't want to pry, despite her suspicions, as she couldn't fail to notice that Melanie would clam up and change the subject at the mere mention of Mitch's name, or of the forthcoming party.

When not talking with Shirley, Melanie spent time round at Anna's playing the latest Beatles album over and over, as she knew Anna was oblivious to her feelings about Mitch and more intent on the party, what she herself would be wearing and what to do with her hair. However, whilst her time with Anna was a pleasant distraction, Melanie drove herself crazy dealing with her thoughts and feelings as she whiled away the interminable hours and days to Saturday.

The day of the party came around at last. Melanie had to play in an inter-school doubles tennis match that afternoon with Alexa, a classmate of hers. Melanie loved sport and was a good all-rounder who represented her house and school in all of the sports she turned her hand to. Tennis wasn't really her favourite, or best of sports even, but she had still managed to scrape into the third pairing for that afternoon's tournament, an event she would normally have entered into with her usual enthusiasm, grit and determination.

However, on that afternoon she couldn't muster any enthusiasm whatsoever for the challenge that lay ahead; her thoughts were elsewhere. Her heart simply wasn't in it, and she just wanted it to be all over with. Try as she might, she couldn't prevent the thought of that evening's party from looming on her mind.

For a number of reasons, Melanie's close friends weren't remotely interested in sport. Unfortunately, Shirley was a little overweight and very self-conscious of her body: she had never been particularly gifted in sport anyway, perpetually being the forlorn figure left standing alone as the final pick when the girls were selecting teammates of choice for their friendly team games. Possessing an unwarranted lack of self-worth, she was constantly comparing herself to the other girls around her and invariably found herself to be wanting, so she naturally shied away from anything which would, in her mind at least, cause her to expose her weaknesses to others, and the resultant embarrassment which would inevitably engulf her afterwards. Whenever she could, therefore, she would persuade her stepmother to write out a sick note for her games teacher, and breathe another sigh of relief as she was excused games to join the huddle of other sick-note girls watching their chums enjoy themselves.

Anna, on the other hand, was far less complicated by nature. A good-looking girl, she was full of self-confidence, fully absorbed in her own image and never happier than when she had the luxury of devoting her time and energy to the most important thing in her life. Outside school hours, she wouldn't have been seen dead in a tracksuit or tacky shorts, never mind donning those silly plimsolls. Running around getting bedraggled and sweaty with hardly any make-up on was not a look she wished to adopt, one which she utterly detested in fact; she resented being forced to endure it, even when she had to. She would be far too busy on a Saturday anyway, getting ready for whatever was coming her way that night. Her clothes would be strewn all over her bed, while she ironed her hair straight and generally made sure she looked drop dead gorgeous from head to toe.

Sammy too wasn't interested in extra-curricular sports, for she considered any activities outside school hours a total waste of time when she could be off doing so many other exciting things that took her fancy. That hidden agenda of hers would frequently be revealed to her friends, as if from nowhere, before they were all caught up in the moment only to find themselves being whisked off on some other madcap escapade dreamed up in Sammy's fertile, and at times reckless, mind. Who knew where she would be or what she would be up to this Saturday afternoon? Probably hanging out with boys and getting up to mischief down town somewhere, Melanie mused as she wandered aimlessly across the playing fields to the nearby tennis courts and adjacent changing rooms. Whatever it was, she knew it would be infinitely preferable to having to go through the motions of this stupid tennis tournament.

In this mood, perhaps it was unsurprising that Melanie made a particularly bad start to the match. She started poorly and got worse as the first set went on and seemingly harmless serve after serve shot past her, to the rising frustration of her partner. She was allowing herself to get inwardly mad for the smallest mistakes, to the extent that she was not concentrating on her shot-making at all.

However, as she was about to serve in the second set, her competitive instincts finally kicked in. It was as if something seemed to click inside her. Normally very competitive in sport, and hating as she did to lose, she realised that she was behaving erratically. She just had to change her mindset. She wasn't used to not being in total control of herself and didn't like the way this stupid crush, because that's all it was after all, she'd decided, was affecting her normally logical decision making and the way she was behaving. Where had her pride and determination gone?

She toughened herself up mentally, dug deep inside, became focused, and somehow raised the level of her play. She came back into the match, playing with sheer willpower and determination. But it was too late. Despite her best efforts, they lost. The bubble she'd been living in that week finally burst as the realisation dawned on her that she had let Alexa and the school down. She was devastated.

Somehow, she managed to hold herself together long enough to congratulate her opponents in time-honoured fashion and say a very brief goodbye to her partner and teammates before swiftly heading away from the court. As she turned the corner however, and was safely out of sight from the others, she could contain her emotions no longer, and the tears of frustration started to roll down her cheeks. All the feelings that had been building up in her came tumbling out in waves of emotion.

Melanie only ever cried alone, putting up a wall against her vulnerability in front of people. Even at this early stage in life she had sufficient self-awareness to see this as a major flaw in her character. That innate sensitivity of hers often allowed her to become overwhelmed by feeling too much. Though she didn't realise it at the time, no matter how hard she tried to overcome this flaw, it was destined to stay with her throughout her life.

When nearing her home, she made a determined effort to put on a reasonably bright face. With a bit of luck, she reasoned, her mother would see any signs of unhappiness as disappointment for losing the match and nothing more. She entered the house and spotted the moving shadow of her mother in the kitchen making tea. It would be the same as every Saturday, sandwiches, and cups of tea in front of the TV, having had their main meal earlier in the day.

She had inherited her love of sport from her father, who she knew would be watching Grandstand in the living room; cricket and tennis in the summer months, football and rugby in the winter, for this was the Saturday routine in the

Jackson household. The thought flitted briefly, almost subconsciously, through Melanie's mind, that she would never be so regimented in her ways when she grew up and had a family of her own. She would make life diverse and entertaining, not boring, and unimaginative as her family and their traditions were.

Melanie shouted a cursory hello from the hallway and said she was off for a bath, taking the stairs two at a time so as not to be waylaid by either of her parents. She lay almost motionless in the bath, surrounded by sweet-smelling bubbles and soothing hot water, and let her mind wander for quite some time; it was peaceful and relaxing and she was beginning to feel calmer.

Her reverie was suddenly broken as she became aware of her mother's voice calling her for tea. Reluctantly, she emerged, wrapped a bathrobe around herself and went downstairs to join her parents.

She responded to her parent's questions about the tennis in the usual robotic voice she kept especially for them. "It was OK, but we lost. Yeah, I'm going with Sammy, Anna and Shirley to the party. No I won't put too much make up on mother, and yes, I will be home for eleven." Her words sounded distant to her, an echo; as if they were being spoken by someone else. Sometimes she felt she was two different people. She loved her parents, especially her father, but in recent times she had gradually come to feel indifferent towards them in relation to their involvement in her life. The person her parents knew was not the same Melanie she really believed she was; deep and passionate, bursting at the seams to enjoy herself and escape the boredom of their mundane life.

As soon as she felt she had given them enough time and information, she excused herself to go and get ready. It was after six, and she was meant to be calling for Anna at seven on their way to Sammy's, then Shirley's, who lived closest to Tony's house and the party. Her hair was still damp from its hurried drying, but at least she didn't need to iron hers, it was naturally thick and straight with a full fringe and, thanks to her mother, she would be wearing her favourite dress. The swirls and colours lifted her spirits. She'd had a complete disaster with it the first time she had worn it, managing somehow to pour a whole bottle of coke down it, but her mother had washed it with care, ironed it and laid it out on her bed for her. Sometimes she did love that mother of hers; she did have her uses from time to time.

Satisfied with the way she looked, and some of her confidence restored, she said her goodbyes to her parents and set off for Anna's house. She found her friend as bubbly as ever. With the care and attention that she gave herself she always looked dazzling, and she knew it.

"How do I look?" she asked Melanie, arching a quizzical eyebrow.

"You look stunning," said Melanie sincerely. Anna threw her arms round Melanie and excitedly announced, "You do too. We're definitely going to get our men tonight!" at which Melanie felt a shiver run through her.

Anna wasn't selfish, but she had no insight into others and their feelings. All week she had been totally oblivious to the turmoil Melanie had been experiencing, and clearly tonight was going to be no different. But Melanie understood her friend and was happy to accept her as she was, because she knew there wasn't an ounce of harm in her, and she really was a loyal pal, in addition to all her other redeeming features. Without further ado and with the formalities completed, the two girls set off on their way, arms linked, to Sammy's house, the next gathering point on the journey before heading off to collect Shirley.

Although the girls never discussed their family lives in any great depth, it was apparent when visiting each other's homes that there were differences, subtle though they were. The style of communication was very different in Shirley's house. Her mother had died long before Shirley had developed any lasting memories of her. Her father had remarried, and his second wife, Elsie, looked after him and his daughter and their home.

Melanie could sense that the relationship between Shirley and her stepmother was different from that between her and her own mother. It was always slightly strained, and although it was obvious that Elsie idolised Shirley's father, it seemed, to Melanie at least, that his daughter just came as part of the package and not her responsibility, other than providing her with food on the table, clean clothes and all the other essentials a lodger might expect.

Shirley never had to contend with nosey or angry parents. Her father cared very much for her and made all the right gestures, but didn't really know how to impose boundaries and had little or no idea as to how to relate to a teenage girl. Consequently, all four girls were usually left very much to their own devices when they were at Shirley's house. In fact, it was often the place where the girls pretended they were going when asked by their own parents.

Shirley wasn't a rebel in any sense of the word, for she had nothing to rebel against, no real house rules. Melanie sensed that her friend was possibly insecure because of this, combined with the lack of a natural mother/daughter relationship. She felt that Shirley had latched onto her friends as her main source of love and attention, and this made Melanie feel very protective towards her.

Having gathered up Shirley, the four friends headed off for the party, Anna her usual excited and exuberant self, Melanie tense and nervous and Sammy casual and laid back as always, while the ever-observant and thoughtful Shirley watched her friends and sensed Melanie's discomfort about the forthcoming evening. She was right to be mindful, for throughout the journey Melanie was indeed giving herself a good talking to. "Just pull yourself together" she told herself. "He either feels the same way about me or he doesn't, and I'll find out one way or the other later this evening." Deep down, she desperately hoped he did feel the same way about her, but if not, she was determined she would just move on and get back to the happy-go-lucky way she had been before.

When they arrived at Tony's house Melanie hung back a bit, but the other three girls, laughing and giggling excitedly amongst themselves, walked straight into the action, with Melanie following behind. She was noticeably more subdued as she edged herself into the hallway, where there were several people she didn't know hanging about.

Not coming across anyone they knew immediately, they moved towards the entrance of the front room and looked in. The place was filling up. There were several people squashed onto a sofa, smoking, drinking and talking amongst themselves, all apparently laughing at something one of them had said, whilst the Beach Boys were playing in the background and a small group of girls were dancing in the middle of the room.

The girls did not know many of those gathered there, and some of them looked a few years older, so they wandered into the kitchen to get drinks and seek out their host. Anna spotted Tony and went up to say hello. A boy who was with him, someone Melanie thought she vaguely recognised from somewhere, immediately asked her to dance. Before she'd had a chance to answer, he grabbed her hand and whisked her into the front room to join the other dancers. She scanned the room discreetly, but there was no sign of Mitch. She heaved a sigh of relief, for the last thing she wanted was for him to see her dancing with somebody else.

When the song ended, the boy put an arm around her, casually but firmly, in an obvious attempt to make sure that nobody else cut in. She felt uncomfortable but as if by the marvel of telepathy, Shirley suddenly appeared by her side. Melanie quickly seized the opportunity to escape. She smiled at the boy and made her excuses, dipping under his arm as she did so.

Only then, to her horror, did she spot Mitch hovering at the entrance to the room. Their eyes met for a second, and there was a fleeting expression in his eyes; was it anger? Or could it possibly be jealousy? She hoped so.

She felt a blush creeping up over her skin and a kind of panic rising up from her stomach. She couldn't face him. She turned her back and looked pleadingly at Shirley as if to say "talk to me!"

That was when she felt a tap on her shoulder. It was Mitch, and she was relieved to see that his manner had changed. He seemed confident and genuinely pleased to see her, and told her he was glad she had come. He smiled at her, an infectious smile, and she smiled back instantly. But she still wasn't sure of his intentions or how he felt. Was he just being sociable and friendly?

She saw a brief look of annoyance cross his face when Anna and Sammy appeared on the scene as if from nowhere and drifted across the room to join her. He didn't know them, they'd moved into his space; they were distracting her from him, and she could see that he wasn't comfortable with them being around. She wanted desperately to get to know him better and be alone with him, but she knew she couldn't be rude to her friends. Her mind was filled with confusion and frustration.

Then suddenly Mitch leant over and touched her ear gently with his mouth as he whispered softly "Do you want to go for a walk? I can meet you outside."

That touch lit a spark deep inside Melanie and, without hesitation she whispered back "Yes, I'd love to". A tingle of excitement mixed with pleasure flowed through her. That was just what she had wanted to hear.

As soon as she could, when Anna had headed off to the kitchen to replenish her drink, Melanie had a quiet word with Sammy, told her where she was going, waited a while until the others were engaged in animated conversation, then quietly left the room, and slipped outside to meet up with Mitch.

But her exit did not go unnoticed. As Anna emerged from the kitchen, where she'd been topping up her drink whilst chatting to anyone who would listen to her, she caught sight of Melanie disappearing through the front door and a quizzical look shot across her face. Where on earth was her friend going?

As she glanced into the front room she saw that Sammy was dancing with a boy, but Shirley was standing by herself on the far side of the room, looking a bit uncomfortable, so she made a beeline for her.

"What's going on, Shirley?" Anna asked her. "I've just seen Melanie disappearing through the front door. What on earth is she up to?"

Shirley shuffled her feet and looked nervously down at the floor before replying. "Erm... I'm not sure really, but, well, before she left she popped over and told Sammy that she was going for a walk with Mitch, but she did leave in a bit of a hurry. She seemed quite excited."

"Excited? But she's never even mentioned him since last week, and that's so unlike her if she's keen on someone. She usually can't wait to give us all the skeet."

"I know" said Shirley, "But then she has been acting so strangely, for her anyway, all week, hasn't she?"

"Oh, I don't know, she seemed all right to me. You'd think I would have noticed if she had," replied Anna. This drew a raised eyebrow from Shirley.

Shirley thought that would be extremely unlikely, but she tactfully dismissed the thought and moved on. "No, she's definitely not been herself Anna. She's talked to me a lot this week and her mind's been all over the place. I'm beginning to think that maybe she really is keen on him. Anyway, she'll tell us all about it when she's ready, I'm sure."

At this, Anna looked a bit hurt. "Well we should know now, shouldn't we Shirl? After all, we're her best friends, and we share everything, don't we? Do you know anything about him?"

"No, of course I don't. How would I? I've never met him, and Melanie hasn't exactly made a song and dance about him, not to me anyway. But you met him last Saturday, didn't you? What did you think of him?"

At this point one of the boys at the party tapped Anna on the shoulder and enquired politely if she'd like to dance, only to be rebuffed and sent packing with his tail between his legs. Anna had much more important matters on her mind, and she wasn't in the mood to be distracted by some silly boy, especially one with pimples and greasy hair, poor lad.

After a brief reflection, Anna turned back to Shirley, a thoughtful look on her face. "Well, I don't know what he's like really when I come to think about it. I never got a real chance to talk to him as I was with his friend Tony, and he walked me home. But I must admit, my first impressions were that he seemed a bit cocky. Most boys are, I know, but he seemed a bit too sure of himself by half, if you know what I mean? And I think he's older than her too. I wouldn't have thought he was her type, to be honest. But it's not like her to hold stuff back from us, is it? What are we going to do about it Shirl?"

Shirley looked at her blankly and shrugged. "Why are you asking me, Anna? I wouldn't have a clue. Maybe it'd be best if we just don't interfere?"

But Anna was having none of this. After taking a few minutes to gather her thoughts, her eyes suddenly lit up with glee as the answer came to her in a flash of inspiration. "Tony!" she exclaimed excitedly. "How stupid am I? Tony's his best mate, and I'm sure he fancies me. Leave it to me. I'll go and chat him up and see what I can find out. Stick with me Shirl. Back soon."

With that, she disappeared towards the kitchen, where she caught sight of her prey and gave him one of her well-practised 'here I am, come and get me' looks. Tony wasn't the brightest on the planet, but then again, he wasn't one of the dimmest either, so he quickly latched on to the fact that his luck just might be in. Hitching his trousers up at the waist, he puffed his chest out and ambled across the room towards where Anna was standing, waiting most invitingly for him. Adopting what he imagined was a casually confident air, he looked her in the eye, smiled, and turned on the charm in his own inimitable fashion.

"All right girl? Knew you couldn't resist me. Want a drink then? Or is it my body you're after?" he asked, with something between a leer and a smirk etched on his features. Though pained by this lack of subtlety, Anna somehow managed not to cringe, and instead put on a damned fine show of being suitably impressed by both his charm and his debonair approach, whilst at the same time thinking to herself what a prat he was. She hoped Melanie realised what a good friend she was.

"Why yes I'd love a drink. Thank you, Tony," she said sweetly, returning his smile. "What have you got to choose from?"

"Oh, there's Babycham, sherry, some of the old girl's white wine?"

"I'll try the white wine please. What is it?"

"Dunno" he replied. "White wine's white wine, isn't it? Wouldn't go near the stuff myself, but you girls seem to like it. I'll get you some then."

With that masterpiece of boyish wisdom left hanging in the air for Anna to savour, he turned tail and wandered across to the drinks table, thinking to himself 'Tony my old son, you handled her well there, looks like you're in with a chance tonight.'

On reaching the table he turned to his mate "Hoy, Dixie, what kind of glass do you stick this muck in then?"

"Don't look at me mate. Thought you were the bloody smartarse round here," said Dixie.

"Thanks mate, really bloody helpful that was. If I wanted a dickhead answer you were the right one to ask, weren't you? Stuff it, this one here'll do." He selected a half-pint glass that looked reasonably clean. Anna was taken slightly aback when she saw the glass he proudly handed to her, but she bit her bottom lip and smiled sweetly at him again.

"Thank you, Tony, that's so kind. I always think wine tastes so much better when it's in a bigger glass, don't you?" The comment was wasted on Tony. Then, almost without pausing, for she was sure she wouldn't be able to take much more of this, she got to the point.

"Where's your friend Mitch then? I thought he'd be at the centre of things. But I can't see him anywhere."

"Mitch? He was knocking about earlier but I think he's popped out with your friend Melanie. He said something about the two of them going for a walk, I think."

"A walk?" Anna continued to probe. "When all the action's going on here? How strange."

"Not really," Tony responded. "I think he just wants to spend some time alone with her. You know, so he can get to know her better. The daft bugger's gone all soft and gooey eyed ever since he met her. Totally out of character, for him, as well. Dozy sod hasn't stopped talking about her all week.

Driven me bloody crackers he has. Anyway, hasn't Melanie filled you in, told you all about him?"

"Well, er... I haven't seen a lot of her this week, and when I have she hasn't mentioned much at all about him, so I thought she wasn't too keen to be honest. She usually gets all excited when she fancies someone, but no, come to think of it, she's hardly mentioned him."

Tony thought this was hilarious. "Oh good. Bloody marvellous, that'll really piss him off then. He thinks she's the best thing since sliced bread."

"Really? Well, if he's that serious about my friend, then you really must tell me more about him. What's he really like? I must say, he seemed a bit cocky to me if I'm honest."

"Cocky? Mitch?" Tony laughed. "Too right he is. That's my mate all right, but don't tell him that. He'll think it's a compliment, won't he? It's not as if he's big-headed or anything, he just gets away with murder, the bugger. And he's certainly got some way with the women. He's a right charmer on the QT, and doesn't he know it. Don't tell him I said that mind. He might be my best mate and all that, but I wouldn't want him to know I'd said anything nice about him." He gave a knowing wink.

Anna still wasn't satisfied. "Really? Has he had lots of girlfriends then?"

"Huh? What do you think? Thinks he's a bleeding romantic, doesn't he? Falls in love with all of them till the next one comes along. Mind, I've never seen him quite like this over a girl. He usually stays well clear of getting too close. So, who knows? Anyway, I thought it was me you were interested in, not bleeding Mitch."

At this, Anna realised it was time to ease off and change

the subject, reasoning that she could always pump him some more later on if she played him along. Swiftly changing tack, she flashed him one of her cutest smiles and wriggled her hips to make sure she had his full attention. Boys were so easy to manipulate. Then she announced, "You know it's you I'm interested in Tony. You're just such a hunk. I chose this dress specially for you because you just swept me off my feet when we met last week, so I just had to make an impression on you." Then, taking half a step backwards, she placed her right hand on her hip, raised her left arm in the air and blew him an air kiss. "Well, here I am. What do you think?"

Tony looked Anna up and down. "You look all right actually. You'll do for me," he said, with a wink and a grin. Anna's jaw dropped, noticeably so, unless your name was Tony. She stared at him disbelievingly, as she heard a voice screaming inside her head, "All right? I look all right? Not bad at all? I've spent two hours in front of a flaming mirror getting ready for his stupid party, and this little...prick, thinks I look all right? Who the hell does he think he is anyway, the slimy little weasel?"

Seeing the look of surprise on Anna's face, however, Tony thought smugly, "Hmmm. Nice one. That seems to have hit the mark then. She must really fancy me", and in the process he failed miserably to take on board that, in reality, he might just as well have committed suicide right there in front of Anna, for in her eyes he was dead and buried anyway. When Anna got over her initial shock she shook herself back to her senses and quickly made her escape.

"Why thanks Tony, you really are too kind," she declared, with a withering smile on her face. "I'm sorry to have to drag myself away from you, but I've left poor Shirley in there all by herself. She's so shy at parties and I did promise I wouldn't be long, so I'd better pop back in and see how she's getting on. Maybe we can catch up later."

"Sure, see you soon," said Tony. Anna turned on her heels and waltzed off furiously in the direction of the front room.

As Anna disappeared, Tony turned back with a confident grin to join his pals gathered at the drinks table.

"You look happy, sunshine. Cracked it then, have you?" asked Dixie.

"Too right I have matey. We're only going to get together later, aren't we? Can't resist me, can they?" He laughed and poured himself another beer from a Party Seven. He'd always thought of himself as being a fairly bright lad, quick on the uptake even, and he certainly was not one of the dimmest on the planet. He might however just have been one of the dimmest at his own party. Or possibly, in common with most men, he would never be blessed with the intellectual capacity required to interpret the signals emitted by the female of the species.

Back in the front room, Anna hurriedly made her way across to Shirley, who looked at her eagerly, trying to assess how things had gone with Tony. "Well, how did you get on then?' she blurted out.

"With that idiot? Don't ask. But just wait until you hear this. Tony reckons that Mitch is cocky and full of himself. And what's more, he just picks girls up and then drops them like a stone when he's fed up with them."

"Really? Are you sure? He sounds awful."

"Of course, I'm sure. I wouldn't lie to you, would I? And

that's what his best friend thinks about him. We really must have a word with Melanie. I don't think he's her type at all and I wouldn't like to see her hurt. Would you? You know how sensitive she can be."

"Oh, I really don't know Anna. I think we need to be careful. Melanie's not stupid, and she's got her head screwed on right when it comes to boys. I really can't see her falling for someone like that. Why don't we just wait and see what she has to say first? I'm sure she'll spill the beans when she's good and ready."

"Humph!" grunted Anna disdainfully. "Well, as far as I'm concerned, she's our friend and she has a right to know what we know. When she's good and ready just might be too late by the sound of things."

Shirley, being Shirley, acquiesced quietly, but at the same time she wondered if Anna might possibly have got hold of the wrong end of the stick again and offered up her own version of events for the consumption of others, believing it to be gospel, or at least the gospel according to Anna. After all, she wasn't the best of listeners if it wasn't herself holding forth, and it wouldn't be the first time she'd managed to get things wrong, bless her.

CHAPTER 10

Mitch and Melanie's prom walk

Meanwhile Melanie had emerged from the house to find Mitch waiting patiently for her, leaning against the railings smoking one of his favoured Player's Medium cigarettes. God, he looked cocky, she thought. But he was gorgeous at the same time.

"Love that flower in your hair, it's so you somehow. And you've got a nice serve by the way, but that backhand needs practice" was his opening gambit.

"You were watching me?" was her astonished reply.

"Just caught the end of your game, actually," he said with a smile. "I was playing football in the grounds next door and wandered over because I thought it was you, and I couldn't turn down the chance of watching you in your cute tennis gear, could I? Gorgeous legs, by the way" he added, raising his eyebrows appreciatively.

Melanie blushed profusely. Thank goodness he had only seen the end of the match. Her hair had been plastered to her head from charging around the court – she must have looked a real mess. Still, at least he liked her legs.

Then, without warning, Mitch's whole demeanour seemed to change. The veil of confidence melted away and, almost shyly, but with deep sincerity in those soft brown eyes, he drew nearer to her. It was as if he'd allowed his natural defences to drop, purposely revealing his inner self to her. He was letting her see the real person behind the cocky young charmer who was normally on view to the rest of the world.

Melanie was almost overwhelmed by this change in him and couldn't take her eyes away from his. He held her gaze with such intensity that she felt overcome, dizzy, and elated all at the same time. Never before had a boy aroused such deep and confusing feelings within her, and those feelings only intensified when he took her gently in his arms, pulled her towards him, and kissed her tenderly, then passionately on the lips. He whispered in her ear "Melanie, you're the most beautiful girl I've seen in my whole life. I think of you constantly, every minute of every day."

A warm glow spread over Melanie, her heart pounding, as she looked up into his eyes again and saw his face, wet from the rain, so handsome in the light reflecting from the street lamp. And a beautiful smile radiated from her, that same smile which had drawn him to her initially and was etched in his mind. The same warm glow spread through Mitch too, as he began to realise she just might feel the same way about him. He started laughing. It was infectious and she laughed with him; she loved his laugh, it made her feel so happy inside.

All too soon, it seemed to Melanie, that almost magical moment had passed, but the feelings remained within her. They went for their walk. It seemed to Melanie as if she was walking on air, and she hardly noticed the light rain that was falling. They held hands and simply couldn't stop smiling at each other. His smile was captivating and spontaneous, and it aroused feelings within her that were more intense than she could ever have imagined possible.

Hand in hand, they walked down to the promenade and onto the beach. She kicked off her sandals and the sand felt good; soft, cold, damp but welcoming beneath her feet. The sky was changing colour and darkening; it had stopped raining and the pair of them quietly absorbed the sights and sounds around them, the dazzling array of coloured lights that were twinkling and shimmering along the full length of the promenade, magically reflected in the thin layer of glistening rain lingering on the road. They heard the sound of the waves gently lapping the sand, and the beautiful sound of silence that engulfed them as they drifted along in a world of their own.

There were several young people meandering along the prom but the beach stretched invitingly before them, so peaceful and blissfully free from anyone who might intrude on their sense of togetherness, seemingly existing in that special world of theirs. The sea was calm and she felt as if it were whispering to her. It was the most romantic moment Melanie had ever experienced.

Her reverie was broken by the sound of Mitch laughing.

"What's so funny?" asked Melanie. They stopped and sat together on the steps leading down to the beach.

"Well... I've just realised I don't know anything about you really, apart from the fact that you're gorgeous, and I just love being with you!"

"Well, my full name is Melanie Jackson, pleased to meet you," she giggled, offering her hand.

"Pleased to meet you too, I'm Tom Mitchell" he laughed. He took her hand gently in his, put it to his mouth and kissed it. She loved his laugh. It made her feel so happy, and she laughed too. "I think I'll call you Mitch. I like it better," she said, almost shyly.

They sat together on the steps for a while, sharing a cigarette as they swapped stories about their lives. He asked her what school she went to, what music she was into and what her interests and passions were. As they eagerly exchanged information, it became obvious that the intensity between them went far beyond just an attraction. The more they talked, the greater the impression Melanie made on Mitch. He sensed how intelligent and well-educated she was; how different she was from any other girl he had ever met. She had definite views and opinions of her own and her fiery passion for life, her expressiveness and clarity of thought shone out like a beacon.

At the same time, Melanie was thinking to herself that this boy could have any girl. What did he see in her? He was cute and good looking, sensitive, and seemed so tender and kind, not how she'd thought he would be. Perhaps his cockiness and the confidence she'd seen oozing out of him earlier was just a front he put on when he was around his friends.

He wrapped an arm around her and smiled. Her heart started to hammer in her chest. Was it natural to feel such an immediate reaction to someone's touch? She could feel it was mutual; she was sure that they could sense it in each other. She could see a deep intensity in this boy's eyes like she'd never seen before in anyone else's.

So strong was her body's reaction that she suddenly had the urge to move away. She stood up swiftly and started to run the short distance to the sea, dislodging the flower from her hair, which floated on the gentle breeze and landed gently on the sand in her wake as she ran, shrieking and laughing with the sudden shock of the cold water as it hit her feet and washed against her legs. Mitch looked at her shapely silhouette against the sky, swaying gracefully in the water, arms raised in the air as if she could hear some intoxicating melody in her head. As if by instinct she turned around to look at him and shouted over, "Aren't you joining me?"

"I'm just admiring the view, it's beautiful from here," he shouted back. After a moment's hesitation, he took his boots off and placed them carefully against the wall, then ran down the sand towards the water. Realising that he had forgotten his socks, he ripped them off and hurled them over his shoulder as he approached the water's edge. They were caught by a wave as it lapped the shore. Melanie dissolved into fits of laughter when she saw the look on his face as they floated past his ankles and drifted out to sea. He stared at her for a moment and then started to laugh with her.

Her hair was being blown by the breeze, and as they moved closer he gently brushed it away from her face and held her close to him. He drew her towards him and kissed her again. In the magic of that moment, her passion caught fire and she kissed him back urgently. She was no longer afraid of her feelings. It felt as if a hundred butterflies were fluttering away in her stomach. She could feel his heart thudding against her, and was so happy in the knowledge that he was feeling it all too.

They stood there holding that embrace for a long time, looking out to sea and smiling. Her feet were numb, but it didn't matter, for the heat he aroused through the rest of her body more than made up for it. She caught her breath and looked out to where the sea met the sky. She imagined she could see for miles, way beyond the horizon, to beyond the point where sea and sky melded seamlessly into one. She was curious to know who was out there, what they were doing, and if they could possibly be feeling as happy as she did right now.

He looked at her and stroked her cheek. She really wanted this, him just holding her and kissing her. It felt like a dream, and one that she never wanted to wake up from.

He lifted her up and spun her round. Her clothes were thoroughly wet from the splashing. His trousers were soaking wet too, but neither of them noticed, lost in the moment as they were.

As they left the water and emerged on to the now warm and welcoming sand, she danced round and round him, spinning around and laughing all the time. He was amazed at how happy, carefree, and wild this crazy girl appeared to be. She seemed almost childlike in her joy and enthusiasm, which made her all the more exciting to be with.

He found a piece of driftwood, knelt down, and drew a heart with it in the sand. She took the wood from him and carefully traced their names within the heart. It was so romantic and such a touching gesture, she thought, but still she shivered as she couldn't help thinking that it would be gone tomorrow, washed away like a dream that wakes you in the night but disappears mysteriously from memory into sleep's hazy mist, as if it had never existed. But she knew that this wasn't a dream and that the memory of these shared moments would remain with her always, never to be forgotten.

All too soon, it seemed, it dawned on them both that time was passing and Mitch realised that he needed to make sure that Melanie was home by a reasonable hour.

"Are you cold?" he asked her. "We'd better head back before your parents start to worry about you. I wouldn't want to get off on the wrong foot with them."

It struck Melanie just how serious he must be about her if he was so concerned about her parents. A smile lit up her face as she snuggled up to him. "How thoughtful Mitch," she whispered.

They reluctantly turned their backs on the seascape which had so captivated them both, clasped hands and walked back up to the steps, where they slipped their shoes back on, oblivious to the sand and grit clinging to their wet feet. Mitch did not even give a second thought to the state his beloved new boots would be in when he eventually arrived home.

They wandered arm in arm along the prom in the direction of Melanie's house, mingling with the holidaymakers strolling along their route, neither of them paying the slightest attention to anyone but themselves. Suddenly, as they were passing a small hotel, Mitch stopped in his tracks and withdrew his arm from her shoulder. Then, with a mischievous glint in his eye, he leapt over the railings of the hotel's garden. "Back in a jiff" she heard him call over his shoulder as he disappeared over the railings and landed fairly and squarely on the grass beyond. She hardly had time to regain her breath and grasp what was happening before a huge, murky figure emerged into view in the doorway of the hotel.

"Hoy! What the hell are you doing, you young sod? That's my bloody garden!" a furious voice boomed out above them. Melanie was frozen to the spot but Mitch's senses, more sharply honed than hers, kicked into gear immediately. "Run, Melanie, run!" he shouted. "I'll catch up with you." He leapt back over the railings clutching his prize, a beautiful rose plucked in haste from the garden. Then he set off in pursuit of Melanie, who by this time was disappearing at a rate of knots. As he caught up with her they began dodging bemused holidaymakers and onlookers, closely followed by the enraged hotelier. But age and a lack of agility were against the man, who soon had to give up the chase.

As Mitch drew near to Melanie he couldn't help but admire her speed and the elegance with which she wove her way between the bodies on the bustling pavement, her young body swaying athletically from side to side.

"Whoa, Melanie, it's over, he's given up, he's knackered" shouted Mitch as he threw an arm around her. He took one last look back as they came to a stop, him laughing uncontrollably at the bewildered look on her face.

"What the hell was that about, you idiot?" she managed to gasp between breaths, her chest heaving with a mixture of mild fear and excitement. "You're crazy, Tom Mitchell, bloody crazy!"

"Oh, and you're not then I suppose, Melanie Jackson?" he replied, tilting his head to one side and raising his eyebrows quizzically in mock disdain before bursting into laughter. Any concerns dissolved instantly as she too saw the funny side of things. Regaining her composure, she tossed her head skywards, looked mockingly down her nose at him, and responded haughtily, "No, Tom Mitchell, I certainly am not. I think you'll find I'm the intelligent one. And don't you forget it. Fat chance of that though!" she added, before dissolving into uncontrollable giggles herself. "But really, what was that all about? I didn't have a clue what was going on. I just ran like hell when you screamed at me."

"Oh, nothing really" he replied, a smile spreading across his face as he slowly withdrew the flower from behind his back. "You lost your flower. It looked lovely on you, so I couldn't let you go home without one, could I?"

He drew her head towards him, gently tilting it to one side and sliding the flower into her hair, then kissed her on the forehead.

"Oh Mitch, you're just so... so romantic" she whispered, and a warm glow spread through her body.

"I know" was his swift response. "Aren't you the lucky one, Jackson?"

When the moment was over Mitch turned back to see the frustrated hotelier in the distance. He was still gazing at the pair of them, hands on hips and a furious expression on his face. Feeling a touch guilty, Mitch threw him an apologetic wave and smiled to himself as the hotelier returned it with a two-fingered salute.

They passed most of the walk home in a strangely satisfying and comforting silence, exchanging the occasional contented smile, both blissfully happy just being together, absorbing and relishing the depth of feelings and emotions the evening had aroused within them. On reaching Melanie's house they settled down together on the wall to savour their final, lingering moments together before Melanie would be forced to break the spell and comply with her curfew.

Mitch gazed longingly into Melanie's eyes, scarcely believing how beautiful she looked in the glow of a nearby street light. Melanie's senses were heightened. She picked up on the almost imperceptible change that had gradually come over Mitch, and wondered what he was thinking as he assumed a more serious look. After a long silence, Mitch, looking hesitant and more than a touch out of his comfort zone, drew in a long, deep breath and gazed deep into Melanie's eyes. In a gentle voice, he finally broke the lingering silence.

"Melanie" he sighed, "I'm not very good at expressing my feelings and, well, erm... well... you really are the most beautiful girl I've ever seen. And you're so different, in so many ways. I just don't have the words to express my feelings. I've never said this to anyone else before, but I think I love you Melanie. I love being with you. I love everything about you. I, er... I didn't think it was possible to feel like this about anyone. Ever." his voice trailed off as he gazed, anxiously, into her eyes, desperately hoping for some kind of positive reaction; willing her to respond.

Melanie's heart soared and skipped a beat. She was giddy with delight. Her mind was racing, her brain scrambled by the emotions tumbling and pounding through her head as she came to realise that this was the real thing; he really did love her, and she loved him. Her head was spinning, her heart was pounding. Every fibre of her young body was tingling. Unable to put her feelings into words, she did what came most naturally to her. She sank into Mitch's waiting arms and responded to his tender kiss with an intensity and passion that not only surprised her but left him in no doubt as to how she truly felt about him.

It was Mitch's turn to experience the feelings of elation as his spirits soared, his pulse raced and he came to realise that his dream girl had fallen hopelessly in love with him too. An intense longing seemed to jangle every nerve in his body. The feeling lingered long after their lips parted, for he would never forget that moment when Melanie sighed, allowed her forehead to come to rest so naturally on his chin, her body leaning against his, before she slowly raised her head, gazed directly into his eyes and whispered, "I think I love you too Mitch. I don't know how. I don't know why. I hardly know you at all, and yet... deep down, I just know I want these feelings to go on forever. You've made me feel things I've never felt before either. I just feel so happy and alive when I'm with you."

Born on different sides of the track, but with eyes only for each other, they gelled perfectly in that moment when they looked lovingly into each other's eyes; two young hearts beating strongly as one in the warm glow of the heady summer moonlight; a soothing summer breeze drifting idly and playfully across their young faces. But it was only a moment, for just then the porch light flickered into life, shaking them back into reality. It was the signal that the witching hour was rapidly approaching and Melanie's mother was preparing for her daughter's return.

They were both in the middle of end-of-term exams and realised it might be a while before they could meet up again, but Mitch promised he would find some way of keeping in touch with her until then. Having said their goodbyes, they reluctantly parted. As Melanie walked towards the front door, she turned to watch Mitch heading homeward, but he was still standing at the gate, and her heart was lifted again as she saw him mouth the words "I love you." She mouthed back "I love you too" and blew a silent kiss that floated gracefully across the night air to the young boy she now knew she loved with all her heart.

As he wandered homewards, with an unusual spring in his stride, Mitch savoured the events of the evening and the feelings their shared passion had aroused in him. He'd never experienced anything approaching true love. He'd seen it at the movies and scoffed at it with his friends, believing it would never happen to him. It was such a shock to his normally carefree system that it took some time for him to come to terms with reality, and accept that love was real. He loved everything about Melanie; she was the perfect girl, beautiful, intelligent, funny, and exciting to be with all at the same time. She made him smile, she made him laugh. She had such a passion for life, a true free spirit, and he knew he really loved her. Being with his mates would take second place from here on.

When Mitch arrived home, his senses still reeling and with a beaming smile on his face, he bumped into his dad in the hallway. His father looked him up and down before pronouncing, "Crikey son, where've you been? Those new boots of yours are in a hell of a mess. What have you got to smile about?"

Mitch's gaze dropped to his cherished new boots, but the grin remained.

"Aw, what the hell Dad, they're only a pair of boots," he said. "I'll survive."

A knowing smile flickered across his father's face as it dawned on him that there had to be a girl involved for his son to act with such good grace. "Fancy a nightcap and a smoke while you tell me all about it son?"

"Yeah, why not Dad? Sounds good to me" said Mitch, and the pair of them headed off into the lounge together.

As Melanie entered her home she was oblivious to the fact that a conversation had been taking place earlier between her mother and father. Her recent behaviour had not gone unnoticed by her parents. They were aware of the change in her, and had decided that they needed to talk to her about whatever it was that seemed to be troubling her.

"It will be some boy" Julia sighed, resigned to the inevitable. "Have a chat with her when she comes home Jim. She listens to you, but I might as well be talking to the wall."

James wasn't too sure about that. His daughter would listen to him if he was helping her with her maths homework or they were discussing some world event on the news, but he doubted that she would listen to his advice on personal matters such as relationships. However, he did not voice these thoughts to his wife. He just waited patiently for

Melanie to come home wondering how he was going to approach the subject

After switching the porch light on to welcome her daughter home, her mother had gone to bed feeling dejected that her daughter wouldn't engage in any conversation with her about her personal life, but then Melanie had always been a secretive and stubborn child at the best of times.

Not long afterwards Melanie came rushing in with a flushed, excited look on her face. "Hi Dad" she exclaimed, initially pleased to see that he had waited up for her on his own and that her mother had already gone to bed.

James dived straight in. "So, who's the boy?" he enquired. He looked at Melanie, eyebrows raised quizzically.

This was not a conversation she wanted with her father, most definitely not now with her emotions so heightened with the events of the evening.

"Who says there's a boy?" she said. "Can we talk about it another time, Dad? I'm not too sure about it all myself yet." The words tumbled instinctively from her lips. She could see that her father was every bit as uncomfortable with the conversation as she was, so she added, "Don't worry Dad. I'm just having fun. There really is nothing to worry about."

"OK, but I just want you to know that your mother and I are here for you if there is anything you would like to talk about. We just don't want you to get hurt."

As if I'd talk to either of you about it, thought Melanie, but she just smiled and kissed him on the top of his head. To all outward appearances, James, seemingly satisfied with that answer, replied "OK, off to bed with you then. It's late and you've got exams coming up. And don't forget to shout goodnight to your mother. She worries about you too, you know."

But James was not stupid. He had noticed the new flower in his daughter's somewhat bedraggled hair and the dried sand on her toes. But he wisely kept his thoughts to himself. He was well aware of his daughter's need to express herself as an individual and explore her own emotions, make her own decisions and ultimately take responsibility for the consequences of her actions. It was all part of the growing-up process, he reasoned, and he appreciated the need for her to start finding her own way in life and learn to deal with the feelings and emotions which were part of growing up.

After Melanie had made her way off up to bed, James poured himself a large whiskey and settled into his favourite armchair, alone with his thoughts.

Up in her room, Melanie decided that she was not only ready to talk to her friends about Mitch but looking forward to it. She felt a blossoming confidence about their relationship. She couldn't wait to tell them all about Mitch and their evening together, to share with them what he was really like and how she'd grown to love him. She was bursting with emotions and dying to share them. Something had wound itself round her heart.

CHAPTER 11

The morning after

When Melanie woke up the morning after the party, thoughts immediately came into her head from the time she'd spent with Mitch when they'd slipped away by themselves and shared such a wonderful evening. An evening alone, just the two of them getting to know each other properly, she thought as she savoured the lovely, delicious memory of how happy she had felt. Mitch's laugh was echoing in her ears and she smiled at the thought. Her body was tingling from head to toe as she lay warm and drowsy under her covers, daydreaming.

She was unaware of the conversation happening in the next bedroom between her parents.

"Did you talk to Melanie last night, Jim?"

"Yes, and I think there's definitely something different about her. Like you said, it's probably some boy that's turned her head, but it was bound to happen, Julia. You know you can't wrap her up in cotton wool. She's too headstrong to listen to us. Never has really. But she's a sensible girl."

Julia wasn't so sure. Her mind went back to her own early teenage years. She knew all too well that some boys could be controlling, manipulative and charming smooth talkers, turning otherwise clear-thinking, intelligent girls into silly, giggling, blushing wrecks in their presence. She also knew how sensitive her daughter was and how deep her feelings could go. She couldn't bear the thought that she might get hurt. But Julia was also resigned to the fact that such things were inevitable in the scheme of teenage life and that it would do absolutely no good talking to her. It would be the same old story, as if her parents had never experienced anything like it, and they'd get that look of hers that says they come from a different planet. She smiled ironically to herself. If only Melanie knew, she thought, as she reminisced about her own youth, which didn't seem that long ago; those heady days of adolescence, fun, laughter, love, hurt and pain.

She also worried that to gain freedom in life, some teenagers automatically rebel against authority figures. Julia wasn't willing to take that risk where Melanie was concerned. Both she and James had always tried to give her a certain amount of freedom to express herself and take control of her own life and its consequences and she didn't want to start imposing strict boundaries now. Her one big regret was that her own daughter didn't feel able, or to have the desire possibly, to share her innermost feelings with her.

Later that morning Melanie left her house in a jubilant frame of mind to collect Anna as usual, and they headed off towards Shirley's house, gossiping about the night before. Anna had promised not to say anything to her about Mitch until they were all together, and she had readily agreed because she didn't want to have to be the one to upset her friend, as she now realised they inevitably would.

The girls loved meeting at Shirley's. She had been given the use of the basement of their big old boarding house, which took in visitors in the summer, and she was allowed to do exactly what she wanted with it, so consequently it was their favourite place in the whole world. The girls had painted the walls and ceiling black and scattered glitter on the floor. When listening to music they used red light bulbs in the lamps, with a small glitterball hooked up to the beamed ceiling, complemented by strings of fairy lights dangling from corner to corner to enhance the mood and atmosphere as they danced around laughing and making silhouettes on the walls.

Shirley and Melanie, the two 'artists' of the group, had painted on the walls; blinding, surreal explosions of psychedelic colours, abstract intense swirls, a kaleidoscope of red, orange, and purple. There were posters torn out of magazines about the Beatles, the Stones, Simon and Garfunkel and Bob Dylan, sitting alongside iconic fashion idols, Twiggy and Jean 'the Shrimp' Shrimpton, portraying 'Swinging London' and all it had to offer young girls. When they were younger they had had their first introduction to alcohol in that very cellar, a half bottle of whiskey mixed with lemonade, which Sammy and Melanie had downed only to be violently sick soon after. But now they had become much more accustomed to alcohol, and they'd started to experiment with smoking, exhaling out of the little window where they could just see the feet of people walking past. They spent endless hours imagining who the feet belonged to and making up stories about them.

They could play loud music in this basement and had held several parties there. Initially they were innocent, all-girl parties full of dancing, music, and laughter. But latterly they had moved on to the introduction of some boys, which involved those games of spin the bottle and postman's knock where the most daring thing a girl had to do was to follow a boy into the corner and let him kiss her, whilst telling him to keep his hands to himself. And of course, if they were lucky, or clever and devious enough, they would make sure they got to kiss the ones they really fancied, the cute-looking boys they were all attracted to, especially if they came with the reputation of being somewhat adventurous. Those who were classed as wet and wimpy were dismissed disdainfully and despatched with the merest peck on the lips to skulk back to their pals, their tails between their legs. Girls could be so harsh at times to unsuspecting, gullible young boys, but to them that was of no consequence

Remnants of Shirley's childhood could be found stuffed away in various cardboard boxes in the corners of the room: toys, stuffed animals, broken dolls, children's books, annuals, dressing-up clothes. The furniture was old, but serviceable, its appearance enhanced by blankets draped tastefully over the old sofas and coloured cushions scattered haphazardly in a Bohemian style, which the girls considered to be extremely becoming and up to date with the fashions they'd seen in the magazines of the time. Music was their constant companion as they gathered in that cellar; a transistor radio served to keep the girls up to date with all the latest new releases which filled the airwaves from dawn to dusk, reaching out to its mainly teenage audience across the land. A treasured record player provided ample opportunity for them to play their ever-growing collection of records, blasting out music at full volume for parties or simply playing their favourite singles or LPs as they passed the time away in animated conversation. There were magazines depicting teenage fashion and agony columns on what to do if your boyfriend is cheating, dumps you or wants sex, which they read and re-read to each other with varying degrees of amusement. This summer they were going to have their first real party, and had already started making plans for it.

None of Melanie's friends were looking forward to having to talk to her about Mitch. It was obvious to them now that she was mad about him, and they had a strong sense that she wouldn't listen. She had always been a determined, independent person and they had no reason to believe that she would pay any attention to anything they had to say.

As the most sensible one, it had been agreed that Shirley should be the first to broach the subject and put the girls' point of view, something which she really wasn't comfortable in doing, even though she realised she was probably the best qualified.

With some tension in the air and hesitation in her voice, she started to speak.

"It's lovely to see you so happy Melanie," she began. "I've

never seen you quite so happy. Mitch must have made some impression on you."

"He has," replied Melanie. "He really has, Shirley. He's just so different from any other boy I've ever met. Last night was just so wonderful. He's just so intense, so loving and thoughtful. And he really does love me. I never thought I'd feel like this over a boy."

"Mmmm... that's what's troubling us a bit, now you mention it" observed Shirley, latching on to the opening Melanie had afforded her. "We're all just a bit concerned actually as, well... from what we've heard, he doesn't seem to be your type. The type of boy you'd fall for."

"You just don't know him, Shirley. None of you do. He's so genuine. He really is. When he's not with the lads he's so different. I've seen the real Mitch."

"Well that's true I suppose. None of us really know him, but...'

The rest of Shirley's response was left hanging in the air, as Anna could contain herself no longer. "But we know what he's like without meeting him. His reputation goes before him. He's a chancer, a player. He breaks girls' hearts. And I know that for a fact as Tony told me, and he's his best friend. Even he didn't have a good word to say about him. Well, hardly anyway," she added hastily after seeing the looks of horror on the other girls' faces as the impact of what she had said struck home.

"That's a bit harsh, Anna" Shirley quickly interjected. "We're all just a bit concerned that we know so little about him, that's all. And you didn't talk to us about him. That's so unlike you. You're always so enthusiastic about exciting things in your life," she added, trying to soften the blow for

Melanie and to take the heat out of the situation. She flashed daggers across the room at Anna.

"I was ready to. In fact, I was bursting to share it all with you today," Melanie said dejectedly. "You just don't understand how I'm feeling. I can't describe it, but I've got my head screwed on too, I wouldn't let myself fall for someone who would treat me badly. You haven't seen the way he was when we were alone, the special moments we had last night, the feelings we shared."

Shirley, sensing the depth of Melanie's feelings, responded sympathetically to her friend "I know, Melanie. It's only because we care so much about you. It's just that you've been acting a bit out of character recently, and it's so unlike you. Sometimes lately you've seemed lost inside that head of yours, as if you can't make sense of your thoughts. We're your best friends. We are just here for you no matter what, but we've noticed a change in you and we're worried as you haven't seemed as happy as usual."

"I just can't believe you're all saying these things to me. Can't you see that I'm happier than I've ever been? Don't you think I've thought it through? You're my friends, and I thought of all people you'd be happy for me. Maybe last week I was preoccupied and had my doubts, but after last night I do know how I feel about him and how he feels about me, I really do!"

In truth, everything had happened so suddenly, and against her better judgement in many ways. Melanie still couldn't quite comprehend how she could feel this way about a boy, or him about her. She still wasn't one hundred percent sure how deep his feelings went for her, but she was learning to trust and believe in him, she thought. Little did she know that she was having the same effect on Mitch.

At this stage, sharing Shirley's concern for their friend, Sammy took over. "Look, we get no pleasure from telling you this. I can deal with boys like that, but you're different, you're much more sensitive than me. I can take them or leave them, and up until now I thought you could too, but now I'm not so sure. I've seen the change in you as well, and I'm concerned for you. We all are. You are part of us, and none of us want to see you hurt, that's all."

"I understand why you think that," said Melanie, "but as far as I'm concerned he proved last night how much I mean to him and I'm different from any other girl he's ever known. Maybe you just don't like him because he snubbed you at the party? It was only because he wanted me to himself. I know he comes across as quite cocky in company, but he's not like that at all really. He's gentle and caring and... oh, I could go on but I know you won't want to hear it."

Her friends looked at each other and could see that it was hopeless. "Well, just don't say we didn't warn you." said Anna in frustration, dismissive as ever, and in truth bored with the topic. "Anyway Sammy, what happened to you last night?"

"I struck lucky and met a boy with a car!" Sammy sensed that enough had been said and wanted to move on for Melanie's sake.

"Ooh!" said Anna, "What kind?"

"I don't know. A big red one, and its dead flash! And he's left school! He's taking me to the pictures on Friday. I'll fill you all in when we meet up on Saturday. What are we doing on Saturday anyway? Any parties likely? More importantly, what shall we do this afternoon? We could listen to the top 40 on the radio, or take a trip up to the holiday camp maybe?" She looked around questioningly at the others.

The holiday camp was where they sometimes hung out in the summer, going swimming in the pool or simply sitting in the café. They'd recently hooked up on a casual basis with a group of the college day boys who also frequented the place, Mark, the ringleader, Phil, Charlie, Pete, and Luke; the camp was one of their regular haunts. They were a disparate bunch of older boys, extremely outgoing, somewhat daring, a touch wild at times even, and good fun to be around for a group of young, easily-influenced teenage girls.

As it happened it was only two short weeks before that they had last been there, sitting drinking Coke, when another cute college boy, who quite clearly had the hots for Melanie, had come over with his friend and started talking to Melanie and Sammy. His name was Johnnie. Melanie had been instantly attracted to his easy manner and nice smile and had felt a slight crush developing. At the time, she'd even felt it might go somewhere as she'd thought he was so friendly and open, but he held no interest for her now, and nor did the camp for that matter. In fact, the camp was the last place she wanted to go, so she managed to persuade them all to pop into town, do a bit of window shopping around the boutiques and spend the rest of their time at one of the town's local cafés.

Felice's was their café of choice, it being the most trendy one. It had pinball machines and a juke box with all the recent chart singles, so it was a gathering place for teenagers, many of whom were among their friends. Most importantly for Melanie, she'd discovered in conversation that it wasn't one of Mitch's haunts, so she knew she could relax there with no likelihood of him or his mates appearing on the scene to cause any embarrassing moments, or give her friends any ammunition to back up their concerns for her, genuine as she knew they were.

The rest of the day passed without any further mention of Mitch, which was a relief for Melanie. When she arrived home later that afternoon in a pensive mood, she was met by the sight of the table, set out for the usual Sunday tea, complete with wilting lettuce. It served to bring home to her once more the dullness of her parents' routine, although they seemed very happy in the life they'd made for themselves, the routines they'd come to welcome and adhere to. She knew she was being unkind to them, but her feelings were heightened by the first flush of young love and the desire to break rules, rush at life and just break free. She simply couldn't understand why her mother didn't want more than this; more excitement, more adventure, a bigger piece of that world out there.

As soon as she could, Melanie went to her room to listen to the radio. She suddenly felt exhausted and emotional, but was still determined that her friends had got it wrong. She could still feel Mitch's lips on hers, his breath as he whispered in her ear the beautiful words he had spoken. Her friends just didn't understand. They had never been in love. She and Mitch had this amazing connection. At the same time a part of her did wonder if he might be dangerous for her, but that only sent a shiver down her spine and heightened the intensity of her feeling.

She closed her eyes as a love song on the radio drifted

across the room; it seemed more relevant, more vivid, than ever before. When nobody else understood the way that she was feeling, these songs did, and she felt they were speaking out to her personally. Songs she had never noticed before, or at least had meant nothing to her up until then, seemed to be expressing every thought she was having, exaggerating every emotion, and helping her to work through and understand them.

Her thoughts drifted to the end of term and the summer holidays, which promised to be eight weeks of pure pleasure. Friends, Mitch, sunshine, all the excitement of a holiday town filled with visitors and the social buzz that went with it. She'd have money to spend from a part-time job she'd managed to secure in a local hotel, and the future looked rosy. If anything, Melanie's friends, and their warnings were pushing Melanie closer to Mitch. She just knew this was real. It was the first time she had felt this way, and she would prove them wrong. Deep down she sensed that Mitch would too, once they got to know him and realised just how different he was from the boy they thought they knew.

Two days later, when Melanie arrived home from school and went into the kitchen, she found her mother standing there, a knowing look on her face and raised eyebrows, waving an envelope in the air. "You've got post, Melanie. Have you got a secret admirer that you've been hiding from us by any chance?"

Blushing, Melanie swiftly responded, "Why on earth would you think that mother? "It's probably just from one of my friends."

"Oh, really darling? And do your friends usually draw hearts and kisses on the back of an envelope?"

Embarrassed, and blushing even more profusely now, Melanie was stumped for an answer. She took the envelope from her mother's hand, placed it casually to one side and sat down at the table without further ado.

"Well, aren't you going to open it then darling?" her mother asked, stifling a smile as she saw her daughter squirming uncomfortably in her chair.

"Of course not, Mother. It's probably just some prankster playing a practical joke anyway. I'll open it later. Can we just drop it now please?"

The meal passed off without any further reference to the matter, with Melanie putting on an almost convincing display of acting normally. But her mind was racing. She was wondering if it was from Mitch, or if not, who else it could possibly be from. As soon as she deemed it reasonable however, she made her excuses, rose from the table, and casually collected the envelope from its resting place before withdrawing upstairs to her room. There she ripped the envelope open, holding her breath as she withdrew the letter and settled down on her bed to read it.

1st July 1967

Dear Melanie

This is the first time I have ever written to any girlfriend so I hope you're impressed. I certainly am! See what an effect you have on me.

I know we haven't known each other for very long but I think I fell in love with you the very first time we met and that's never happened to me before. I know we can't meet up again until next week but I'm missing you already and next week seems such a long time away so I thought I'd write to you. I hope you're missing me too and looking forward to seeing me again.

The very first time I saw you my heart skipped a beat and I couldn't take my eyes off you. I was so pleased when you smiled back at me across the dance floor the other week and I was so happy when I realised you might fancy me too. It took me a little time to pluck up the courage to ask you to dance as I've never actually danced before, not like that anyway, but when I did you were really lovely and never laughed at me once! Bet you felt like it though.

And then the other night on the beach with you! I loved every minute of being in your company and you were so much fun to be with.

You have such beautiful eyes and a fabulous smile. I could just stare into your eyes for hours and just swoon. (I know you like poetry so I hope you like that one, I picked it up from one of the poems we're doing at school for GCE's) And you said you like my eyes too. Do they really make you go weak at the knees or were you just saying that to make me feel good? Nobody's ever said that to me before, so it's really quite exciting. And you are definitely the best kisser of all the girlfriends I've ever had, and I've had a few, not that I'm bragging of course. But your lips are so soft and tender and when we kiss you give me goose bumps and make me feel tingly all over! Nobody's ever done that to me before either.

Of all the things in the world there are two that I really love the most but guess what, you come out on top because I love you the best. That makes Manchester United only runners up! So that's how much I love you. Aren't you the lucky one!

I know you can't make it this week because of your school disco and I don't know what group is on at the Palace next week, but I thought it might be nice to meet up there. I could meet you on the steps outside about half eight if that's OK. I'll be with the boys but I'll be easy to spot. I'll be the tall, good looking one and I'll be wearing my Cuban heel boots so you'll have to stand on your toes to kiss me!

My mates all think I'm soppy and give me some stick because they can't understand why I'd rather be with you than with them, but I don't care because you're such good fun to be with. Anyway, I think they all secretly fancy you too and they're just jealous! I'll probably pop to the Woody with them first for a couple of pints before we head down to the Palace. If it's a nice night perhaps we could have a walk along the prom first or maybe just sit on the steps outside and just have a chat together before we go in.

The beer's quite good at the Palace and we never have a problem getting served. I don't know what you drink yet but I don't suppose you drink beer. Most girls I know seem to like Sherry or Babycham for some unknown reason. Yeugh!

This is the longest letter I've ever written so I think I must really love you. As we both like the Beatles I'm sending this letter with 'All my Loving' and with love 'From Me to You'. I know, I'm just so romantic.

Love

Mitch

p.s. these are my thumbprints in ink. Please send me yours if you love me.

Melanie read the letter over excitedly, again and again, and couldn't help smiling and laughing each time she did so. She had had love letters from young admirers before, but never one quite like this one; cocky, amusing and somehow so romantic and unusual all at the same time. He loved her more than Manchester United? For heaven's sake! What kind of compliment was that to give to a girl? He really was a one-off. But beneath it all she could sense how genuine he was and how expressive, and her heart warmed to him. In her excitement, she couldn't wait to reply and to let him know just how much she loved him too.

3rd July 1967

Dear Mitch

Thank you for your letter. It was really unexpected, and so good to hear from you.

I can't believe you think you have fallen in love with me! It's 11 o'clock and I've just got into bed. I have twenty German words to learn by tomorrow but I don't care, I'd rather write to you instead. (I hate German anyway!) Sorry about the writing but it's quite dark.

You won't know this, but I saw you a few weeks ago at the Palace and I thought you were the cutest guy I'd ever seen. Tall, dark hair, deep eyes and I know other girls thought you were good looking too. Unfortunately, I didn't know your name or anything about you then.

I went again the next week in the hope of seeing you. My mum had just bought me a dress I really wanted. It is an orange and purple mini dress. I wore it and was so excited because I thought I might see you and was so unhappy you weren't there.

So, that moment a couple of weeks ago, I knew someone

was watching me intently from the side of the dance floor but it was dark and I couldn't make out who it was. When I turned around and looked closely it was you, and when I realised you were smiling at me I was so happy I got butterflies in my stomach, and you just looked at me with this amazing sparkle in your eyes. When you asked me to dance I felt like I could have stayed on the dance floor with you forever, and I was so upset when you just walked off, I didn't think I'd see you again.

I've had a few boyfriends but none that made me feel like you did. I was in my own world when you kissed me later that night nothing and nobody else mattered.

I was quite worried about going to Tony's party though, as I wasn't sure how you felt, but I ended up having the best time ever with you down on the beach.

Actually, I thought you were a bit big headed (but then all boys are) so was really surprised to get such a romantic letter from you.

I can't believe you love me more than Manchester United! That's really got to be the biggest compliment ever! All boys love football, I think it's boring but it's always on in our house as my dad loves football. He supports Liverpool. I used to find it a real drag but now I just go down town and hang out with my friends. We usually go to one of the local cafes for a coke, but I've never seen you or your friends in any of them.

I really can't believe you feel the same way as me. Of course I want to meet you again, but as you know I can't make this weekend as it's our school dance, I wish you could come, but it's strictly for our school and boys from the college. It won't be the same for me without you there, but I'm meant to be going to the Palace with my friends the following week. They don't like me being with you, but maybe we could 'accidentally' bump into each other and I would love to go for a walk with you. And I love beer! In fact, I drink anything, but I'll have to be careful as my dad might be picking me up and he was suspicious a few weeks ago when I got in the car after getting a bit drunk at a party.

Did you watch Top of the Pops the other night? That song by Percy something gave me goose bumps and I just love the Hollies. I don't like that Jimmy Savile though, he gives me the creeps!

I was just so embarrassed at school the other day. I was just daydreaming and doodling in Physics when the teacher came up to me and told me off for not paying attention. I had only gone and written 'I love Mich' on my pencil case, which he held up in class and said 'Well, isn't Mich the lucky one!' I could have died (and I spelt your name wrong!)

I've got to go now, counting the days til we meet again and 'do you want to know a secret?' I think I love you too.

Lots of love

Melanie Xxxx

p.s. I couldn't find any ink, so I pricked my thumb and tried to do my thumbprint for you in blood!

Mitch received the letter the following day and anxiously ripped it open, as he knew it just had to be from Melanie. His eyes lit up when he saw her response. That is until he reached the end of the letter. "Huh!" he muttered. "She only *thinks* she loves me?" What was up with the girl? Couldn't she see how sincere he was? He would have to find some way of getting into that dance and then they'd see what she thought of those college boys. But he could tell in his heart that she did indeed love him, for he knew her well enough to know that she was quite shy about expressing her feelings and it must have taken a lot for her to commit them to paper. That school dance was definitely on his agenda now.

CHAPTER 12

The end of term approaches

The girls were already experiencing the thrills of the new world that were opening up to them, a world which afforded so many opportunities for them to spread their wings and become immersed in the social whirl that was becoming available to them outside the school environment. They were graduating away from the rather tame and somewhat restrained atmosphere they'd previously experienced at school discos, which Miss Latimer would dutifully supervise with her beady eyes, ably assisted by a range of her equally-vigilant colleagues.

However, whilst the girls considered these more formal

discos as dull as dishwater and way behind the times, carefully arranged and heavily supervised as they were, they realised that they did indeed serve a useful purpose. For they were attended by the pupils of the nearby private school for boys, the College, and thus provided the girls with their opportunity to mix with boys of their own age in a convivial social setting. Soon they were discovering the fun of weighing up who was cute and who was not, who was hot, who was not and, even more daringly, who was sexy, a new word that had entered their vocabulary, and one which quickly became established as the ultimate accolade that could be bestowed upon a boy. And there was so much for the girls to weigh up and chatter about for days afterwards, providing endless hours of gossip and excited chit chat from dawn to dusk and often beyond for huddles of excited young females vying with each other to voice their opinions to whoever was prepared to listen. Every one of them became immersed in the thrill and delight of this enthralling experience, and it was happening at school, of all places. How heavenly it seemed to them; school would never be the same again. A corner had been turned, and to hell with Miss Latimer, they were absolutely going to make the most of it.

Secret notes and love letters between the girls and boys of the two schools was a time-honoured tradition, but it was new to Melanie's age group. The mantle was passed down to Lower Five from the older girls, and they saw Melanie and Sammy as a natural choice to carry out this custom, delivering and collecting the post at secretly-arranged drop-off points or at a hastily-organised after-school rendezvous. Occasionally, when the missives assumed a degree of urgency that warranted such risk-taking, the two girls would dutifully weigh up their options, throw caution to the wind and take it in turn to 'disappear', with the other one covering during a free period or lessons in the afternoon.

These two were more than happy to take on this role of the 'go-betweeners' as they would become known. They were excited by the prospect and prepared to take on the responsibility and confidentiality required. They were young enough to be a little bit in awe of the older girls and therefore put themselves at risk for them, yet at the same time they were old enough to understand the importance of their position. The realisation that they might now be included as recipients of such letters was an added incentive.

Imagine the anticipation as they collected them, the hopes and disappointments, the fun of passing them onto their friends, the ups, and downs, the promise of relationships and romances that it would all entail. It was a rite of passage for the two of them, a transition in social status, and they weren't going to let anyone down.

Anna and Shirley had not been included in this new part of their school life, Shirley because she would have deemed such actions as inappropriate and too risky. However, she still had her own secret hopes that a letter would land her way, so she wasn't above allowing others to take risks on her behalf. After all, some of the boys were so cute, sexy even – although that was a term Shirley couldn't quite bring herself to use in front of others, at this early stage at least.

Anna was not to be trusted with confidential matters, and her lunchtimes and free periods were far too precious to her anyway. She spent her free time devouring magazines left behind in the art room by sixth formers, and discussing the latest fashions with some of the older girls. She just couldn't get enough when it came to tips on looking good.

This 'passion post', as it became known, did indeed start to include letters for Sammy and Melanie, as the pair came into contact with boys from the College more often.

The Monday morning following Tony's party was no different from any other school day, except that it was the last week of term. The general buzz of conversation was louder and more animated than usual as Melanie climbed aboard the school bus and took her seat next to Sammy. She had watched Sammy grow from a quiet, subdued child to the self-assured extrovert she had become, and she never tired of looking at her pretty face every morning with its warm smile.

Sammy's mother had married and had her daughter when she was very young. Sammy had three younger brothers, the youngest of whom was hardly more than a baby. Her mother devoted all her time to child care. With never a moment to herself, she seemed permanently distracted, disorganised and disjointed. Her father ran his own business, worked long hours and was hardly ever there. When he was home he rarely participated in family life. In fact, he appeared to cause more conflict when he was home by upsetting the normal family routines whilst Sammy's mother tried hopelessly to calm all the emotional undercurrents of a busy household.

To Melanie they appeared to be a very religious family, as they were of the Catholic faith and went to church regularly, something she hadn't done herself since the early days of her attendance at Sunday school, which, as far as Melanie could remember, had been more of a social occasion than a religious one.

Sammy had attended a convent school in her junior years and some of the stories she had shared with Melanie amazed her. She was staggered to hear about the strictness, the punishments and the feelings of isolation. Melanie had always thought it strange that Sammy sat alone in the classroom whilst everyone else participated in the usual daily chaos of the morning assembly where the girls whispered and giggled to each other as the teachers, throwing their gowns up over their shoulders, rushed in and tried to shush them before the Headmistress took her place on the stage. When she had brought the question up once, Sammy had explained that she was excluded from morning assembly as the school's religion and hers held different beliefs. Melanie didn't really understand this concept but she did wonder if the extreme rebellious streak she saw in her friend was a reaction to these experiences and influences in her early life.

Melanie loved to study and learn new things, but she couldn't help but rebel against the constraints and petty rules that were regularly imposed. She and Sammy were forever being called in to see the Headmistress or being placed in detention for simple things like not wearing proper uniform, using make up, wearing jewellery, having their skirts too short, smoking, skiving, or generally playing up in class. They shared an instinctive defiance to authoritarian figures and a refusal to conform just for the sake of it. They were both naturally clever, but as they moved into their teens their reports were starting to deteriorate. They were a contradiction. They participated in all the activities that school had to offer, such as drama, art, and sport and they had initiated a guitar class and a chess club, but they were so full of life and intellectual capacity that they could not help but question everything they deemed unfair or unnecessary, to the annoyance of most of their teachers.

Melanie's mother had certainly noticed the change in comments on her daughter's school reports lately: Melanie 'could do better', 'doesn't give her all'. She needed to contain her rebellious streak, stop messing around and use the intelligence she was possessed with. Such comments had never featured previously.

The sixties were a time of change for women, and Julia was conscious that Melanie would have many more opportunities than she had had in her life. She had already heard about feminism creating new possibilities for women in education and the workplace. She knew that if her Melanie could go on to higher education she could make something of herself, and consider a career that Julia herself could only have dreamt about, instead of settling for the traditional role of wife and mother. Julia knew that Melanie possessed all her own qualities and more – intelligence, a free-thinking attitude, a strong character with already defined opinions – and she would be able to demonstrate those qualities in this changing world if only she could emerge from this rebellious period.

Melanie secretly admired two of her teachers, although she would never admit to it. They were her Latin teacher and her Maths teacher, both strict disciplinarians. They were both married, and Melanie couldn't even begin to contemplate what their husbands must be like. She imagined small, downtrodden men completely ruled by these large ugly women whenever they left the school behind and gave them some family time, which didn't seem to be that often. But strangely, and for reasons she couldn't even fathom herself, she had grown to respect both teachers in her own way. She recognised that each of them ultimately had the students' best interests at heart. They were exceptional teachers in their fields, whose sole intent was to give their all, and they tried to run the school with perfection, even if that involved ruling with an iron rod.

Melanie was mystified by this view that she had of them, as these were not women who conformed to the stereotypical role of a wife that she was used to. She admired their strength of character, and the fact that they had careers and a purpose in life; that they never for a split second doubted who they were or what their destiny was. She was slowly, almost subconsciously, becoming aware of the shifting values from the conservative and traditional perceptions of her mother's generation to the current more enlightened way of thinking, whereby young women had greater expectations than to spend their lives chained to the house and bringing up a family.

Anna had no interest in the educational side of school. Indeed, she had no aspirations whatsoever in furthering herself academically. She couldn't wait to finish school the following year and find a job that paid some real money. She imagined herself working in one of the new, flourishing boutiques, surrounded by lovely clothes and accessories as she dished out her advice and superior knowledge to other young girls.

Shirley was quiet and studious, but she had little ambition or vision for how her future would be shaped, unlike Sammy and Melanie, who already knew they were going to escape the Island and go on to higher education. Although Island life was exciting to them now, and offered everything they could possibly wish for, including a high level of freedom for girls so young, they were also becoming aware that there was even more out there to experience. Indeed, they regularly discussed how they would both go off to be students in 'Swinging' London. They had read magazine articles avidly on the fashion boutiques of Carnaby Street and the Kings Road, the pure decadence of the music scene and free love, although they weren't too sure exactly what that was. To them London seemed to be such a shining, fashionable, and hip city scene that they longed to be part of, and they couldn't wait to get there.

CHAPTER 13

The end of term dance

There was a tangible air of excitement amongst all the pupils now that the long school holidays were in sight and the end of term dance was looming so close. School was jumping with life, and the passion post escalated to dizzy heights that week. Sammy and Melanie had their work cut out collecting and delivering all the notes and letters without being caught, although there was a distinct relaxation in the teachers' approach to life as the long summer awaited them as well.

The young college boys' ardour was growing, with a flurry of vital information, secret assignations, and arrangements to be made, telephone numbers, addresses, and dates with girls they admired to be organised furtively before this lifeline of communication was to be cut from them. There were also plenty of requests to meet up at the school dance, and the girls would chatter incessantly about it; the delight of being able to discard their school uniforms and replace them with the latest miniskirts, bell bottoms and psychedelic dresses, to let their hair hang long and straight and make up to be applied, focusing on dark eyeliner and pale lips, a look that was not only all the rage at the time but also released them from the conventionality of the school uniform and shouted individuality and freedom.

The four girls all had their fair share of written requests from the college boys and laughed as they showed each other some of the inept attempts to ask for a date or a dance. Girls were sneaking off at lunchtime in droves to meet boys at various places on the beach and trying to hide amongst the rocks, and teachers could sometimes be seen patrolling the little promenade in their gowns, most of them half-heartedly, being only too aware that boys meeting girls was as old as time and that any punishment dished out at this stage of term was futile.

As the day of the dance arrived, Melanie's friends couldn't fail to notice that she lacked the enthusiasm of everyone else. More than anything she wanted to see Mitch, but she knew he would not be there. In fact, Melanie was secretly building up doubts again in her head. When she was with him, she believed in everything he said. She knew he meant it when he told her she was beautiful and he loved her, but when she had been apart from him for a while, doubts would creep in, not helped by the negative attitude of her friends. Still feeling a certain amount of insecurity about their blossoming relationship, she knew there would be lots of other dances going on elsewhere that night, and she worried that Mitch might be off to one of them with his mates and be exposed to the temptation of other girls. It gave her a tight feeling in her throat when she thought about it.

Sammy and Anna kept reminding her of the number of other boys who fancied her and all the post she'd received from a whole list of eager suitors. In the end, she could not help being swept along with their enthusiasm, although her heart was not truly in it. Sammy and Melanie had already agreed to swap clothes. Sammy was going to wear the coveted orange mini skirt and Melanie the gorgeous, swirly, floaty bell bottoms, which lifted her spirits when she put them on. To round off her look for the evening she put plaits in her hair again and added the now-familiar flower.

The hall began to fill up and the sounds of the disco came blasting out, with their all-time favourite songs of the Beatles. But it was relatively early and the four girls had not yet hit the dance floor. They loved to stand and watch, surveying the scene and laughing at the ineptitude of some of the boys on the dance floor, their attempts at dancing to some extent a reflection of their personalities. There were the awkward, shy ones, shuffling embarrassedly on the spot, some rigid, others with arms and legs flailing, or bobbing up and down supposedly in time to the music. Then there were the flamboyant types - 'I'm a natural, get a load of this, why don't you?' - strutting around like Mick Jagger, full of confidence, or in some cases alcohol.

There was always an element of competition that crept in, an attempt to be better than the other boys, when they failed to realise that all the girls were giggling at them. All they wanted was someone who looked comfortable and confident, and looked like he was having fun. From time to time the four girls, including Melanie, couldn't help but fall about laughing at some of the boys' awkwardness and general lack of social skills.

Girls could be so cruel, a trait often displayed by Anna, who always initially looked aloof and dismissive if a boy she didn't fancy came up to speak to her. She had no intention of dancing with any boy until she had at least seen him in action and considered him to be a relatively skilled dancer. There was no way she was going to be shown up on the dance floor.

As their eyes scanned the room, Sammy suddenly touched Melanie's arm to get her attention, as the music was so loud. "Look, there's Johnnie," she shouted. "Now he is cute, you've said so yourself. You quite fancy him Mellie, and he's looking over this way. I bet you could have him if you wanted. Let's dance and see." She took Melanie's arm, dragging her onto the dance floor before she had time to object.

Melanie started to dance half-heartedly with Sammy, thinking she'd rather be somewhere else. She could see out of the corner of her eye that Johnnie was looking at her, and sure enough it wasn't long before he was beside her with his friend asking them both to dance. Melanie smiled at him politely. He really was attractive. As the music came to an end, he tried to put his arm around her, but she slipped from his grasp and then, seeing his look of dismay and feeling guilty, said she would dance with him later. An empty promise, as it turned out.

"What are you doing?" murmured Sammy insistently. "He's gorgeous." But even as she spoke her eyes turned to look at something over Melanie's shoulder and her expression changed.

"What is it?' Melanie enquired, seeing the startled look on Sammy's face. But before she had time to turn around she felt a familiar presence behind her and a hand slipped round her waist. She found herself being spun round and staring into Mitch's big grin and soft brown eyes.

Her heart did a flip and she turned to jelly. "How the hell..." she began.

"I've been watching you," he said. "You're really not enjoying this, are you? I've got a surprise waiting outside for you. Are you coming?"

In amazement, Melanie turned and looked at Sammy, who was standing alongside, her hips still swaying in time to the music and with a broad, knowing smile on her own face.

"Go for it girl," whispered Sammy into her best friend's ear. "He must really think a lot of you to turn up here. No one will notice you've gone. See you on the last bus."

Unlike her other friends, Sammy thought deep down that Melanie should follow her heart and see where it led. She knew that if it did all come crashing down she would be there for Melanie, and at least she would have experienced something she thought was magical that she would only live to regret otherwise. Better to have loved and lost, and all that.

Not needing any further encouragement, Melanie let Mitch lead her by the hand away from the hall and out of the school building, excitement bubbling up inside her. On seeing their friend leave so unexpectedly with Mitch, Shirley and Anna left the dance floor and rushed over to Sammy.

"Where's Melanie heading off to? What on earth are that pair up to?" asked Shirley, a note of concern in her voice.

"Oh, Casanova came and whisked her off to heaven," replied Sammy with a smile.

"What? How the hell did he get in here, and why would she want to miss all this?" Anna shouted above the noise of the music, gesturing to the buzzing scene all around them. "Oh, I remember now. She loves him, and he loves her, supposedly," she added sarcastically.

Sammy pointed to a group of college boys standing near the entrance "He came in with them," she said. "He must know them somehow. God, he's got some nerve! Fancy gate-crashing a school dance like that."

Once they had emerged from the dance, Mitch led Melanie over to a motor bike parked by the pavement just outside the school. He hitched up his trousers, gripped the handle bars in his left hand, swung his leg nonchalantly over the saddle and leant backwards. The bike wobbled, but he maintained his composure and his cocky smile as he gestured for Melanie to join him. She stifled a giggle. He looked so gorgeous in this portrayal of a tough, bad boy, which only excited her more.

"Where did you get it from? Can you really ride it?" she asked, with an incredulous look on her face.

"Of course I can" he smiled with a sparkle in his eyes, "Jump on, Jackson!"

For an instant Melanie hesitated. She'd never been on a motor bike before, so she was tentative, but she tried to hide it. As she climbed on nervously behind him, Mitch reached behind, grabbed her arms and pulled them round his waist.

"Hold on to me tight," he shouted over his shoulder. "You'll be fine." He did not have to ask twice. Melanie could feel her heart starting to race again as she felt his body so close to hers. She leant against him as they took off, her senses immediately heightened by this new experience. She felt more alive than she had ever felt before.

Shirley and Anna, who had rushed outside to try and find out what the hell was going on, stood transfixed in the doorway. They watched with mouths agape as Mitch and Melanie roared off from the school and into the summer evening.

"Just what does she see in him and why would she want to go off on that dirty, smelly machine?" asked Anna, shaking her head from side to side in disbelief. She turned on her heel to head back inside.

Maybe it was something to do with the fact that he was so good looking, a real charmer with an endearing cheekiness and an aura that spells danger, thought Shirley. That would attract the free-spirited Melanie. But she kept those thoughts to herself, as she knew that they would be wasted on Anna.

As for Melanie, she had never felt so exhilarated. A wave of freedom surged through her as they blasted along the road with the wind blowing through her hair, weaving around bends as the sea passed by on one side and fields whizzed past on the other. They were truly in a world of their own. She could feel her cheeks flushed by the fresh air and could hear Mitch's laughter being carried away on the breeze, as she laughed out aloud along with him, her senses heightened by the roar of the engine as they hurtled along at breakneck speed, her heart beating wildly and her senses completely blown away by the whole experience. She hugged him tighter, thrilled and excited by the speed and danger, while Mitch revelled in having this lovely girl on the bike with him.

He came to a stop when they had reached a headland. "Your turn now," he urged, looking round and smiling at Melanie.

"No, I couldn't!" she gasped.

But he was having none of it. "Of course you can. It's easy" he reassured her. He swapped places with her and let her ride with him on the back helping her steer. She was wobbling like mad at first, nerves getting the better of her, but he oozed confidence and made her feel secure enough to open the throttle a bit.

All went reasonably well until, without warning, the bike careered off the stone path, rode onto the grass and veered crazily across some hillocks before the pair of them eventually managed to get it under control somehow and it came to a standstill. They were both breathing hard and laughing, revelling in the thrill and excitement of the whole experience. As they dismounted, still laughing, Melanie trembling with a combination of shock and excitement, he grabbed her hand reassuringly and they wandered off along the water's edge, with Melanie still feeling stunned and euphoric from the ride of her life.

Suddenly he stopped and leaned towards her, a bemused expression on his face.

"What is it that makes you so interesting and different from all the other girls I've met?" he whispered as he moved even closer. Their lips brushed, light as a feather, then he kissed her gently. "You are beautiful, Melanie Jackson. I don't know what you've done to me but you'll be my downfall, that's for sure."

As they lay down on the grass together, staring into the evening sky and watching the sun going down, he leant on one elbow and stared into her face, tracing the outline of her cheek gently with his other hand. It was a magical and peaceful moment.

"Melanie, I want you to know that there have been other girls before, but whatever anyone might tell you, they have meant nothing, absolutely nothing," he said. "There is only one who has any place in my heart. I'm looking at her right now, and she's making me dizzy."

"You make me dizzy too, Mitch. I really didn't mean to feel this way. It's just happened to me, like I've been struck by lightning. And when I'm with you it's the craziest, most amazing feeling in the whole world, just you and me together like this. And nothing else matters but this."

For a while they were lost in time, lying close to each other in a beautiful silence, with only the distant sound of the sea joining in with their thoughts. "I can see fire and passion in those tantalizing eyes of yours. I dream about those eyes, you know," whispered Mitch as he leant over and looked deep into her eyes. "Melanie, I love you."

Melanie, smiling at the sweetest words she had ever heard, suddenly pressed her lips to his. Tenderly, he put his hand on the back of her head and they kissed softly. Then his hand gripped her hair as he pulled her more tightly to him and he melted into her kiss.

Suddenly the noise of a passing car startled Melanie.

"Oh God, what time is it? I have to catch the bus!" she exclaimed.

Mitch laughed and tried to draw her closer to him, but she pulled away. "No Mitch. I'm serious. I really do have to go' she said. She kissed his smile briefly, then jumped up and brushed the loose grass away from her clothes. He jumped up alongside her, turned to her as if he wanted to say something more but couldn't find the words, so he simply smiled and said "Don't worry. I'll get you home". Then he wrapped his arms around her.

"No, you don't understand. I have to be on the bus. My dad is picking me up from the bus station!" she blurted out. Mitch couldn't help but be amused by this, but when he saw the worried look on her face he capitulated. "It's OK, don't panic. Jump on the bike. We'll chase the bus. It'll be fun! Just you wait and see."

True enough, once they were back on the bike she relaxed as she clung on tightly to him once more and felt the thrill again of the machine accelerating away into the darkness. They had discovered a shared passion for living on the edge, revelling in the exhilarating thrills of speed and danger. Hurtling along once more, ignoring speed limits through the little villages as they went, they caught up and overtook the bus just before it entered town, and Mitch pulled into the stop ahead.

"Thanks for this evening, for coming to take me away from that boring old dance and giving me such a mad, crazy time," said Melanie. "I can't begin to tell you how much this evening has meant to me. It's been the best ever." Then she jumped hastily off the bike, blew a kiss goodbye, and flagged the bus down.

She skipped onto the bus in a state of pure elation, adrenalin flowing through her veins. "Quick" she said to Anna. "Let me sit in the window seat." Just in time she saw Mitch overtaking the bus, and she pressed her face against the window and blew him another kiss. He returned the gesture with a flamboyant wave of his hand.

"Look at the state of you!" said Anna, furiously trying to get a comb through Melanie's hair. "What will your dad say? Calm down, for goodness sake. Where the hell have you been? You've got about two minutes to look presentable, so pull yourself together!"

"Hi girls" said Melanie's dad cheerily as they jumped into the car. "Good evening, was it?"

"It was fab thanks, Mr Jackson" answered Anna. Melanie was sitting there with a far-away look on her face, thoughts racing through her mind of the magical adventure she had just been on. "I'm sure Melanie can't wait to tell you all about it when you get home." Anna pulled a face at Melanie.

James could see his daughter's dreamy expression in the rear-view mirror as car headlights lit up her face intermittently. He knew that someone had taken over her heart, and he had lost her. The child had gone and he couldn't pull her back into the safety of her childhood and the family, however much he wanted to. She was away in a fantasy world and completely lost inside her own head.

CHAPTER 14

Planning for a party

The end of term had come and gone and Melanie had been working for three days helping in the kitchen and as a waitress in one of the large Victorian hotels on the seafront. It was packed with visitors, as were the many other hotels and boarding houses that occupied the full length of the promenade. They were interspersed with cafés, souvenir shops, pubs, amusement arcades, and dance halls; everything to keep the visitors entertained and encourage them to part with their money.

Melanie had been a little shy on her first day, as she didn't know anyone, and it always took her a while to get to know strangers, but now she was really enjoying it. All the holidaymakers were in a happy holiday frame of mind and the other staff were all friendly, most of them young and just over for the summer months to soak up as much of the holiday atmosphere and social scene as they could before they went back to their relatively boring lives back home.

It was early afternoon when Melanie finished her shift, and she was in good spirits as she looked forward to the lazy summer afternoon and the free time which lay ahead of her. She smiled at a group of young visitors chattering happily away amongst themselves as she passed them in the lobby and made her way outside. Blinking as she emerged from the dark confines of the building into the dazzling sunlight, she reached into her bag for her sunglasses and slipped them on as she skipped lightly down the steps, taking deep breaths of the pure sea air. What a wonderful day it was, and how great it felt to be alive. The rest of this glorious day was hers to enjoy at her leisure in the company of her best friends. She set off to visit Shirley, who lived just along the prom from where she was working.

"Wow, look at you, all sexy in that uniform," came a familiar voice from out of the blue. She was taken aback at first, but her face quickly lit up and her blushes rapidly disappeared as she realised it was Mitch, who had been standing large as life at the bottom of the steps. True to form he had a big smile on his face.

She was wearing her uniform, a short black skirt complemented by a white blouse, and her hair was tied back in a high ponytail with a big black velvet bow. She knew she wore it well from the admiring gazes she unfailingly received on a daily basis from the teenage boys staying at the hotel, but it still thrilled her to hear Mitch complimenting her so enthusiastically. Sexy? He had never said that before. At the same time, she could see that he meant it as his eyes wandered appreciatively over her young body.

"Hi, what are you doing here?" she managed to say as calmly as possible whilst her heart leapt into her throat and the now familiar knots started twisting in her stomach. When would her body start behaving itself when he was around?

"I can come and meet my girl, can't I? And take her for a walk. Unless you fancy a drink somewhere that is?"

He looked tanned and handsome in a white T-shirt and jeans, and the urge to take him up on his offer was strong, but her friends were expecting her.

"I'm meant to be going straight to Shirley's to talk about the arrangements for our big party" she said, not wanting to hurt his feelings as he'd obviously had his heart set on spending the afternoon with her. She could sense from the look on his face that he was disappointed with this response.

"Ah yes, the party," he said, with a note of amused sarcasm in his voice.

"You are coming, aren't you?" asked Melanie nervously. Her spirits sank on seeing his reaction. This couldn't be happening, surely, after all the effort and hard work they had put into the party. It would all seem pointless without him there. A thought flashed through her mind: and so would her life.

Before she had time to gather her senses, she blurted out, "Please Mitch, you will come, won't you? I'd so like you to be there, and it is our first proper party."

"Of course I will. Wild horses wouldn't keep me from anywhere you are going to be," Mitch replied, sensing how much it meant to her. "I'll be there for you, one way or another."

"What do you mean, one way or another?"

"Oh, it doesn't matter. Just forget it, it's not important. I'll explain some other time."

"No. Tell me now Mitch. Please, it's important to me" she implored.

After some hesitation, Mitch decided to come clean after all.

"OK. You probably won't understand, but it's all just so difficult for me."

"Why is it difficult for you?"

"Well, the boys aren't really too keen on your lot. You know, your girlfriends and that college lot that always seem to be hanging around you. To be honest, I'm not so keen myself. I'm not stupid. I can tell that the girls aren't best pleased when I'm around you. It's obvious from the looks on their faces whenever I appear on the scene, especially that Anna, Miss High and Mighty. Who the hell does she think she is anyway? And those college lads are just a bunch of toffee-nosed prats with their heads stuck up their own arses most of the time."

Melanie sensed his strength of feeling and frustration. "But it is important, Mitch. It's so important. It is to me anyway. I didn't realise they'd made that kind of impression on you, or treated you and your friends so badly. I know the college boys can seem a bit full of themselves, but the girls aren't like that. Really, they're not. They'll be fine once they get to know you better, and see the real you. It's just that they've never seen me like this before with any boy. It's so unlike me. They heard some rumours about you, if you must know, about how you never stay with one girl for long. They know how sensitive I can be and they're just being protective as they don't want to see me being hurt if I become too attached to you and things go wrong between us, if that makes sense. They'll come around in time. Really, they will, you'll see."

Mitch smiled at this and nodded gently, as if he understood, although Melanie could see that he wasn't really convinced. Then he softened and, looking longingly into her eyes whilst holding her gaze, he added "If I'm honest, and looking back on it, I'd have to admit those rumours are right Melanie. I haven't stayed with any girl for long. But only because I've never met any girl before that I've wanted to stay with, one who's made me feel the way you do. Before I met you, I'd laugh when people said they were in love, but now I know how it feels to love somebody. I can't explain it, but you're the most wonderful thing that's happened to me and I never want to let you go, ever. It really doesn't matter to me what your friends think. As long as you love me, and want to be with me, then that's all I need to know."

"That's just so wonderful for me to hear, and it means so much to me. You must know I love you too, Mitch. I can't hide it and I can't explain it either. You have the same effect on me, and I've never felt this way about anyone else. I struggle to understand it myself, so it's not surprising how the girls are struggling to come to terms with it and the change in me. But I still don't really understand why things are so difficult for you and why you said you'd find a way to be at our party one way or another. What else is there that you're not telling me?"

God, this girl was so perceptive, Mitch thought to himself. She wasn't going to let go of this until he gave her an explanation.

"OK, you win. If you must know, the boys are giving me a really hard time about you as well. Don't get me wrong, it's got nothing to do with you. They all like you. You're not like your mates. You've got no airs and graces, take everyone at face value, and they can see the attraction, but, apart from Dixie strangely enough, the dozy oafs just can't understand why I'd want to spend so much time with you, rather than be off out on the pop with them. I'm getting so much stick it's unbelievable. They don't want to waste a night at the party, so they've organised a big lads' night out on the same evening, and they expect me to be with them. And to be honest, it's not just the party. It's their whole attitude. None of them has ever fallen for a girl like I have for you. They just don't see the point of it and why anyone would want to spend their time with some girl rather than being with the gang. It's not something I can discuss with them. They'd just take the piss. But it's got to the point where I feel as if I'm on the verge of becoming a bit of an outsider, if you know what I mean? Somehow or other, between now and then I've got to find a way of keeping them on board and still getting to the party to be with you. I know it sounds daft, but it seems to me that you're experiencing something similar with your friends too?"

Now it all became clear to Melanie. Why he usually appeared on the scene in tow with the boys, why they hadn't yet ventured on a proper date just by themselves.

"You're right. Now I look at it I think it maybe explains the girls' behaviour towards me and you as well. I've sensed somehow that they seem to resent me not spending my own time with them, as part of the group. Although nothing's ever been said, of course, it wouldn't be the done thing with us. That might explain part of their attitude towards you as well. Maybe they resent you taking me away from them, now I come to think of it. How weird. Why didn't I think of that?"

"I don't know, but it sounds as if we might be in the same boat. At least we'll be in it together! Come on then. I guess you'd better shoot along and join them or they'll be wondering what's up. Let me walk you to Shirley's, the long way around."

Without further ado, he smiled, grabbed hold of her hand and, without warning, spotting a gap in the traffic, he started to run across the prom. Melanie kept alongside him, shock and excitement rushing through her as the pair of them darted daringly from side to side to avoid the oncoming traffic and horse trams, laughing as they charged across the busy road, car horns blasting furious warnings as they weaved their way across to the beach.

Slightly breathless, Melanie removed her sandals. She had been on her feet for hours and welcomed the soft sand as it started to creep up between her toes, gently massaging them as she walked.

Finally, they stopped and sat against the sea wall, and she could feel his eyes on her.

"By the way, you look beautiful, as always. I love your hair like that," he said. He leant forward until their lips were almost touching. It felt so good to be with him after what seemed to her like four very long days. It was so comforting nestled in close to his body, warm and contented, just sitting close to him.

He removed a wisp of hair that had blown across her face and she closed her eyes as he gently stroked her cheek and jawline with the tips of his fingers. Her body shivered involuntarily, even though it was a beautiful, warm day. He looked deep into her eyes, and with such a tender voice said, "Melanie, what is this all about, you and me? Why do you affect me the way you do?" She smiled back at him, leant towards him and they kissed as the world seemingly faded into insignificance.

As they parted, gazing longingly into each other's eyes, Melanie thought to herself how strange love was. She still couldn't work this boy out. He was so unlike anyone she'd ever met before; a strange mixture of tough on the outside when in the company of his pals and the softer, more sensitive side he revealed when alone with her. And yet, inexplicably as it seemed to her, she couldn't help but be drawn by both sides of his personality.

Eventually, he broke the dreamy moment. "Come on then, suppose you'd better get to your friends," he said. "I've things to do as well." But he didn't elaborate on what the things were, and she didn't like to ask.

"See you here Saturday then" he said outside Shirley's. He pulled her to him for the last time, planted a kiss on her forehead and took off back along the prom. She stared after him briefly. What a puzzle he was. He could be so gentle and loving, but there was this other side to him which was throwing her off balance at every turn.

Mitch's thoughts were much less complicated. All he

could think about, as he looked back and saw her disappearing into the hotel's revolving door, was that beautiful young body and those amazing legs of hers.

"You're late" Anna said curtly as Melanie entered the basement of the hotel which Shirley's step mum and dad owned and tried to adjust to the dim light.

"Yes. Mitch met me from work," she answered, with a big smile on her face.

Anna rolled her eyes at the others and groaned inwardly. She could not contain herself any longer. "Melanie Jackson, just because you've got a crush on some boy it's not the be all and end all of life, you know. You've changed, and I for one don't like the new you. That Mitch is no good for you. I don't know why you don't listen to us. We all used to have such a laugh, and now you just walk round in a daze all the time looking all dreamy. What happened to that girl we used to know, who was never going to let a boy make a fool of her?"

Exasperated by Anna's attitude, Melanie was unable to contain her frustration. "He's not making a fool of me and it's not just a crush, Anna. It's so much more than that. I don't just fancy him because I think he's cute. This is different. It's inside me and it's magical. It's like entering a whole new world. It's so intense and emotional. I'm really sorry. I know I'm acting irrationally, but I just can't think straight. My heart starts to race when he's around. Do none of you understand how I'm feeling? It's the greatest high I've ever experienced, and all you can do is make snide remarks to me and be offhand with him. It's not fair. He doesn't deserve it, and neither do I for that matter."

"Humph! If you say so" said Anna dismissively. Shirley

had listened quietly to this exchange and could see a look of hurt cross Melanie's face. Her heart went out to her. It was obvious that she at least thought she loved Mitch, whether he was good for her or not, and it was obviously upsetting for her that her friends, Anna in particular, were so against him. Shirley knew that Melanie desperately wanted her friends to understand how she was feeling, how important it all was to her. But, in her heart she too felt uncomfortable at Melanie's extraordinary high spirits. She understood her friend so well, and knew that her emotions and sensitivity went deep, that she felt things more than most. She also knew from past experience that where there was a high there was every possibility of there being a crashing low to follow, should things not work out between her and Mitch.

Even Anna, thoughtless as she could be, was aware of Melanie's inclination to dwell on every aspect of her emotions, and in her own way she was just as concerned for what she saw as her friend's inevitable downfall. However, having been spoilt in life, she simply didn't have the compassion or patience to try and resolve other people's personal problems, for Anna had inherited her characteristics from her mother, who was forthright, larger than life and with a quick sense of humour. She was a teenage copy of her mother. In fact, they were so alike that they often clashed, and you could feel the tension between them, especially as Anna got older and was trying to assert herself and strive for independence. As a family, they were very well off and Anna never went without. Her father, a handsome and easy-going man, worked abroad, and on his visits home he would lavish gifts on his only daughter as she sat on his knee, playing the daddy's girl card, and looking at him with those big eyes. Her mother bore a certain amount of envy of the affection he bestowed on his daughter, but she was not an affectionate woman herself and so they just got on with what was a very ordinary, but acceptable marriage, as so many did at that time.

In Anna's mind, she had done her bit for Melanie and offered her advice, so that was it as far as she was concerned. But Shirley was a totally different kettle of fish. More sensitive than Anna, and by nature more protective of Melanie, she sensed the atmosphere that had developed between Anna and Melanie, so she quickly stepped in to change the subject.

"Anyway, look what my dad managed to borrow for me!" she squealed excitedly.

"What is it? Wow, a strobe light!" exclaimed Anna, her enthusiasm rekindled. "Oh wow, I just love those. They have an amazing effect on the way you look on the dance floor. Just how good are we going to look when we're all dolled up and dancing, girls?"

"Yes, but don't wear anything white, because it will shine right through as if you are not wearing anything," explained Sammy, who had experienced that embarrassing situation first hand.

"Oh yes, and don't wear black either as it highlights any bits of fluff and makes you look like you've got dandruff" said Anna, at which they all fell apart laughing, until Melanie suddenly remarked "Oh no! I've just put a deposit down on a black and white mini dress and I'm picking it up Friday when I get paid! It's absolutely the very latest fashion."

"You'll just have to hope the black and white bits are all

in the right places and don't stand too near the light then," Sammy joked.

Before long they were frolicking around the room to the beat of the music from the record player in the corner, excitedly passing on tips, hints, and new moves they'd picked up from Top of the Pops and some of the older girls at school. In the midst of all this Sammy came up with the idea of them all lining up and trying out one particular move in unison, the 'one hundred and eighty degree spin', as demonstrated only that week on Top of the Pops.

"It's quite a simple move really" explained Sammy. "Just watch me and I'll show you how it's done. She positioned herself in the middle of the room. "Watch closely now. You cross your left leg over your right like so, then swivel your body around to face in the opposite direction, dance for a little while with your back to your partner, then do the same again and swivel back so you're facing them." She completed the whole manoeuvre with consummate ease and grace. "There, told you" she exclaimed in triumph. "Now, all line up and we'll do it together."

Suitably impressed, the others joined her in a line and waited eagerly for her instructions. "All together now, one, two, three, spin" and they all spun together, successfully completing their initial spin, giggling as they all carried on dancing, but by this time facing the opposite wall.

"Wow, you're right, it is easy" said Melanie. "Let's swivel back again. One, two, three, spin." It was indeed easy, for three of them at least, but poor old Shirley simply couldn't get the hang of it and, halfway through, disaster struck. She tumbled helplessly sideways, taking the rest of the girls with her as they collapsed in a jumble of arms and legs onto one of the battered old couches.

Once harmony was restored, the four girls settled back again into their normally comfortable relationships, chatting away together happily, and busying themselves with their plans for their big event. Once again, the quiet, unassuming Shirley, albeit inadvertently, had stepped in and saved the day – much to Melanie's relief.

CHAPTER 15

The Gang of Four's big party night

It was the day of the party. The basement was ready in all its glory. The girls had fixed the glitter ball up in front of the strobe light so it would light up in flashes, and the effect was dazzling. Red bulbs beamed out from the lamps that lit the corners of the large basement room, and they had allocated a space as a dance floor by partitioning it off with some of the old furniture that they'd pulled out from the dark recesses of the basement.

Shirley's stepmother had mixed a huge bowl of non-alcoholic punch for the party, along with several soft drinks all laid out on a table, but the girls were well prepared for this, and had a bottle of brandy and a bottle of vodka already hidden away ready to add to the punch to make a decent drink for everyone. They were sure that others would be bringing various types of alcohol secreted upon their persons too.

Soon there was a group of young people mingling in the basement, mainly girlfriends from school giggling away and chatting about the usual subject, boys – who fancied who, who was fit and who wasn't – and exchanging compliments on each other's clothes, hairstyles and make-up. Gradually, the room filled up until it was wall to wall with teenagers, and someone cranked the music up to full volume. Drink of all descriptions was being sneaked in surreptitiously and consumed in great quantities, and the atmosphere was smoky from cigarettes and joss sticks. Friends had invited friends, so that in the end there were people there whom the girls didn't even know, but soon would.

The strobe light was flashing away to the beat of the music, while all the other lights had been switched off, so that it illuminated the makeshift dance floor. The slow-motion effect it produced on the dancing figures was hypnotic, creating an illusion of stop-go movements, of flickering silhouettes of bodies.

Melanie was trying to hold a conversation above the sound of the music with Johnnie and his mate in a corner, although her mind was wandering and she felt restless. She was waiting for the arrival of Mitch, and her heart was going into overdrive at the thought. She tried her best to concentrate on what Johnnie was saying, but all the time she was wondering where Mitch was, and tingling with anticipation. The party had been going at full tilt for some time now and it was getting quite late, so she couldn't help nervously looking over to the doorway every few seconds.

Then there was a loud commotion and Mitch appeared on the scene with several friends, all in boisterous mood. They had had more than a few drinks by the look of things. Shirley's heart dropped. She was dreading gate-crashers, and although they seemed to have come with Mitch, the behaviour of a couple of them was already close to being out of control.

Mitch spotted Melanie immediately, and made his way over to where she was standing, only to be stopped in his tracks by Johnnie's mate, who by this time was slightly inebriated himself, and took it upon himself to step between the pair. He looked Mitch up and down scathingly and declared in a voice loud enough for others around to hear "So, you're the famous Mitch then, are you? You're a very lucky boy. Our Melanie here is quite a catch. No hard feelings you understand but, quite frankly, I don't know what she sees in you, old chap. Still, each to their own, I suppose." He smirked cockily to his college-boy friends standing by, and offered Mitch his hand to shake. "I'm Percy, by the way."

Mitch's hackles rose, but he caught sight of the anxious look on Melanie's face and, to his credit, managed somehow to retain his composure and self-control. He ignored the hand, although he kept his eyes on Percy. The grin left Percy's face and his college pals reacted with smirks and stifled laughter. "Yes, I am a lucky boy, aren't I Percy?" said Mitch. "I'd like to say it's been a real pleasure meeting you. I'd like to say it, but..." he trailed off, shaking his head disarmingly and leaving Percy lost for words.

"May I have this dance?" he asked Melanie in the most charming manner he could muster. They made their way to the dance floor, where he pulled her against him and wrapped his arms around her.

Those feelings of nervousness and excitement rose once again inside her. The sheer elation of this boy's closeness was having the usual effect on her – the butterflies, the tingling. She was proud of the way he'd handled himself. He was dangerous and very flirtatious, but she didn't care in that moment; she had never felt the way she did right then. She reached up and slid her arms around his neck as a slow song emanated from the speakers.

Those thoughts were enhanced when, inspired by the strains of one of his favourite songs, 'Groovy Kind of Love', Mitch started murmuring the words softly into her ear: "When you're close to me, I can feel your heart beat, I can hear you breathing in my ear..." She knew that those words, that song, were permeating her brain, and she would never forget it, ever.

When I kiss your lips, ooh I start to shiver, can't control the quivering inside

Wouldn't you agree, baby you and me, got a groovy kind of love

We got a groovy kind of love.

Yes, they really did have a groovy kind of love, she thought, and it was such a wonderful feeling.

For a while they were lost in each other, dancing close in their own inner world, feeling the heat of each other's bodies, both overwhelmed by their depth of feeling and, in their own way both scared by it; Melanie because she was disposing of any shield and letting her guard down completely, believing in the words he spoke and the love he said he had for her and Mitch because this wasn't the way he thought he should be. He should be the man about town along with his mates, but all he really wanted was to be with this beautiful, sweet, exciting girl who made him feel crazy, as if he was going out of his mind.

"Is there anything to drink?" Mitch enquired when the music eventually paused, looking around the dimly-lit basement.

"Yes, we've got some punch and it's got vodka and rum in it" Melanie said as they drifted to the side of the dance floor. He let Melanie pour two tumblers of the disgusting-looking stuff, although he would have much preferred a beer. She placed them on a table and then he pulled her with him onto a nearby battered old couch which let off puffs of dust and a few feathers into the air as they sank into it. He kissed her neck.

"Ah, I'd forgotten how good you smell, sweet with a hint of orange blossom. Unlike this furniture!" he added. She closed her eyes briefly and just enjoyed the feeling of being with him.

Whilst they were enjoying their drink, Melanie couldn't help but notice that Sammy seemed to have consumed a large quantity of alcohol. She was all over the dance floor, gesticulating and laughing. Shirley went over to remonstrate with her, but Sammy just said "For God's sake lighten up Shirley and have a drink, why don't you? It's a party and a bloody good one too." She thrust a bottle of what appeared to be neat vodka in front of Shirley's face. Shirley attempted a swig, as she didn't want to appear boring, but was nearly sick as the pungent spirit hit her throat. She then watched with some trepidation as Sammy staggered haphazardly across the dance floor, climbed onto a table and started dancing precariously near the edge.

As if from nowhere, Mitch's mate Jack, the joker of the pack, suddenly appeared on the scene and, clearly a bit drunk himself, thought it would be funny to shake the table in accompaniment to the music, with the inevitable outcome being that Sammy lost her balance and fell. Fortunately for her she landed in Jack's arms, following which the pair of them staggered drunkenly off together into a corner of the room, laughing and giggling.

"Do you ever get like that?" enquired Mitch.

"I have done a couple of times" admitted Melanie, "But when it comes to alcohol I like to retain at least some form of control over my actions."

"That's a shame," he joked.

Just then a rumpus broke out on the far side of the room. Alcohol had started to take its toll on a couple of Mitch's mates, who were becoming more boisterous by the minute. Mitch could see trouble developing when the pair started shouting and gesticulating to him from across the room, where they were stationed close to the staircase leading out of the basement. Melanie could see it was bothering him, so they rose and made their way across to join his mates. Jack shouted across to Mitch, "This is a bloody juvenile's party. Come on Mitch, let's go where there's some real action and some decent ale."

When they reached him, it turned out that he was

annoyed because Sammy had passed out on him before he could, as he put it, 'get anywhere' with her.

Melanie could see that Mitch was in a dilemma. They could both see that if the boys didn't leave fairly soon, with Mitch in tow, there was every chance that trouble could break out, as some college boys were gathering close at hand, looking a touch menacing. There was no love lost between the High School boys and them, and both sets had consumed considerable amounts of alcohol by this time. Melanie could see that Mitch was clearly torn between calming the situation down by succumbing to peer pressure and acquiescing to their wishes or letting them get on with it. The last thing she wanted was for any trouble to break out at Shirley's house, so she asked Mitch to have a word with the boys to see if he could calm them down.

Unfortunately, his intervention was doomed to failure. As he drew near to his mates he felt a tap on his shoulder and turned to find Percy, clearly the worse for drink and still brooding on their earlier meeting. He lunged forward and gripped Mitch by the throat.

"Not so fucking clever now are you, smartarse?" he blurted out, anger written all over his face.

Mitch stepped adroitly backwards and knocked Percy's hand away with a swift upward thrust. "Just calm down Percy" he said, looking him straight in the eye and raising the palms of both hands in the air as a conciliatory gesture. "We don't want to cause any trouble for the girls now, do we?"

But Percy was having none of it. "That's typical of you and your bloody shower of yobs. All mouth and no balls when it comes down to it, aren't you? You're all just a bunch of cowards!" He lunged towards Mitch again. Showing remarkable restraint, Mitch neatly sidestepped his lunge and again raised his hands in an effort to calm the situation, but Percy's anger rose at being made to look a fool once more.

"Melanie's a fucking idiot going out with trash like you. She needs her fucking head examined!" he cursed.

That did it. Mitch shook his head slowly from side to side, exhaled deeply and half turned away, as if making to leave. Then he swivelled back around and hit Percy square on the nose with all the force he could muster. Percy collapsed into the arms of his college pals. Mitch stood there for a short while, feet planted wide and looking at each of the college lads in turn, daring them to try their luck as well, but there were no takers.

Fortunately, Mark and some of his friends, sensing further trouble, then stepped in to calm things down. Although the fracas was brief, it had caused a stir, and Mitch could see the troubled look on Melanie's face as he glanced briefly in her direction before ushering his own mates towards the stairs so that they could leave the scene before any further trouble reared its head. He mouthed a silent 'sorry' to Melanie and beckoned to her to follow him, which she duly did. Not having witnessed such violence at close quarters before, Melanie made her way up the stairs alongside Mitch with a strange mixture of shock and excitement welling up inside her at the same time.

When they reached the top of the stairs and emerged into the cool night air outside, Mitch paused to light up two calming cigarettes, passing one to Melanie and sucking in a large, soothing draught. Melanie could see her hands were still shaking from the shock of it all.

"I'm so, so sorry Melanie. I was trying to calm him down but he was having none of it. I could see there was no way he was going to stop, but I was fine until he insulted you, then something inside me just kind of snapped. I really am so sorry. Please apologise to Shirley for me."

"It's OK Mitch. I know you did your best. He just pushed you to your limits and, who knows, it could have got a lot worse if you hadn't sorted him out. It certainly took the heat out of things, and gosh, that was some punch you hit him with." She was unable to hide the excitement in her voice. "What does it matter anyway? There's no real damage done, apart from to Percy's pride, and his nose for that matter. It serves him right, he's always been pompous and arrogant and that might take him down a peg or two. What are we going to do now?" She looked at him with those gorgeous, mesmerizing eyes.

"I'm sorry Melanie, I'll have to go. I obviously can't go back into the party now and you'll need to head back down there, see how things are and smooth things over with Shirley. Will you meet me later? Go on, please, sneak out and meet me, I'll meet you outside your parent's house."

"I'm staying here at the hotel tonight" said Melanie, "All four of us are."

"Even better. I'll meet you on the beach opposite at one o'clock. Please be there, I really have to go."

She didn't answer him this time, just gave a nod of her head, feeling deflated. She saw him smile to his mates as they walked over, grabbed him good naturedly by the arm and left.

"They've won" she thought. "He'd rather go off with them than be with me." She saw Mitch being physically bustled along the pavement, although he was putting up no resistance and laughing along with the banter. Their eyes met for the briefest moment and she saw a look of something, a shrug, some sort of apology, but then he was gone.

Melanie dutifully returned to the party, which had calmed down already, apart from some excited chatter about the brief encounter between Percy and Mitch, which was undoubtedly the talking point of the evening. Mark had spotted Melanie returning to the party and when he saw that she was upset he wandered over to check that she was all right. Melanie was pleased to have somebody to talk to, and even more pleased when she found that he'd brought a drink with him.

Mark had a real soft spot for Melanie and felt protective towards her. He knew instinctively that she didn't feel the same way. He desperately wanted to be more than a friend to her, but to her he was just like a brother. In a weak moment, he'd once told her how much he loved her, but after seeing her expression of complete bewilderment he had never mentioned it again. After that he had settled for being her friend and being able to spend time in her company.

"Are you OK?" he asked.

Melanie could see he was genuinely concerned. "Yes, I'm fine Mark, just a bit shaken up. I thought there was going to be some real trouble there, as there's no love lost between that lot, so thanks for stepping in and calming things down."

Mark just smiled and shook his head, then laughingly responded, "Forget it. After all, why ruin a good party just because that prick Percy had his nose squashed? Serves him right, it's been coming for a long time. If you're sure you're okay I'll get back to the lads.' He smiled and moved off to join his friends, but not before adding "Oh, and if there's any more trouble you know where I am. You know you can always turn to me." really wishing she would, she was so beautiful in his eyes.

Melanie kept a low profile for the rest of the evening until Shirley's father dutifully appeared in the doorway to the basement close to midnight to check how things were going and to wind down the party. The noise wasn't a problem because the hotel was still busy with guests returning after a night out and laughter and conversations were floating out from the piano bar upstairs. But he felt it was late enough for his fifteen-year-old daughter and her friends. A lot of the older party goers had already moved on to discos or more house parties and the younger ones had already been collected or set off for home.

Even though the place looked like a war zone, Shirley's dad said the girls might as well get to bed and clear up in the morning. "Is Sammy OK?" Mr Crossley asked uncertainly as he pointed to her figure stretched out as she lay horizontal on one of the couches.

"Yes, she's fine, just exhausted. We'll get her to bed, don't worry," the girls advised him. Reassured by this, and satisfied that he'd done his duty, Mr Crossley turned on his heel and made his way upstairs to join his wife for a well-earned drink himself and a bit of relaxation listening to the piano player. He had been on reception duty for most of the evening, and now it was the turn of the night porter to clock on for duty.

Later on, the four girls were ensconced up in Shirley's bedroom, contemplating the party and the evening's events.

"Well, that was a success" said Anna. "What a great evening, wasn't it?"

But Melanie's mind was wandering. Why had Mitch just gone like that? She had been keeping her emotions in check, but as she let herself think about it all she became close to tears and the alcohol she had consumed wasn't helping as her heart began to ache. The look he gave her as he left was etched on her mind. She thought he looked apologetic. Now she was trying to analyse it. Was he really sorry? She had to go and meet him to put her mind at rest if nothing else. Her mind was in a whirl. She knew he didn't want to appear soppy or stupid in front of his friends; he was being teased and had given in to peer pressure, that was all. He did love her. He had told her often enough. Even just tonight he had whispered that song in her ear. Knowing full well by now that Mitch was part of a gang of young boys who were used to ripping each other apart, she reasoned that he just didn't know how to behave with her when the lads were around, and his awkwardness had clearly shown through a couple of hours earlier. She would go and meet him, at least see what he had to say.

Suddenly however, and without warning, there was that questioning voice inside her head again: "He's never actually taken you on a proper date though, has he? He just turns up, usually with his mates in tow, and takes you over like a possession." "What's it got to do with you? Go away" she said to that voice of reason, "I don't want to listen to you." For in her heart Melanie knew that there was never any doubt that she would go and meet him. She just had to make it clear in her mind.

She turned to her friends for some reassurance. "He

seems ashamed of me in front of his mates, although he tells me I'm beautiful," she whispered to Shirley.

"You are beautiful Melanie, and he thinks so too. I've seen the way he looks at you," Shirley replied, slightly wistfully. "I wish I had a boy as good looking as him who'd look longingly at me like that."

Her friends' views were mixed. Anna was adamant that she shouldn't give him the time of day. "If he's not prepared to stay at the party and be with you when we've gone to so much trouble then he's not worth it. He would have stayed if he really loved you," she said.

Sammy, who wasn't really capable of processing the conversation, just waved drunkenly into the air and said "Go, just go. Go and get your man."

Shirley laughed, but as well as being concerned for her friend's welfare, she was worried that Melanie would be caught by the night porter and get into trouble.

"Don't worry Shirley, I won't land you in it," Melanie reassured her. "I'll go out the back way and if I'm seen I'll say you are asleep and don't know anything about it."

As 1 am approached, Melanie sneaked out of the rear of the hotel into the back lane. It was very dark and she had to edge herself along the wall to the end. As she emerged onto the prom she was amazed to see how busy it still was. She had never been out this late, but there were still plenty of holidaymakers around, laughing and shouting as they made their way back to their hotels or headed towards the newly-built casino which was open late into the night.

Mitch was waiting for her opposite the hotel, down on the beach as promised. He had his back to her and was casually throwing stones into the sea. As Melanie approached and called to him, he turned and immediately noticed the strained expression on that beautiful face.

"You look as if you're afraid of something" he said. "Are you all right?" He tried to take her hand, but she pulled away.

"It's just how much I'm falling for you, and I'm scared of getting hurt. You behave differently sometimes and it confuses me," said Melanie. Even as she said it her resolve was weakened by the crestfallen, bewildered look on his face.

"You won't hurt me, will you?" she whispered, so quietly her words almost floated away with the sea breeze.

"I'm sorry. You must know I'd never do anything to hurt you," he replied. Those were the words she needed to hear, but as he said them she took a step backwards. She wasn't ready to give in and forgive him that easily.

He hadn't seen her stubborn streak up until now. "Please don't fight me, I'm confused too" he said, pulling her into his arms and kissing her neck. "Please don't doubt me either. I love you, Melanie. I'd be lost without you."

She could feel his hand on her back pressing her to him, feel its heat through the thin material of her dress. Finally, she began to relax, but not before pushing him for more answers.

"Then why did you go off with the boys and leave me on my own at the party when you knew I'd been looking forward to spending the whole evening with you?"

"I'm sorry Melanie, really I am. I didn't think I'd be welcome back at the party after what happened, especially as your friends don't seem to like me anyway. I felt I just had to go with the boys and get them away from the party as I knew they were brewing for trouble. I had to go with them. You don't understand the shit I get, especially when it comes to you."

She turned her face to him and he kissed her, gently to begin with, but she could feel the passion rising in her, and when they finally broke apart they were both breathing hard. They sat again on the steps leading from the beach. Those steps were getting to be a habit, their special place, and tonight Melanie could see that the stars were out in abundance as she stared upwards at the beautiful sky.

"Are you cold?" asked Mitch. "This should warm you up a bit." He handed her a bottle which contained some spirit or other and she downed a large mouthful gratefully. Cold? Hardly. She could feel the heat radiating from his body as they sat closely together. Her heart raced and her legs shook.

"I love your dress, by the way, what there is of it," he murmured as he kissed one of her bare shoulders. Resistance was futile. Her heart melted, and she gave in to her feelings.

"You have such passion in you for someone so young," he said.

The alcohol was making her light-headed. She heard herself saying "I am a passionate girl. I'm passionate about a lot of things. I love fashion and music, but I'm also passionate about winning in sport, animal welfare, oh and maths! And George Harrison. Oh, and you." She giggled.

Mitch grinned. "My dad says I'm going to be a famous mathematician one day. You won't be laughing at me then. Dad says there's a beautiful logic to maths. You think you know exactly where you are but it's always full of patterns and riddles. Just as my head is now." She took another swig from the bottle. Mitch simply smiled and nodded in agreement, for he realised that the alcohol was taking effect on Melanie and it was probably nearly time to take her back to the hotel and her friends.

They could hear music floating out from one of the hotels. The whole length of the prom was alive with all sorts of venues, all fit to bursting. It was the height of summer and anything went. He led her up onto the promenade walkway, held her hands and started to move in time to the beat. She was embarrassed and shy at first with all the passers-by looking on, but they just looked on them with fondness or amusement, and gradually she lost her inhibitions and started to dance too, captivated by him. He was so charismatic and so much fun. Without thinking, she jumped into his arms, giggling uncontrollably, her face flushed with excitement. He twirled her round in the air in his arms and hugged her close to him before putting her down.

A slow, rhythmic beat now emanated from the hotel's open doors and they drifted into a slow dance as she held his gaze, caught in the moment. He looked longingly at her as her face lit up with the sheer delight of it all and she gazed around her and up at the distant blanket of stars that covered the sky.

"I wish we could just stay here all night," she said happily in his ear.

"I think your friends would have something to say about that. I don't want to get into their bad books any more than I am already, so I think I'd better behave like a gentleman and get you back."

Suddenly Melanie spotted something and froze. Her dreamy expression changed to one of horror, and she turned and ran for the steps back down to the beach. Mitch was mystified by her behaviour and, as she crouched down behind the sea wall, he joined her.

"What the hell's up with you Melanie? What's going on?"

"Oh God, it's my parents" she whispered. "They're walking along the prom towards us."

"Shit, did they see you?" said Mitch.

"I don't know" she hissed back. "I've only just spotted them. They're so close, they might have done. Oh no, what if they have?"

The next couple of minutes seemed to take forever to pass. Finally, Melanie took a deep breath and began to calm down. She had taken a brief peek through the railings above her head and seen the figures of her parents ambling slowly into the distance.

"I guess not" she said finally, nervous laughter rising up inside her. "They were coming out of the casino. I'd forgotten, but they told me they've been there once before. I never thought I'd see them out and about on the town at this time. Phew! That was a close call."

Yet a realisation was developing in Melanie's mind of the scene she had just witnessed, one that would be imprinted in her mind's eye for ever; her mother looking modern and pretty in a long hippyish dress, her parents holding hands and smiling and chatting away intimately, sharing a moment between them without a care in the world and as if there was no one else in their lives. It was something she had never witnessed before. They looked young and happy, not how she thought of them at all, and it suddenly dawned on Melanie that her parents' life together wasn't mundane after all. They loved each other and were genuinely happy together. And her mother had been walking barefoot, carrying her sandals, just as Melanie herself did. 'Wow, how weird is that?' she thought.

She shared none of these thoughts with Mitch. As he saw the relief register on her face, closely followed by that wonderful smile of hers, he could not help but see what a gorgeous creature she was.

"God you're beautiful," he said. "I could stay here all night with you, but I'd better behave myself and get you back to the hotel before anything else happens."

Melanie was feeling braver now, and the effects of the alcohol and that strong instinctive attraction she had for him were making her feel bolder than she usually was.

"OK. But I've put my trust back in you, Tom Mitchell. You had better not break my heart."

"I won't. Promise. Come on, let's go."

As he saw her safely across the road and to the back door of the hotel, she felt like she was in heaven, lost in a warm place somewhere in time and space and floating on air. She was exhilarated by the new feelings of freedom and independence that she had just experienced, and she felt capable of anything, including manoeuvring her way up the back staircase without waking anyone, sliding into bed, and dropping off to sleep without trying to analyse her feelings, which she managed to do for once, aided undoubtedly by the rather large amount of alcohol she'd managed to consume.

The next morning, she awoke to Sammy's plaintive moaning. "Oh God. What did I do last night?" came her wail from the bottom double bunk bed in the corner. "My mind's a total blank. I'm confused and my head hurts like Hell. What DID I do last night?" Sammy groaned as patchy memories started flooding that painful space where her brain should be.

"Apart from dancing on a table, drinking copious amounts of vodka with Jack and snogging the face off him, you mean?" chided Anna.

"Oh, don't be so cruel. I wasn't that bad, was I?"

"Yes!" came the unanimous, amused response. "But don't worry" Shirley added considerately, "you passed out before anything too bad could happen!"

"Oh no. How embarrassing is that? Anyway, how did you get on with Mitch?" enquired Sammy to Melanie, who was lying sleepily next to her in the double bed.

As Melanie gradually came to, stretched her body out lazily and looked inside her head for an answer, she realised that she felt really alive, full of teenage passion and desire. She had experienced something totally new and exciting; her perspective had altered and she felt she was moving towards something, but something she couldn't quite put her finger on. She was lost in her thoughts.

Sammy, having waited so long for a response, enquired of nobody in particular, "Am I missing something here?"

"Not a lot Sam," Anna piped up. She leaned over and peered down at them from the top bunk opposite them. "That is if you discount the fact that Melanie's Mitch only went and punched the lights out of Percy. Oh, and that was just before he went and left Melanie on her own and disappeared off with his mates looking for a better party somewhere else."

"What? Mitch had a fight with Percy? Percy Tomkinson?

You're joking, aren't you?"

"Why would I joke about it? It was quite exciting. The best bit of the party. And Percy wasn't half taken down a peg or two in front of his mates. I was quite taken with Mitch, actually. He can really handle himself. I have to admit he went up a bit in my estimation at the time, but that was before he showed his true colours and swanned off into the night with his mates."

"Oh, my God! That's awful, simply awful. Poor Melanie!" said Sammy, genuinely concerned. She turned to her friend.

"Poor Melanie?" snorted Anna contemptuously. "Don't waste your sympathy there. Poor Melanie here sneaked out and met him on the beach at one o'clock this morning. And God only knows what time she got back, or what she got up to for that matter. And it's all back on with lover boy, judging by the look on her face anyway, all smug, lying there. He's leading you astray and I just hope you know what you're doing. Melanie Jackson. You've never done anything like that before."

Melanie had to acknowledge that one, but it had all been so exciting. It might have been the first time she had seriously broken any rules, but it certainly wouldn't be the last.

"I'm really not sure that I do know what I'm doing" Melanie replied, and left it at that as she didn't want to have another confrontation with Anna. She was young and these were new and intense feelings. All she knew right then was that she felt truly happy.

As it happened, Mitch woke up that morning with similar feelings. He wasn't confused about Melanie, or his feelings for her, as the previous evening had finished on such a high note. What confused him was the attitude of his mates. How could he reconcile being in love and wanting to spend more time with Melanie with the taunting and the pressure his pals were putting him under? He wasn't comfortable with feeling like an outsider. It was way outside his comfort zone, and he was genuinely struggling to come to terms with it.

CHAPTER 16

Love blossoms

After her heady experience down at the beach, there was another shifting of Melanie's perceptions. She no longer felt innocent, and she was high on love. She recognised the passionate feelings stirring inside her as desire. She had seen those films where lovers looked dreamily into each other's eyes, a smouldering tension that lay just beneath the surface, a subtle portrayal of passion and lust and now she understood that look, those feelings. During those sunny summer days of 1967 Melanie and Mitch fell truly and deeply in love, intoxicated by their feelings for each other and the sheer joy and excitement of their summer romance.

Melanie, who had initially been intrigued by Mitch and his beguiling ways, so different to any other boy she had met previously, became increasingly attracted to him as their relationship continued to develop. She became so convinced that she was in love with him that she displaced her friends, kept secrets from them and developed a life which she hid from her friends as well as her parents. The only exception was Saturdays, which were sacrosanct to the girls and to the boys as well. But even then, Mitch and Melanie would somehow find a way to meet up 'accidentally', usually at the Palace.

They met up at every opportunity, Melanie walking down to see him when he came out of work on occasions, pretending all the while she was off to Shirley's in case her mother was in prying mode, but eventually throwing caution to the wind by the fact that she no longer alerted Shirley to her devious behaviour.

At other times she waited restlessly but eagerly at her bedroom window, knowing he had promised to walk past after work, excitement building whenever she saw his figure approaching. Sometimes he'd be with Tony but, even then, he somehow managed to do something to set her heart on fire; looking up at her and blowing her a kiss behind Tony's back, or gesturing with his arms in the shape of a heart.

Deep down there remained a certain amount of conflict in Melanie's head between her sense of reasoning and the wilder instincts and feelings of passion he brought out in her. But she always quelled any unwelcome thoughts, and when she was with him she could think of nothing else. When she wasn't with him she thought of him constantly, wondering where he was, what he was doing, wishing she could be with him.

Her stubborn and rebellious streak came to the fore

when she had been grounded for staying out way too late one night and worrying her mother and father half to death in the process, something she had never done before. She seethed with indignation and frustration, furious that her parents could impose such a restriction on her. How dare they! She determined that they weren't going to prevent her from seeing Mitch and one day managed to get a message to him at work through her trusted friend Shirley to let him know she'd been grounded but that she'd find a way to meet him on the beach later that night, already planning her escape route in her head.

She was angry and desperate and her teenage logic was, "My parents are already punishing me, what else can they do to me?"

Later that evening, in fiercely determined mode, she climbed gingerly out of her bedroom window, even though there was a considerable drop to the ground, but knowing it was the only way out, as the stairs creaked and her parents had only just gone to bed. She somehow managed to scramble, somewhat indelicately, down the drainpipe alongside her window before letting go and tumbling the last few feet down to the ground below, thankfully without incurring any injury other than to her dignity. Having reached terra firma relatively unscathed, she breathed a huge sigh of relief. That was the hard bit, for she knew she could easily sneak back in later via the garage door at the back that was never locked. She was confident that by that time her parents would be fast asleep, and her night time escapade would remain blissfully undetected.

Wrong! Unfortunately for her, Jim was sitting on her bed when she sneaked back in at 2 am with his head in his hands, fear and disappointment written all over his face. Melanie, full of remorse, broke down. She was genuinely mortified, profusely apologetic, so sorry to have caused so much worry, promised she would never do it again and meant it, but she was still immature, not really old enough to appreciate any danger associated with her actions, or how distraught her parents really were. It was an empty promise, one that was to be broken regularly in the coming months.

Every encounter and shared experience with Mitch, however brief, heightened her senses, made her feel truly alive; a new excitement in her previously relatively sheltered life. He seemed so confident and worldly wise in her eyes by comparison to the other boys she'd ever met. Rebellious, defiant, but strangely deep, gentle, affectionate, and passionate.

Mitch too, maintained a certain amount of secrecy about their meetings, still aware of the tauntings he would get from his mates that he'd gone soft in the head. But to them both it was real. Serious. He had found an amazing girl and the pull was so strong, arousing so much passion in him, although he knew he had to take it slowly. To him she was a beautiful person inside and out. Beautiful, caring, thoughtful, intelligent, challenging, cute, adorable, thought-provoking, complex, sensual, loving, funny, so exciting to be with, to name but a few of her many attributes. She really was a one-off. He loved her, wanted to be with her, just wanted her.

They sincerely believed that theirs was a true love, that they would never be parted, they belonged together; soulmates in the truest sense of the word.

They sat in little summer cafés and talked about the hopes, dreams, and future adventures they would have in the lives which stretched out before them, the struggles they were both experiencing with peer-pressure, their fears, their different backgrounds, and the respective relationships they had with their parents.

Melanie had strong, although youthful, opinions on the world. In her mind so many things could be changed for the better if everyone would stop putting themselves first. Her simple vision was an end to world hunger and poverty, and helping those less fortunate. Her generation could create a world full of love and peace. They could change the world where others had failed, they were young and idealistic, and they would lead the way.

Mitch and Melanie were like-minded individuals, both filled with excitement and positivity about the future, and enthusiastic about any challenges along the way. This was a time for adventure and exploration, filled with opportunities, freedom, and inspiration. They were certain they would maintain their love for each other. Their friendships, they acknowledged, although strong now, might be broken and doubtless there would be many new friends along the way: the discord they both experienced at home and school, those restrictions would be gone, but they were convinced that as a couple they were made to last. The intensity of their relationship scared Melanie from time to time, but Mitch always reassured her that he wanted her and only her. "You're safe with me Melanie. We are forever," he would whisper in her ear.

They enjoyed going to the pictures together to see the latest movies, *To Sir with Love* and *Bonnie and Clyde*, to name but two. Ground-making though the movies may have been, they simply enjoyed being together, sitting close to each other in the dimly-lit theatre, with the slightest of touches on the arm, both wanting more, getting closer, oblivious to the film and those around them, softly whispering in each other's ears. Clasping hands, experiencing such a feeling of intimacy yet in a public place. Turning to each other, faces and lips so close, Melanie's heart beating so loudly in her ears she was sure everyone else would hear it during the quieter moments in the cinema.

Sometimes they walked together along the river during his brief lunch breaks, Melanie having finished her summer job. They were walking hand-in-hand together one day when Mitch stopped and drew her to him. The next minute he found himself flat on his back. It all happened so fast. Two young boys were tearing along the towpath on their bikes and managed to strike Mitch as they hurtled past. He fell on his back, sliding on the grass, and Melanie tripped and landed on top of him. He was winded, and just lay there looking up into her face with that soft, sweet smile. Her hair tumbled forward, gently brushing his nose. He was entranced as he gazed into those perfect blue eyes. He gently pulled her towards him to meet his lips, a kiss so tender and yet passionate at the same time. She couldn't get enough of him and returned his kiss with another, until it dawned on them that the two youngsters were still looking at them, nudging each other and making childish remarks as kids are prone to do.

The young lads eventually got the message and carried on their way, leaving behind them nothing but the sound of the trickling water. Mitch put his arms round Melanie's waist and looked deeply into her eyes before declaring, totally out of the blue, "One day I'm going to marry you, Melanie Jackson."

Melanie was stunned, and initially she wasn't sure if he was joking or serious. She managed to keep her cool, even though inside the butterflies were stirring again.

"Oh really?" she laughed.

"Well, perhaps I should say I'm going to ask you to marry me. Maybe I was being a bit presumptuous," he added with a smile.

"Yes, maybe you were" she replied teasingly. She reached up and put her arms round his neck. Their faces touched, and she gave in to yet another beautiful kiss that sent her spinning on the spot.

Mitch gazed intently into her eyes when they drew apart. "Well?" he said.

"Well what?" she asked, looking innocently at him.

"What will your answer be, Jackson?"

She still wasn't sure whether he was being serious, but she couldn't resist any more. "Of course I'll marry you, Mitchell" she said, and she genuinely believed it. They were under each other's spell, and it certainly felt serious.

Against all the odds that summer, Mitch and Melanie kept their new-found love for each other alive. Their blossoming relationship was full of sweetness, warmth and the burning intensity of new feelings never felt in such depth before. They both believed with all their hearts they were destined to be together.

Mitch had so much to deal with, the stick from his

mates, the rift that was ever increasing between himself and his mother, making his home life intolerable, not to mention having to work such long hours in his summer job whilst desperately trying to meet up with Melanie whenever he could. Melanie had her own problems. Although her friends were much kinder and gentler on her, they were still always on at her about how they believed Mitch wasn't what he seemed and said she was losing self-control, consumed by him as she was. On top of this she had to deal with her parents, always there in the background, keeping a quiet but firm eye on her.

Soon summer was coming to an end, and the school holidays were drawing to a close. Since Melanie would only be allowed out at weekends when term started, their last midweek date was to be a party in Peel. The girls had recently met a friend of Mitch's, Dixie, who initially appeared rough and ready, but who was polite and gracious to the girls, unlike most of Mitch's friends, and they all came to have a soft spot for him. More importantly, Dixie had a car and was driving them to Peel. Mitch had managed to persuade Melanie to bring Shirley along at Dixie's insistence, as he had a bit of a crush on her.

Melanie was now confident in their all-consuming relationship and looking forward to the evening. Shirley was more than willing to go to the party with her. She had missed her company. She knew that Melanie had been neglecting her friends and exactly what had been on her agenda, but she wasn't judging, for she had never seen her friend so happy

As she got ready for the evening ahead, flushed with excitement, Melanie was blissfully unaware that events later that night would soon change everything between them, turning her world upside down in the process, and testing their fairytale romance to the limit.

CHAPTER 17

Dixie

Dixie was a relatively new addition to the boys but, as time passed, he became an integral member of the group. Tony and Dixie knew each other well from time they had spent together as army cadets in their younger days. Although Dixie was a year older than the other boys, Mitch also knew him and his family well as they'd attended the same primary school and lived close to each other when they were young.

Dixie's mum, Doris, was a real character. She was a hard-living, outgoing widow with a vibrant personality, who always had a warm welcome and a hearty, deep-throated laugh for all the customers who frequented the fish shop she ran, including Mitch when he popped in every week to pick up the family's order. From a very early age he had warmed to her, wishing all mums could be like her.

Dixie had inherited many of his mum's characteristics, not least her extrovert character, sense of fun and lack of inhibitions. Taken at face value, he was a yard dog of the first order, and was often perceived by others as an irresponsible buffoon. He preferred to portray a tough, brash exterior to the outside world, but underneath it all, once you got to know him on a one-to-one basis, he had a heart of gold. He also had a sensitive side, which he was careful to conceal from strangers, which was a pity in many ways as few people got to know the real Dixie the way Mitch did. Long boozy nights spent round at Dixie's house with him and his mum were sheer joy for a young teenager, as Doris had an open mind and was happy to let the boys relax and enjoy themselves with no restrictions. "Smoke, drink, do what you want boys. Have fun and enjoy yourselves. Believe me, life's too short not to, and I should know," she was fond of saying, as she knocked back another large swig of rum.

Dixie had had a tough life, having lost his dad, a hard-drinking Navy man, at an early age. In his early teens, Dixie had been involved in a serious accident when a pillion passenger on his older brother Steve's motor bike. He had suffered a serious leg injury which had resulted in a major operation to save his leg. Now he had to wear a built-up shoe on one foot, forcing him to walk with a pronounced limp for the rest of his life. His inability to take part in sport with the other lads, or any other strenuous activities for that matter, meant that he had piled on the weight in his early teenage years, but he was never heard to complain about his lot in life.

Dixie was not blessed with naturally good looks, and he had a tendency to be coarse at times, even in mixed company, so he was not the most attractive proposition to the opposite sex. However, Mitch knew from their long chats that deep down he yearned for female company, although he did not speak of this to the other lads. Mitch was comfortable when he was alone with Dixie and they became confidants of sorts, with a mutual trust between them. In quieter moments, the yard dog would disappear and the sensitive side of Dixie would prevail. As time passed Mitch grew to confide in him whenever he sought to clear his thoughts and feelings for one girlfriend or another, and Dixie was a good listener.

Being a little older than the others, Dixie had managed to pass his driving test when he was sixteen, the legal age for driving on the island. As a result, a whole new world opened up to him and his friends. Dixie's mum was happy for him to use her car, which she had little need for, so the boys had transport. They could now extend their activities to all parts of the Island; pubs, dance halls, parties anywhere, were now all within their reach, and they were not slow to take advantage.

Mitch had just turned fifteen when Dixie took it upon himself to teach him to drive in Doris's car. The fact that Mitch wasn't legally old enough to drive a vehicle on the open roads, had no driving licence and consequently wasn't insured, was of little or no consequence to either Dixie or Mitch; they would simply jump in the car and shoot off wherever and whenever the mood took them. Despite his young age and Dixie's somewhat unorthodox approach to instruction, Mitch turned out to be a competent and confident driver, better in fact than Dixie, who went on to write off three cars in fairly quick succession for his mother, fortunately without injury to him, his mates, or anyone else in the process.

He might well have written off more than three cars if it hadn't been for Mitch stepping into the breach and assuming driving duties on the way home from their many alcoholic-fuelled evenings out around the Island. Although the boys knew that Mitch's alcoholic consumption was on a par with Dixie's, they also knew that his eyesight was vastly superior. On the balance of probabilities therefore, they reasoned that with Mitch driving they were less likely to end up overturned in a ditch somewhere.

Amongst her other attributes, Doris was an enlightened, extremely tolerant and forgiving person, and never took umbrage with either Dixie or the boys following their madcap episodes. In fact, much to Mitch's surprise, Dixie's mum was both delighted and proud when she heard he had learnt to drive her car.

"Well done Mitch. Fancy you being able to drive at your age. I bet your mum is really proud of you. You know I don't like driving so you'll be able to drive me into town and back, now won't you?" was her immediate reaction.

Dixie's older brother Steve had a very similar outlook on life; it was he who taught Mitch how to ride a motorbike around the same time. Mitch was enthralled by the sheer joy and freedom to be found in hurtling along the Island's roads at breakneck speed at every opportunity on Steve's gleaming Triumph. These were heady days for all the boys, now that their band of four had become a band of five.

For the last two summers Mitch had managed to get a

job working at the local laundry, which needed extra staff to cope with increased demand brought about by the heavy influx of visitors. The work was both laborious and monotonous, and the hours were long, with staff often required to work from eight in the morning until sometimes as late as ten in the evening, as well as putting in a Saturday shift finishing after lunch. Working conditions were poor and the foreman had targets to meet, so he was demanding, to put it mildly. His wrath would descend on anyone caught talking to a workmate, or sneaking a couple of minutes longer on their break. But the pay was good, especially for a young lad, and you simply had to get on and make the most of it whilst the season lasted.

Mitch's role consisted of shaking out pillowcases and stretching them on a compressed-air operated rack ready for pressing through the large pressing machines. Throughout the day large wooden bogies filled to the brim with soaking pillowcases would roll continuously up alongside him, one after the other. No sooner would one be empty than the next one would appear with its load of washing waiting for him to dive in, shake, press, and stretch. Every day was an interminable drag. Thanks to his working hours, Mitch was struggling to catch up with the boys and his beloved Melanie. He and Tony, who by this time had left school and become an apprentice engineer at the laundry, had to rely for transport on the works van that picked the workforce up of a morning and dropped them off at predetermined collection and drop-off points when shifts were finished unless they chose to walk to the Woody on their way home, passing Melanie's house as they did so, to get a couple of pints in the men's bar before last orders came around. There just wasn't enough time to get home, get changed and freshen up before heading down to the Palace, so its delights had to be savoured at weekends only.

One day, however, Mitch had something to look forward to, for Dixie had just taken delivery of a brand-new car, a special treat from his mum. It came complete with a wooden rally-style steering wheel. Mitch was naturally chuffed for his buddy, as the new acquisition meant that the lads would never be short of transport in future, and he also knew it wouldn't be long before he got the chance to try it out for himself. But the big thing he was looking forward to was the evening which lay ahead.

The laundry shift was finishing at half past seven that evening and he'd arranged for himself and Dixie to pick up Melanie and Shirley and drive them down to a party that was being held in Peel, about ten miles away. He was getting a mid-week chance to spend the evening with his girl, a rare treat indeed, and something to occupy his thoughts throughout his shift. He knew Dixie was looking forward to it as well, as not only would he be able to take his new vehicle for a spin but Mitch knew he was also harbouring thoughts about getting off with Shirley during the course of the evening. Mitch knew that Shirley didn't have the same idea and was never likely to, but there was no point disillusioning his mate and spoiling what should be a good night.

The morning shift dragged on as usual, so Mitch was delighted when he heard the klaxon sound the call for the lunch break. Quickly gathering his sandwich box, he made his way out into the bright sunlight, where he was somewhat surprised to see Dixie sitting outside in his new vehicle, proud as punch and with a big smile plastered all over his face.

"Jump in, matey," he said. "Fancy going for a quick spin then?"

"Too right I do" replied Mitch, laughing as he jumped into the empty passenger seat.

Dixie was grinning like a Cheshire cat. "What do you think of her then? Like the steering wheel or what?"

"It's a cracker Dix. I haven't got much time mind, we only get half an hour so you'd better put your foot down."

"Watch my smoke, sunshine" was Dixie's response as he gunned the car down the side road heading for the far end of the building and the main road where they could put the new acquisition through its paces. As they turned onto the open road, tyres screeching as they gripped the tarmac hard, Mitch grinned and nodded in appreciation. "Wow Dixie, it's the biz" he said. "I can't wait to give it a whirl myself, you jammy beggar."

Dixie was in his element and the car performed beautifully as he gave it full throttle on the winding road and threw it hard into corners to see how hard he could push it. Mitch was thrilled at how the car performed as well, but after a while he looked at his watch and realised that time was creeping on and he needed to get back to work. "You'd better turn her round up the road here Dix and head back or I'm going to be late" he said. "What time are you picking me up tonight then? If you pick me up straight from work then we'll save some time and get out earlier."

"What's on tonight then? I didn't know we had anything planned" Dixie replied.

"You dozy pillock!" said Mitch. "We're supposed to be picking up Melanie and Shirley and going to that party in Peel, remember?"

Dixie clearly didn't remember, as in response he simply shrugged his shoulders and shook his head and thought for a few moments before he replied, "Now you mention it yes, I do remember, but I'm not really up for a party. I think I'd rather just pop into town and have a few pints with the lads."

Mitch was taken aback. He couldn't bear the thought of ruining his plans for the coming evening. He was desperate to see Melanie and spend some precious time with her before the weekend, and the party beckoned tantalisingly. So, thinking on his feet, he played his trump card. "OK mate. I understand, but it would be a pity if you were to miss out on a night with Shirley when you could have her all to yourself, wouldn't it? It's up to you," he added, seeing Dixie wavering. "No skin off my nose matey."

Mitch knew instinctively that he'd struck a chord and he could sense his mate's brain ticking over as Dixie mulled this over. Mitch could be an annoying little prick at times, but there again, he could well be right. It would indeed be a pity to forego the chance of copping off with Shirley.

"OK, OK" Dixie sighed. "I'll give it a go, if only to shut you up, you pillock."

"That'll do me" Mitch responded, a smile back on his face again as they arrived back at the laundry. "I've got every faith in you my boy. Meet me outside here at half seven then, and don't be late. I've got to go now, get back into work. See you later then Dix."

With that he turned and left, whistling happily to himself as he made his way back into work, still chuckling at the way he'd managed to sway good old Dixie.

CHAPTER 18

Party night in Peel

As soon as the klaxon sounded for the end of shift that evening, Mitch grabbed his things and made straight for the exit, hastily clocking off before heading out expectantly into the evening sunlight. There was a bounce in his stride, and his confidence was rewarded when he spotted Dixie in his car, engine running ready for the off. "Yes!" he said to himself, clenched fist pumping the air. "Good old Dixie, I knew he wouldn't let me down." With a big grin on his face he made his way swiftly to the car, grabbed open the passenger door, leaned his head in and opened his mouth as if to speak. But before he could utter so much as a word, Dixie piped up and cut him short.

"Shut it arsehole. Don't even think about giving me

stick. Keep your smartarse remarks to yourself or we're not going anywhere. Right?"

Mitch burst out laughing at his mate's remarks, but at the same time he couldn't resist having a gentle dig. "OK Dix, you win. I won't say a word. Promise. After all, it's your car, so you call the shots buddy." He laughed.

Fortunately, his laughter was matched by Dixie's, who was in a good mood himself, all things being considered. He'd been expecting Mitch's playful banter and piss-taking and happily played along with it. They were off to a party, and there was always the prospect of hitting it off with the lovely Shirley.

"Right Dix, enough messing about, let's get me home. I need to change and freshen up. I've arranged to pick Melanie and Shirley up at around eight so you need to get your finger out bud." With that Dixie popped the car into gear and off they headed with big grins on their faces.

With Mitch duly smartened up and in his party gear, best boots and all, the pair set off to pick up the girls from Melanie's house. The two girls were waiting up the road from Melanie's front gate, away from any potential prying eyes, and chatting away excitely. Mitch couldn't contain himself at the sight of Melanie.

"Wow! Look at my girl Dix. What a stunner." And Dix could only nod his head appreciatively as his eyes lit on Melanie dressed in a clinging white blouse which highlighted her deeply-tanned skin and was complemented by the shortest of deep blue miniskirts. Her black hair tumbled playfully across her shoulders and face in the light summer breeze.

But Dixie's real interest was in the girl who stood beside

her. "I'll settle for Shirley though mate. She's a belter," he said.

Mitch smiled knowingly. "I'll sit in the back with Melanie then, and Shirley can sit up front with you Dix" he swiftly replied, with a broad grin on his face.

The car drew to a halt and he jumped out to welcome the girls. "You've drawn the short straw I'm afraid, Shirley," said Mitch. "You've got the front seat with Dixie. And as for you Jackson, you are just so lucky. You're in the back with me. Come on then, jump in girls."

He opened the back door for Melanie and without further ado the girls got into the car. Melanie was showing more enthusiasm than Shirley, but Shirley quite liked Dixie on the quiet, although she'd never mentioned it to any of her friends. He could be boisterous at times, a bit rough and ready maybe, but Shirley had a wise head on her shoulders and knew that underneath that hard exterior there was a softer, gentler side once you got to know him. And he'd always behaved like a gentleman in her presence.

Dixie put his foot to the floor, and within a quarter of an hour they were approaching the outskirts of Peel, the main town on the west coast of the island, its port and harbour a thriving base for the island's fishing fleet. As they approached their destination they could see the sun starting to set ahead of them, casting a beautiful red glow across the evening skies above the town.

Mitch and Melanie were cuddled up close in the back of the car, comfortable in each other's company, but their shared mellowness was abruptly broken by Dixie.

"Where's this bloody party then Mitch? Give us a clue, why don't you?"

"Dix, you really are such a romantic, aren't you? It's at Herb's mum's café on the main drag in town. They live in the flat upstairs and the café's shut of an evening so his mum's letting him hold the party there. You can park up outside if it's not busy mate, save us walking."

Shortly afterwards Dixie pulled the car into the side of the road and parked up outside the café. As the four of them jumped out of the car they could hear the unmistakable sound of The Who's latest record blasting out from inside the café, indicating that the party was well and truly under way. They hurriedly made their way through the front door to be greeted by a cacophony of sound and a mass of teenagers, bobbing, weaving, and swaying in time with the beat of the music and shouting to make themselves heard above the din.

The four of them stood just inside the door for a few minutes, taking in the scene in front of them and soaking up the atmosphere, before Mitch nodded in the direction of the bar which had been set up on the counter at the far end of the room. With Mitch leading the way and the others following they jostled their way gingerly through the mass of heaving bodies until they reached their objective, where Mitch and Dixie deposited the cans of beer they'd brought along with them. Spotting a bottle of vodka on the counter, Mitch poured a couple of large vodka and cokes for the girls, split open two cans of beer for himself and Dixie and distributed them to his eager friends, for whom the party was just beginning.

Making up for lost time, Mitch and Dixie quickly downed another couple of drinks, chatting away animatedly with passing friends and acquaintances as they did so, before the four of them eventually made their way onto the crowded dance floor. Fuelled by a few pints of bitter as he was by this time, even Dixie made a reasonable attempt at dancing, in his view at least. Shirley didn't care that he wasn't as good on the dance floor as he imagined. For once she'd let her reserve drop, having sunk a few vodkas more than she usually would, and she was having a ball, much to Melanie's amazement and delight, as she caught sight of her friend letting her hair down for once and really getting into the swing of things.

After a while Mitch tired of dancing. It was good fun, but all he wanted to do was spend some time with his girl. During a brief break in the music he leaned over to Melanie, drew her close to him and whispered in her ear. "How about we get out of here, go for a walk, just the two of us?"

Melanie didn't need a second invitation and he could see by her sparkling eyes that she was just as keen as he was to be alone together. Holding her hand, he led her across the crowded floor and out into the fresh air and peace and tranquillity away from the bustling throng still partying enthusiastically in the cafe.

Lost in their own little world, they wandered down to the harbour, only a short stroll from the main street where they'd been partying just a few minutes previously. The scene that met them as they turned the corner onto the quayside itself was idyllic, almost breathtaking. There was hardly a soul in sight and the lights reflected from the boats tied up against each side of the harbour wall flickered and shimmied playfully across the water as the boats themselves bobbed up and down gently from side to side on the incoming tide. Hand in hand they sauntered along the quayside before sitting down on one of the conveniently-placed benches which lined the harbour. They sat there for some time, Melanie snuggled up to Mitch with her head nestled on his shoulder, his protective arm around her, as they savoured the scene.

After a short while, having shared a cigarette together, Mitch noticed Melanie shiver and realised that the night air was growing colder, so he suggested heading back to grab a couple of more drinks at the party. Melanie agreed, somewhat reluctantly, but she too was starting to feel the cold. It was comforting to feel Mitch's arm holding her close as they meandered back along the quayside, chatting away happily.

When they got back to the party, Mitch suddenly had an idea. The car was parked up outside – why not make use of it? Turning to Dixie, he asked him for the keys.

"Where are you off to then?" Dixie asked.

"Nowhere Dix, just off to sit in the car that's all. I thought it would be good to have a bit of private time with Melanie. It's turning a bit cold outside now, but the car will be warm and cosy." "Aha, I see" said Dixie knowingly. "You don't need the keys mate. I didn't lock it. Crack on and I'll see you later. Enjoy" he added, smiling to himself as the pair turned and walked away.

When they emerged from the café, dusk was turning gradually into night and the light was fading fast. The pair climbed into the back of the car together. It wasn't yet dark enough to prevent Mitch from gazing adoringly into Melanie's eyes and marvelling at how beautiful she was, in every way imaginable. She picked up on his mood, and that wonderful smile of hers beamed lovingly back at him. Filled with a warm glow of contentment, she nestled closer to him, her head resting on his shoulder, her hair brushing his cheek as she playfully kissed his chin before tenderly undoing a button on his shirt and pressing her hand gently against his skin. He let out a gasp as the thrill of her fingers sensually caressing him surged through his body. His head arched back, his eyes closed and his body quivered involuntarily as he savoured the sensations rippling through him. Slowly he opened his eyes and smiled as he saw the mischievous glint in Melanie's eyes.

His heart was pounding as he drew her body closer to him and embraced her in his arms, kissing her passionately. Melanie abandoned her inhibitions. Her resolve melted away, her whole being aroused, as she too was gripped by the passion of that moment. Euphoria swept through her as Mitch smothered her with kisses; her senses reeled as his lips eagerly explored her own, brushing briefly across her cheek, so passionately, yet tender at the same time. A shiver ran down her spine as he ran his lips tantalisingly along the sensitive skin of her neck. Excitement consumed her, and all sense of normality abandoned her as his hand moved to explore her body.

Mitch placed one hand in the small of her back, drawing her body ever closer to him. She initially tensed as she realised that he was unbuttoning her blouse, but she put up no resistance as slowly, button by button her firm young breasts were revealed to him. The moment took her breath away, her mind and body out of control, her eyes closed, just feeling the sensations. A sigh of delight escaped from her lips as she felt his other hand sensually caressing her sensitive, silken skin, his lips tracing patterns as they glided across her exposed shoulder. Her body was on fire, an entity of its own, separated somehow from her mind, the intensity of her feelings pulsing through her; she knew she'd lost herself, but willingly gave in to the depth of the sensations engulfing her. Aroused as she was by his passion, the intimacy of his touch on her skin, she was intoxicated, dizzy with excitement. Feeling emotionally vulnerable, strangely distant from herself, stimulated by feelings she'd never experienced before, she tried to catch her breath, calm her breathing. But she couldn't. She didn't want to for she knew she wanted more, much more. She didn't want these feelings to stop, ever.

Mitch too was consumed with a mixture of passion and lust, his body burning with desire. His breathing was shallow one moment and inexplicably deep the next as he was swept along on a wonderful wave of emotions. His body and mind were racked with excitement and expectation as he experienced feelings he'd only dreamed of previously. His heart was racing and every fibre of his body was alive to Melanie's touch.

Cocooned as they were in their own world, they failed to notice the beam of light that suddenly shone through the car's passenger window as if from nowhere, piercing the darkness and focusing on them like a spotlight and encapsulating them in its beam. Then there came a loud tapping on the window, accompanied by a gruff male voice which boomed out "Stop whatever it is you're doing in there and open this window. Now!"

Shocked into action, the pair shot bolt upright, mouths agape. "What the...?" Mitch gasped, shielding his eyes, and squinting through his raised fingers to see where the light was coming from. Alongside him Melanie was in a state of panic as she frantically struggled to cover her embarrassment by wrapping her blouse around herself, her hands trembling.

"Open this window now. Do you hear me? I won't ask you again." The light was lowered, mercifully pointing down at the road outside, and a man's face appeared close to the glass, peering into the gloom. Mitch lowered his hands and blinked his eyelids furiously as his vision adjusted and he peered out. A sense of panic swept through him too. He sat motionless for a few seconds, frozen to the spot as he realised that the face before him was topped by a helmet.

"Shit, it's a bloody copper," he said. "Get yourself covered up." He turned back and began to wind the window down.

The officer was leaning forward, his hands resting on the car's bodywork. The three stripes on his sleeve revealed that he was a sergeant. He stared menacingly at Mitch, who stared back, his mind racing. Then he saw that the policeman was smiling. "Do you realise this car is illegally parked, young fellow m'lad?" he said.

A wave of relief engulfed Mitch. He puffed out his cheeks, let out an audible sigh, shook his head slowly from side to side and stammered "Erm... er... no I didn't officer".

"Well it is son. So, you need to move it pretty damn smartish before I decide to book you."

"I would if I could officer," Mitch replied, "But – er – it's not my car."

"Oh really?" the sergeant replied somewhat mockingly. "Well whose car is it then son? And more importantly, what are you doing in it? As if I need to ask."

"Well, it was getting a bit cold outside so we thought

we'd sit in here for a while."

The sergeant laughed quietly and shook his head. "Really son? Is that what they call it these days then?"

Mitch stared at the floor in embarrassment, fearing the direction the conversation was going.

"What's your name then son, and how old are you?" asked the officer.

There was no point trying to bluff it out. "It's Mitchell, officer, Tom Mitchell. And I'm sixteen."

"OK." The officer turned his attention to Melanie, who was squirming with embarrassment and shaking like a leaf, filled with dread at the thought of how this would play out with her mum and dad. "And how about you then young lady? What's your name?"

In a trembling voice, Melanie replied 'Melanie Jackson, Officer."

"And how old are you then Melanie?"

"I'm er, fourteen. Nearly fifteen actually."

"Fourteen?" the sergeant enquired, raising an eyebrow. He had assumed her to be older.

Mitch's head swivelled abruptly to look at her. "Fourteen?" he mouthed at her. She nodded awkwardly before turning back to the officer, who had turned back to Mitch.

"So, whose car is it then son? And where's the owner?"

"It's my mate's car, and he's just at the party in the café there."

"OK, well you'd better get yourself in there and get him out here son, and make it pronto." Mitch hastily jumped out of the car and headed off in the direction of the café, leaving the door of the car open.

Once Mitch was out of earshot the sergeant spoke directly to Melanie, diverting his gaze to avoid causing her any further embarrassment.

"And you, young lady, had better make yourself respectable before your young friend gets back with the owner of this vehicle. Think yourself lucky I chanced along here when I did, and thank your lucky stars I won't be reporting this little matter to your parents."

At this the tension drained from Melanie's body. She breathed a sigh of relief.

"Thank you, officer" she replied.

"Don't just thank me young lady, listen and take heed. You're much too young to be getting up to things like this. Young boys are all the same, and they all want the same thing, believe me, so you just watch your step in future. I'll wait on the pavement over there while you make yourself decent."

Melanie nodded and thanked him again before he wandered off, satisfied at Melanie's reaction.

But Melanie knew that her feelings for Mitch were far too strong to let her take the police officer's advice. He had awakened sensations in her that she had never known existed, and never wanted to go away.

When Mitch made his way into the café he had to search for a while before he found Dixie in amongst the bodies which were still feverishly dancing. He had to take a second look to make sure it was him. Dixie was in a passionate embrace with Shirley. Dixie, with a woman? What a night this was turning into.

He pushed over to shake his friend out of his romantic interlude. "Hoy, lover boy" he shouted in Dixie's ear as he tapped him on the shoulder "Break it up mate. We've got a big problem."

A look of fury flashed across Dixie's face for a brief moment, whilst Shirley was overcome by embarrassment, feverishly brushing her hair into place as the couple parted and unable to look Mitch in the eye. Knowing there was no time for formalities, Mitch made a quick apology before leading them off the floor to where they could talk.

"What the hell's going on?" Dixie asked, realising that something must have seriously gone awry for his mate to be acting like this.

"Long story, Dix" Mitch sighed. "Top and bottom is me and Melanie were in the back of the car having a bit of a romantic interlude when a copper rolled up, knocked on the window and started banging on about how the car's illegally parked. Amongst other things" he added ruefully. "Anyway, he only wants the thing moving, pronto, doesn't he? And he's not a happy bunny I can tell you, so the sooner we get back out there the better."

"What?" gasped Dixie. "I thought you said it was all right to park there?"

"Well how the hell was I supposed to know? I don't live here, do I? Anyway, when did you start listening to me, dickhead?"

Shirley intervened at this point. "For heaven's sake you two, stop arguing. It doesn't matter whose fault it is, does it? Just let's all get out there and get it sorted. Where's Melanie anyway?"

"She's fine, she's in the car. Shirley's right Dix, we need to get back out there and sort it."

"Sort it?" snorted Dixie. I've had half a dozen pints. He'll probably arrest me if I go anywhere near the car. You'll have to drive mate."

Mitch gave him a withering look before responding "I can't bloody drive, can I you pillock? He gave me a right grilling. I had to come clean. He knows it's not my car. And I haven't passed my test yet have I? I couldn't bloody lie to him, could I? You'll have to drive," he added pointedly. "You'll just have to bluff it out Dixie. I'll go ahead of you, distract him, then you can just apologise, jump in the car and we'll head off. Get a grip, come on, there's no other option." With this he turned on his heel and gestured impatiently for Dixie and Shirley to follow as he headed for the door.

Dixie shook his head in dismay and reluctantly followed his pal, cursing his luck, and trying desperately to shake off the effects of the beers he'd consumed. Despite his best efforts, however, he was conscious that the beer was having an effect upon him. He emerged from the café and saw that Mitch was already deep in conversation with the policeman, whose back was towards him. The sergeant was writing in his notebook. This was starting to look serious. Pausing briefly to take a deep breath and compose himself, he headed towards the pair of them with a heavy heart.

But as the sergeant turned and saw Dixie, his face lit up. "Dixie! Long time no see. How's your mum doing son?"

Dixie couldn't believe his luck. He knew this officer very well; he was a friend of the family.

"Erm, she's fine thanks Rob. How're things with you? I'd forgotten you'd been posted to Peel."

The sergeant leaned closer to Dixie. "I may be a friend of the family Dixie, but best if you call me sergeant when

I'm on duty son" he said, winking conspiratorially as he did so.

"Sure thing Rob, er, sorry, sergeant" Dixie quickly corrected himself.

"Right, let's get down to business then. Is this your car Dixie?"

"Yes, it is. I only picked it up from the garage today actually."

"Well, it's parked illegally and it's causing an obstruction, so you're going to have to move it son. I can't let you leave it here any longer I'm afraid. Have you been drinking by any chance?"

"Er, yes I've had a couple of pints."

"Really? I thought you might have done as it happens," the sergeant responded, a knowing look on his face. "Well perhaps it would be best if you got you and your friends here back home to Douglas without having any more then son. You'd best take it easy mind, seeing as you've had a couple. And if you happen to get stopped tell them to get in touch with me and I'll sort it."

With that he pointedly slipped his notebook back into his top pocket and winked at Dixie. We'll say no more about it then son, and tell your mum I was asking for her, won't you?"

"I sure will sergeant. Thanks a lot." Dixie heaved a sigh of relief and climbed into the driver's seat, quickly followed by Shirley, who jumped into the passenger seat.

Mitch was still trying to come to terms with what he'd just witnessed, and was marvelling at how things had turned out. He was just about to climb into the car himself, when he was stopped by the sergeant.

"Not so fast young man. I haven't finished with you yet" he said ominously, closing the back door of the car.

Mitch's mood of elation swiftly evaporated, to be replaced by the familiar state of mild panic. What was coming now? It certainly didn't look good from where he was standing.

The sergeant glared at him for what seemed to Mitch like an eternity, but couldn't have been more than ten seconds in reality, before launching into his lecture, his voice stern and full of contempt.

"As for you son, I just don't believe you. What the hell do you think you're up to, playing the big man like that? That young girl you're with isn't much more than a child. Neither are you, come to that. You should be ashamed of yourself. Do you think it's OK to take advantage of a young girl like that? And in the back of a car? On the main road through town for heaven's sake? What kind of way is that to behave?"

Mitch made to answer, but the sergeant stopped him in his tracks. "Don't even think about it son, you'll only make things worse. You've got nothing to say that I want to hear, so keep it shut and listen. If I ever, and I mean ever, catch you up to anything like that again on my patch I'll have you down the station as quick as look at you. I'm not taking this any further for that young girl's sake, not yours. Understand?"

Mitch nodded and managed to utter a brief 'sorry' before the sergeant continued.

"Right. Bear in mind what I've said, and don't take it lightly son, because I won't if I catch you up to any of your shenanigans again, believe me." With that he took a step back and nodded towards the car "Right, get in the car and be on your way before I change my mind."

Mitch didn't need a second invitation. Suitably rebuked, and humbled as he was, he was only too grateful to take the officer at his word and make his escape.

A wave of relief swept over him as he climbed into the back of the car and slammed the door behind him, to be met by three concerned faces.

"What the hell was that all about?" Dixie asked.

"Don't ask Dix. Just drive. Let's get out of here while we can. I'll fill you in sometime."

Dixie could sense how deflated Mitch was so he kept quiet, put the car in gear and drove off slowly down the road, nodding to the sergeant as he went and thanking his lucky stars it had been Rob and not some eager young bobby who had chanced upon them. 'If you can't be good, be lucky, as they say' he thought to himself.

The mood in the car as they made their way homeward was subdued, with Mitch even more morose than the others. Dixie and Shirley made small talk between themselves but Melanie was well aware of Mitch's mood as she tried to snuggle up to him.

"What did the sergeant have to say?" she whispered in his ear. "Do you want to talk about it?"

Mitch simply shrugged and heaved a weary sigh. "No, not really Melanie. He was just banging on about shenanigans in a car on the main road. Gave me a bit of a bollocking, that's all. It's no big deal. Can we just leave it there?" Then he slumped into silence again, the events of the evening churning around in his head. Melanie sensed he wanted to be left alone with his thoughts, so she said nothing more for a while. Then Mitch turned to look her in the eye, a puzzled expression on his face.

"What's up Mitch?" she asked. "Something's troubling you, I can tell."

"Nothing. Nothing important anyway. It's just, well... are you really only fourteen?"

"Well I'll be fifteen in a few weeks," she replied defiantly, but feeling hurt at the same time. "Why? Is it a problem? What difference does it make?"

Seeing the hurt look on her face. Mitch backed off. "No, it's not a problem as such. It's just a surprise that's all. I thought you were the same age as me, or thereabouts. I just never realised you weren't. You look older, you act older. I just thought you were older. Why didn't you tell me anyway?"

"You never asked, did you? I didn't think it was important. I'm old enough to know I love you. Isn't that all that matters?"

On seeing how emotional Melanie was, and spotting the crestfallen look on her face, Mitch couldn't bring himself to pursue the matter further. He loved her and did not want to see her upset, so he swiftly changed tack.

"No, of course it doesn't matter. It was just a surprise. No big deal. Have I told you you're gorgeous? You really do have the most beautiful blue eyes and you are so pretty." He flashed her the broadest grin he could muster. "You're beautiful, Melanie Jackson, just beautiful."

"And you're a charmer Tom Mitchell. A real charmer." A smile of relief spread over her face.

"Oh, I am, am I? And is there anything else you like about me then?"

"Oh, I don't know. I love your laugh. I like your smile, your dark floppy hair, the way you kiss me. Oh, and your boots of course. They're the best bit" she giggled, as she squeezed his hand and leant in close to his body again under his protective arm.

Mitch smiled and hugged her closely to him. But underneath that confident and happy front he was putting on for her he was uneasy. She was only fourteen. It did matter, to him at least. It mattered more than he was prepared to admit to Melanie, maybe even more than he was prepared to admit to himself at the time, but he knew he couldn't let Melanie see that. He simply couldn't bear to see her upset.

They were nearly home by now, and the rest of the journey was uneventful. When they were close to Melanie's house they dropped both the girls off as Shirley was staying the night. Mitch got out and walked them the short distance to the front gate, then as he was walking back to the car Melanie called after him: he turned back to see her standing by the front gate under the soft glow of the nearby street lamp. She really was so beautiful, he thought as he slowly made his way back towards her.

"What about my goodnight kiss?" she called, and he couldn't help but laugh at the beguiling little pout which had formed on her lips.

"How could I forget that?" he said, replicating her frown before laughingly embracing her in his arms.

"So, when will I see you again?" she asked, the smile back on her face.

"I don't know. I've got a couple of late night shifts this week and I'm in on Saturday morning too."

"How about Saturday night? Will you be going to the Palace with the girls?"

She nodded. "Yes, we'll be there. There's a band on that Shirley wants to see."

"OK, tell you what, I haven't seen the boys for a while, what with working and everything. I'll grab a couple of pints with them at the Woody before we all head on down there. Be around nine, half nine I guess. How's that sound? On our steps"

"Sounds good to me" she smiled, and with that Mitch kissed her on the cheek and headed back to the car, blowing her a kiss as he clambered back in alongside Dixie.

Melanie felt some misgivings as Mitch turned and walked to the car. For some reason that she couldn't quite put her finger on, she sensed a difference in him. His attitude, his quietness on the way home, and that last somewhat offhand response from him worried her. But she did not want to make an issue of it by questioning him, so she simply nodded in agreement before blowing him a kiss back and waving as the car drove away.

Mitch said little on the short trip to his house and Dixie's thoughts were on Shirley, but when they arrived there Dixie piped up, "Everything OK matey? Want to talk about it?"

"No Dix. It's been a long day and I'm up early for work in the morning so I need some kip. Tell you what though, I'm finished at eight tomorrow night so I'll get the van to drop me off at your place and we'll see if we can get your ma to let us have some of that special rum she's got. We can have a good natter then. How does that sound?"

"Yeah, sounds good to me. See you then, and I'll tell you all about Shirley. Think I might have cracked it there mate."

"OK Dix. I'll see you then."

Mitch climbed out of the car and waved Dixie off. Then he sat on the wall outside his house, smoking a fag, alone with his thoughts at last.

After he'd finished his cigarette he flicked it casually into the gutter outside the front gate, which he knew would please his mother no end, and headed into the house. Before heading off to bed he poured himself a nightcap from his dad's whiskey and downed it in one before trudging wearily up the stairs to his bedroom. It was going to be a long night. His head was buzzing and his brain hurt. The events of the evening had left his emotions raw, and sleep would be a long time coming.

CHAPTER 19

One mixed-up kid

As Mitch lay tossing and turning in bed that night his mind was a maelstrom of what ifs, whys and wherefores. The space in his head that was supposed to be occupied by a brain had gone into meltdown; it was filled with problems, but solutions escaped him. With working such long hours his spare time had become spread too thinly, a problem he'd been trying to juggle unsuccessfully for some time.

Like most teenagers, he could be quite self-centred at times, his lifestyle, needs and desires taking priority in his mind over anyone else's. Sometimes it was all about him; how his life was affected by others and the unwanted pressures that were inevitably brought to bear on him. On the one hand, he had the boys pressurising him, making demands on him, expecting him to spend his time out drinking and having a ball with them, giving him endless stick for choosing somebody else's company above theirs. What was so much harder for them to take on board was the fact that he was putting a girl above them. Then there was Melanie. To her credit, she wasn't making demands upon him, more the reverse, for in her case it was mutual, as Mitch himself was unable to resist the chance to be with her at every opportunity. Melanie aroused passions in him that he'd never experienced previously with any girl. Tonight, she'd shown him just how passionate and adventurous she could be. But she'd also dropped a bombshell on him, the bombshell which had blown his mind. She was only fourteen! He just couldn't take that on board. So many unanswered questions flitted in and out of his head. How could that be? She didn't look fourteen. She certainly didn't act like she was fourteen. How hadn't he realised? Why hadn't she told him? Why hadn't anyone told him? The boys couldn't have known, that's for sure. He imagined the stick they would have given him had they known; they would probably have accused him of cradle snatching.

It was the early hours of the morning before he eventually fell into a troubled sleep. The daylight breaking through his bedroom woke him from his slumber only a few hours later. Unusually for him he dragged himself out of bed and headed off to the bathroom, his mother's normal wake-up call unnecessary for once as he knew there was no sleep left in him. As he peered bleary-eyed into the mirror above the sink in the bathroom he shook his head miserably from side to side, still battling to make sense of the confusion of thoughts coursing through his scrambled brain.

Shortly afterwards, he wearily climbed aboard the van that would transport him to what he knew would be the longest day he'd ever endured at the laundry. Normally the trip would be quite good fun as the crowd that travelled with him were a lively bunch, mainly women, so the trip would be filled with ribald jokes, good-hearted banter, and laughter, which Mitch would readily enter into. But today he had too much going on in his head to listen to mindless chatter, and he spent the trip in silence, ignoring what was going on around him.

Sure enough, the morning seemed never-ending as he mindlessly ploughed through bogie after bogie filled to the brim with soaking pillowcases. He couldn't concentrate, didn't want to even, and unusually for him picked up two bollockings from Jimmy the foreman for holding up the pressing department through his slow work rate. But whatever Jimmy said was wasted on Mitch. He just shrugged and continued going through the motions.

The klaxon for lunch came as a welcome relief but failed to lighten his mood. He didn't want company, didn't want to talk, to the extent that he pointedly avoided Tony and wandered off by himself down by the river where he could be alone with his thoughts for half an hour and the sound of the water trickling over the stones was soothing if nothing else.

However hard he tried, he just couldn't shake off the mood that had descended upon him, like a dark cloud slowly smothering the sky before a storm, a doom-laden warning signalling that there was worse to come on the horizon. The rest of the day followed on seamlessly in similar vein from the morning shift with Mitch unable to concentrate, his mind elsewhere, morosely pondering how life had taken such a mind-boggling twist, how his whole life had been turned on its head. Why was life so complicated all of a sudden? How the hell was he going to solve the predicament he was in? Why was this happening to him? More importantly, what about Melanie, the girl he knew he loved, adored even? Yes, she was perfect, and yet? And yet, she was only fourteen, so young, so beautiful, yet so young, He somehow struggled through the excruciatingly boring and seemingly endless hours of the afternoon and evening shifts in the same frame of mind, operating on auto pilot. When clocking-off time came at last and he was finally released from the drudgery of the day, he still had no answers to the problems and questions wreaking havoc with his head, but at least his time was now his own again. No longer chained to a laundry press, he made his way out into the evening sunlight and stood for a moment breathing in the fresh air and savouring the warmth of the sun on his face. The tension which had been gripping him slowly left his body as he made his way to the van and clambered on board for the trip to Dixie's.

On the journey, he was struck by a sudden clarity of thought, an insight which had been sadly missing since the previous evening. His face lit up for the first time that day as he realised that he would find the answer to his problems at Dixie's. He would get pissed. No, better than that, he would get absolutely hammered. That usually solved most things, didn't it? For the time being anyway, a voice in his head responded. That was that sorted then. He smiled to himself and settled back comfortably in his seat, the first time he'd relaxed all day.

It was with a lighter heart and a clearer head that Mitch jumped out of the van, made his way round to Dixie's mum's ever-open back door and headed inside, to find Dixie sitting in the lounge finishing off a cup of tea.

"Hi Mitch, old son. How's it going mate?" he asked Mitch.

"Could be better mate, could be better. Where's your ma then?"

"Oh, she's off to bingo for the night so we've got the place to ourselves."

"Great, couldn't be better. Get the old rum out then buddy, and the coke. I've had a shit day and I'm ready for a drink."

Dixie chuckled to himself as he got up from his chair and made for his mum's well-stocked drinks cupboard. Typical Mitch he thought, no standing on ceremony, no small talk, just straight in there and get the drinks out. But Dixie was more perceptive than the rest of the gang gave him credit for, apart from Mitch. As he poured the first of what would turn out to be many rum and cokes, he sensed that Mitch wasn't his normal bouncy self. And he had said things could be better. If he had had a shit day, best let him get a couple in him and open up, if he wanted to that was.

The two friends settled down in their armchairs and chatted about nothing in particular until, at last, Mitch began to relax. Dixie, sensing the timing was right, posed the question which had been troubling him since the previous evening in Peel.

"So, what happened with the copper last night then mate? He seemed to put the fear of god into you."

Mitch stared at him blankly for a moment or two,

pondering briefly how much he should disclose, weighing up the pros and cons. But his need to share his thoughts and feelings with someone ultimately outweighed his natural reservations about discussing his feelings.

"This goes no further Dix, I mean that. It stays between you and me," he said.

"OK mate, no problem, mum's the word." Dixie winked and tapped the side of his nose knowingly.

"OK then. Well, we were in the car weren't we and... things got a bit hot, if you know what I mean. Anyway, your mate the copper turns up, doesn't he? Flashing his torch in on us in the back seat and banging on the window. Scared the bloody life out of me. Scared the life out of both of us. Then he banged on about the car being parked illegally and he wanted it shifting immediately. I knew he meant business when he made me come and get you. It's a good job he knew you though Dix. A right bit of luck that was."

"Too right mate, what a relief that was. Thought I was going to lose my licence until I realised who it was. Anyway, what was that all about when he gave you the third degree outside the car?"

Mitch hesitated again before responding. "Oh, he gave me a right bollocking about how ashamed of myself I should be, cavorting with such a young girl in the back of a car on the main road. Told me he was only letting me off for her sake not mine."

"Bloody hell mate, that's a bit heavy-handed, isn't it? What the hell were the pair of you up to in there?"

"It wasn't too heavy fortunately Dix. But it could have been if he'd turned up a bit later. That's the scary thing. Scares me anyway Dix. Big time."

Dixie looked at him quizzically before responding. "What do you mean scary? How's it scary?"

"I'll tell you how it's bloody scary. He asked us all sorts of questions when we were in the car before making me come and get you, the big one being how old were we."

Dixie jumped in at this point. "Why's that scary? He couldn't take you down the station and charge you for fooling about in the back of a car with a girl. Thought you knew that mate."

Mitch sighed, his patience becoming a bit strained by this time "Are you going to keep interrupting me, you pillock? Or are you going to let me finish?"

"OK, OK, sorry, crack on then sunshine."

"Yes, I did know that he couldn't charge me. But what I didn't know was that Melanie's only fourteen. That's the scary bit. She's not fifteen for another few weeks."

Disbelief registered on Dixie's face. "Really? I mean, seriously?"

Mitch leaned forward to emphasise his point, frustration clearly written all over his face "Yes, seriously. It's not something I'd joke about is it, dipshit?"

"Shit, that is serious. I'd never have known. I thought she was about the same age as you. She looks and acts so much older. Look, do you want to talk about it? How do you feel mate? You can tell me you know, get it off your chest. It won't go any further, you know that"

"How the hell do you think I feel? I'm devastated. You know how much she means to me."

"Yeah, well, you weren't to know. None of us were for that matter. Are you all right? What are you going to do about it? How do you really feel?"

Realising that Dixie only meant well, Mitch calmed down. "How the hell do I know, Dix? She's beautiful. I love her. I'm in love with her. That's all I know and I just can't think straight at the moment."

"Well, you need to get your head together. You do know you could get into deep shit if you go too far with someone that young, don't you?"

"Don't think I don't know that Dix. And after last night that's the really scary bit. I can't begin to tell you the effect she has on me when I'm with her. I just can't help myself."

"Humph. You're going to have to sunshine, if you want to avoid big trouble that is. Know what I mean?"

Mitch knew only too well what Dixie meant, but not wanting to get involved too deeply in that line of conversation, he merely took a deep breath and looked up at the ceiling, running the fingers of both hands through his hair, before letting out a huge sigh and nodding by way of agreement. But Dixie had switched into big brother mode by this time as he warmed to his theme.

"So, really, what are you going to do about it then matey?" he enquired. "Are you going to dump her before it becomes too serious, or what?"

"Dump her? How the hell can I just dump her? Are you for real, Dix?"

"I'm only thinking of you buddy. It's not going to get any easier. If you want to get out now's the time to do it. The longer it goes on the worse it will get. For both of you."

Mitch sank his head wearily into his hands before slowly raising it again to look Dixie directly in the eye. "Look, I know you mean well Dix, but you're not helping, really you're not. That hasn't entered my head. I'm not sure I could do it anyway. She'd be so hurt, I know she would, and to be honest I'm not sure I've got the bottle to do that to her. Or how the hell I'd do it, come to think about it. Let's just drop it, shall we?"

Dixie nodded in agreement, but not before adding one final piece of advice "OK. I understand, I'm just saying, that's all. Whatever you do though, do right by her. She's a lovely girl and she loves you." Seeing the look on Mitch's face he backed off, and raised both palms by way of acquiescence. "OK, enough said, sorry mate" he said.

A brief smile flickered across Mitch's face. "Anyway Dix" he said, as he leaned back in his chair, "Changing the subject, how'd things go with you and Shirley last night then? It looked as if you were in there."

Dixie perked up at this. "Yeah. It went really well, thanks mate. Got on like a house on fire, didn't we? I think I could be well in there. I'm seeing her again at the weekend as it happens."

"Really?" Mitch grinned. "Looks like you've got a problem as well then, Dix my old mate."

Dixie's eyes narrowed. "Problem? What problem? What the hell are you on about?"

"Well, far be it from me to point out the obvious to one so worldly wise as you Dix, but possibly it hasn't dawned upon you yet that Melanie and Shirley are in the same class at school? That much I do know, so she can't be much older than Melanie. How weird is that then?"

Mitch could have bitten his lip as soon as he saw the devastated look of realisation spread across his friend's face. "Sorry mate" he blurted out. "I was just lashing out there. That was uncalled for, but I guess you're better finding out now rather than later. I know what that feels like. Here, let's have another drink." He poured two more large rum and cokes.

Much later that evening Mitch made his way home in a drunken haze. His problems hadn't gone away – far from it, they were merely in abeyance – but at least the alcohol would ensure he had no trouble getting off to sleep that night.

CHAPTER 20

Saturday night and Sunday morning

Friday and Saturday passed relatively uneventfully for Mitch. He was more settled, having put his problems on the back burner for the time being at least. He knew those problems still needed to be addressed, but for now he'd stored them away, neatly packaged in one of those little boxes in the male brain which come in handy when anything needs to be filed under the heading of 'for attention later'. 'Later' in his mind was Saturday night, when he would meet up with Melanie at the Palace and talk things through with her, dealing with everything in an adult way. He could see no point doing his head in worrying about it in the meantime. File it, box it off, and face up to it again come Saturday night was his thinking.

And that was how he coped for those two days. But time is relentless and Saturday evening inevitably sneaked up on him, accompanied by an ever-increasing sense of unease. He would normally catch up with the boys around eight o'clock, but dinner was later than usual and there was no way he was going out on a Saturday night session without some food in his stomach to soak up the amount of alcohol they normally quaffed on the week's big night out. It was closer to half eight therefore as he eventually made it to the Woody, not in the best frame of mind. He had probably missed out on a couple of pints already, and that feeling of foreboding about facing up to Melanie later that evening was building up inside him now he'd remembered the combination lock to the box in which he'd filed his worries in that head of his.

As he stepped through the door into the men's bar at the Woody that sense of foreboding was immediately ratcheted up. The boys were all there, sitting at their usual table in the far corner of the room, and they spotted him entering almost immediately. Their faces lit up, but the smile on his own face disappeared quickly as Tony shouted across the bar "Hoy, Mitch. You're late stranger. Where've you been then? Down the junior girls' school checking out the talent or what?" The whole bar joined in with ribald comments coming from all sides. Some joker at the bar added to the merriment when he shouted across "Yeah, he likes them young I'm told. Younger the better eh Mitch?" This comment was met with raucous laughter all around.

Mitch was furious as he caught Dixie in his gaze. "You

bastard!" he mouthed at him, but Dixie simply shrugged his shoulders and winced apologetically before Mitch turned to the bar in disgust to get himself a drink. Fuck them all, he thought. Determination was building up inside him. Bollocks to them. If they thought they were going to wind him up the whole night, they had another think coming. He could brazen it out with the best of them, and he would. He stood resolutely at the bar, his back to all of them and downed his first pint in one, wiping his mouth with the back of one hand and slamming his empty glass on the bar with the other. The barmaid, having taken pity on him, was in the process of pulling him another pint when Dixie appeared, looking suitably sheepish.

"Let me get that one in Mitch. Sorry mate, I never expected them to give you so much stick" he said, nodding at the barmaid to fill his own glass up as he did so and sticking some money on the bar.

"Piss off you prick" came Mitch's response. "I trusted you. You... arsehole! And this is what I get. You're a twat Dix, a first-class twat."

"Calm down Mitch, calm down for heaven's sake. I haven't told them anything about Peel. All I did was mention that you'd found out Melanie was only fourteen. That's all, honestly mate. And they were going to find that out eventually anyway, weren't they?"

"Oh yeah, they'd have found out eventually. When I was good and ready, they'd have found out. From me though, not from bloody you, you dozy sod. And guess what? I wouldn't have had to go through this then would I, you pillock?"

Dixie could do no more than agree. "Yeah, you're right. Bit of a cock up. Sorry mate. Come on, come over and have a drink, they'll pack it in shortly. Let them have their bit of fun. We'll face them together. I'll sort them."

"Too right you will Dix, and pretty damn quick as well before I bring them up to speed about you and Shirley. See how you like that, will we?" He threw Dixie yet another withering glance and prepared to face the music. "Come on then dickhead, let's go over and join them. And you'd better watch what you say Dix, or you're in deep shit, believe me."

Mitch turned away abruptly and headed back across the room, Dixie following forlornly behind him, pulling a face, and shaking his head vigorously in a furious attempt to let the boys know that enough was enough, it was time to wind their necks in and back off.

Fortunately, the boys had already picked up on Mitch's mood and sensed they had gone too far. Tony piped up, "All right feller, just having a bit of a laugh, weren't we? You can take a bit of a joke, can't you?" He threw an arm playfully around Mitch. "Come on, sit down, it's good to see you out with the lads again. Thought we'd lost you there for a while didn't we boys?"

"Yeah" said Jack. "Good to see you Mitch. Sit down, it's my round, just going to get them in. Fancy another pint then mate?"

Mitch's face softened. "Yeah, OK Jack. Cheers mate, good to see you as well. You bunch of tossers just hit on a nerve there. Touchy subject, that's all." And they all nodded in agreement as Ray chimed in "Aye well, you weren't the only one. None of us knew Melanie was only fourteen either. Let's face it, who would?" he added, looking round the table at the others, who all shook their heads

That little interlude being concluded the boys got down

to some serious drinking again, downing pints as if they'd just been invented. But Mitch was conscious that time was slipping by, and he needed to see Melanie.

"Right boys, where are we off to tonight then? The Palace, is it?" he asked.

"No" came the swift reply from Jack. "My brother's playing in a band at the Villiers tonight so that's where we're heading. Better get a move on chaps, don't want to miss him, do we?"

Mitch cringed on hearing this. The Villiers – what was he supposed to do now? But he didn't get much time to ponder the situation as everybody then rose and headed for the door "Come on Mitch. Get that pint down you mate. We need to head off" Jack shouted over his shoulder as he was leaving.

Mitch hesitated briefly before concluding that he would have to go along with them. If he left them now in the middle of a night out when he hadn't seen them all together for such a long time he would be ostracised. And quite possibly, not turning up to meet Melanie might be the lesser of two evils. He hadn't made a firm arrangement after all. And he ought to be reasonably sober when he did meet her, as there was some serious talking to be done. He would have to try and slip away later and catch up with Melanie.

Down at the Villiers, the place was heaving, the band was good, and the ale was soon disappearing fast. Mitch kept sneaking anxious looks at his watch as the night wore on but eventually he realised it was a futile exercise. The night was slipping away from him, and there was no way he'd get to the Palace in time to see Melanie. All he could do now was to try and put things right with her somehow in the week. Part of him was saddened, but he also felt a strange sense of relief at the same time. The difficult conversation could be put on the back burner for the time being. He was out with the lads, part of the gang again, and it felt good. For the first time in a while, he didn't feel like an outsider. The ale was flowing, it was good craic, nobody was giving him stick and his guilt at letting Melanie down was receding further into the background with every pint he drank.

Tony was now surveying the talent on the dance floor. One girl stood out from the crowd and caught his eye, so he decided it was time to chance his arm.

"Come on then feller" he said, turning to Mitch and nudging his arm, "I need you to get up on the floor. There's a bird over there, the one in the red top." He indicated an attractive blonde girl dancing nearby with a tall redhead. "Can't take her eyes off me, can she? Keeps looking over here and smiling at me."

Mitch cast a casual glance in her direction before declaring "Nah mate, I'm not up for dancing. I'm enjoying having a few beers with the boys here. Settle down and get some more ale in you."

"Aw, come on Mitch, give us a break, will you? I can't go up there by myself, can I? And you can have her mate, she looks quite fit."

"Bollocks To, I'm not interested in her mate. I'm not here on the pull, am I? One of the lads might get up there with you."

"You're joking, aren't you, sunshine? They're all pissed. Come on, give it a go. Help me out here matey."

Mitch took a deep breath, shook his head, and

reluctantly trooped off onto the floor with Tony, but not before adding "You owe me for this buddy. I'm telling you."

Tony grinned. "Yeah, yeah. Heard it all before. Come on, get your arse out here. You never know, you might even enjoy yourself."

As it turned out, Tony had been right. The blonde girl's face lit up when Tony approached her, and the redhead smiled when Mitch tapped her on the shoulder and asked her to join him for a dance. But while Tony and his blonde hit it off straight away, Mitch was merely going through the motions. Even so he couldn't help noticing that the redhead was a good dancer, and quite a looker. And he couldn't simply walk away and leave her on her own whilst Tony was clinging to her friend like a limpet, so he carried on dancing and chatting for a couple more dances before taking the initiative and suggesting they find a table and get a drink.

When the pair of them were at the bar getting a round in, Tony turned to Mitch and asked, "So how are you getting on with Sarah then, matey?"

"Oh, is that her name? I told you, I couldn't give a toss."

"Charming, bloody charming," Tony replied. "Look, the thing is mate, I need a favour."

"What bloody favour? I know you and your favours," said Mitch.

"Calm down. It's no big deal mate. It's just that I'm getting on really well with Angie. She's hot stuff and, well, I'm walking her home when this place finishes, so how's about you come with Sarah?"

"You're joking, aren't you? I don't know the bloody girl."

Tony could see he was on dodgy ground but ploughed on anyway "Aw, come on mate. Do us a favour, can't you? I'd do the same for you. They live fairly close to each other, but not that close if you know what I mean. And anyway, I could do with some time on my own with Angie."

On seeing the pleading look on his mate's face Mitch gave in, but not without some reluctance. "OK, OK. You win. I don't know, the bloody things I do for you mate. It's last orders anyway so you can get this round in then. I'm stuffed if I'm paying for it now. And you can bring the drinks over yourself" he added as he turned and walked away.

Shortly afterwards time was called at the bar, the band played its final number and the foursome emerged onto the promenade. On seeing Angie and Tony holding hands, Sarah took the plunge and linked arms with Mitch, who cringed awkwardly, hoping she hadn't noticed his discomfort. This was all he needed. He stared nervously around, fearful that one of Melanie's friends might spot them or, worse still, Melanie even. How the hell would he explain it if she did? But then he realised that at this hour Melanie and her friends would more than likely be home. Even so he could not fully relax, nor could he stop cursing Tony for getting him into such a predicament.

Having said their goodbyes to Tony and Angie, Mitch accompanied Sarah to her house, careful to keep their conversation to small talk. The last thing he wanted was for Sarah to get the wrong idea about his intentions. When they arrived at her house he simply exchanged a few pleasantries, thanked her for a lovely evening, and breathed a sigh of relief as he set off for home. After all, it could have been worse. He had handled the situation with Sarah reasonably well, and they hadn't bumped into anyone he knew on the way home.

When he reached home and made his way up to his room he was sure he was in for another restless night, but in fact, thanks to a combination of the alcohol, the events of the evening and the confusion of thoughts going through his mind he was so worn out that he sank into a deep sleep shortly after his head hit the pillow.

But that was only a relatively short reprieve, for the next morning came around all too quickly. When he woke, it took a little while for him to gather his scrambled thoughts. His head ached from the alcohol he'd consumed last night. That was the first thing he was aware of as his head cleared. What day was it? Oh yes, it was Sunday, his day off. Well at least that was something he thought, as a brief smile flickered across his face. No pillowcases to shake out for a whole day. Heaven.

But it didn't take long for that smile to disappear. As he lay back in bed, his mind clicked into gear and he started recalling the events of the previous evening as images and recollections flashed relentlessly through his brain. How he'd cringed with embarrassment at the Woody as everyone had taken the piss out of him over Melanie. Melanie? Oh no, he'd been supposed to meet her, hadn't he? But he hadn't made it. What would she think? How would she feel? How was he going to handle the whole Melanie thing? How that idiot Tony had embroiled him in a situation with that other girl, what was her name? Oh, Sarah, that was it. At least he'd come out of that one relatively unscathed he thought, not that that was much consolation. 'Relationships' he thought, 'who needs them? They're all so damned complicated anyway.' Life used to be so simple and now everything just seemed to be so complicated. He loved

Melanie, but she was so much younger than him. And it wasn't just the age difference. Dixie was right, it was her age, fourteen for heaven's sake? How could he continue to go out with a fourteen-year old girl? Why oh why couldn't she be older? What was he going to do?

How was he going to handle it? Could he really talk to her, tell her face to face how big a problem it was for him, for her even?

He was cursing Dixie and his damned shock tactics, but deep down he knew he was right. In his heart he loved her, but sadly in his head he knew he had to be realistic. Yet how on earth could he explain that to Melanie, his beautiful Melanie, his dream girl? He couldn't. He just knew he couldn't bear the thought of seeing her so upset. She was so sensitive, so emotional and he just couldn't imagine himself having the courage to do it. The next day was again spent wrestling with his worries. No matter how hard he tried, how much he chewed it over, he couldn't find an answer. Deep down he felt he could not let Melanie go. He couldn't imagine a life without her in it now, but there again he couldn't imagine a life with her in it, and the complications it would cause.

It began to dawn on him that he was just too young and inexperienced to cope with the complexities and irrationalities of love, let alone resolve the problems which have confounded and bewildered the minds of adult men and women throughout the world since time immemorial.

Throughout the day, Mitch struggled manfully to battle his demons and cope with the conflicting voices in his head, but to no avail. In the end, he opted for his tried and trusted way of dealing with problems - pack them away, put them on the back burner. It was summer, the pubs were open and that was where he headed.

Sure enough, after a couple of pints he had decided a way forward. For now, he'd do nothing. He'd tackle his problems when he had to. The last thing he wanted was a confrontation with Melanie; he could not face the thought of having to look her in the eye and try and explain his feelings to her when he couldn't even explain them to himself. He would leave it for a while, clear his thoughts; ring her maybe, later in the week. With that thought firmly fixed in his head he downed the rest of his pint and headed home.

CHAPTER 21

The heartbreak begins

Melanie had not set eyes on Mitch in ten days, since he had dropped her off after the party in Peel, and the time had passed agonisingly slowly. She had been left feeling deflated and confused by his mood on the journey back in the car that evening, his aloofness when he'd said goodnight, and his rather awkward promise to meet up with her on the Saturday. She felt this change in his attitude was somehow related to the incident with the policeman, but couldn't understand why that would concern someone like Mitch, usually so sure of himself, and why it should impact on their relationship. That evening had been so exciting and aroused such depth of passion and feeling inside her that she knew with the innocence and certainty of youth that she loved him, and thought he loved her. What else mattered?

They had agreed to meet on the steps at the Palace. She had ventured outside countless times on that Saturday but he had not shown up, and it had left her reeling, feeling both puzzled and panicky. She was desperate to find him and missed him so much, but there had been no contact. She had spent evenings wandering along the prom in the hope of seeing him out with his friends, but it was as if he had disappeared off the face of the earth. She felt abandoned, distraught and uncomprehending.

Why had he disappeared from her life? He must have had his reasons. She knew his summer job meant he was working a six-day week from eight in the morning until late – although that didn't explain how or why he had seemingly vanished off the face of the planet – but she didn't feel confident enough to just turn up either in his lunch hour or after work out of the blue. She did stand at her bedroom window regularly in the evenings to see if he walked past but not once did he show up. She needed to see him, needed to know what was going on, needed to talk to him, get an explanation, so that everything was right and beautiful between them again.

Another Saturday came along and the girls were at the Palace once again. Melanie was desperately hoping to see Mitch. Her mind was in turmoil, but despite herself she was searching the room for a glimpse of him, not sure what she would do or say if he was there. There was a note of desperation in her voice as she whispered to Sammy. "Oh god, is he here? What do I do if he is?"

Then she saw him sitting at a table with a group of people. It was dimly lit, but she instantly recognised him.

He was talking to an attractive girl with red hair – and not just talking. Even in the dark, she could see that he knew her, they looked intimate. Then they stood up, and the girl took him by the hand and led him towards the dance floor. Melanie's brain went into meltdown. Her Mitch, the boy who loved her, the boy she loved, was with somebody else.

Stunned, she dropped her gaze. Her brain couldn't take in the messages her eyes were conveying. Was this really happening? She had to get out, get away from the shock of what she had seen. She ran out of the room, out of the building and into the fresh air outside. As it hit her, she breathed in gulps and her body started to shake involuntarily as she began to sob uncontrollably.

She leaned against a wall, slid down to the ground and crumpled into a heap. She could not take in what she had just witnessed. The hope she had held in her heart over the past ten days vanished and all those emotions which she had bottled up came flooding out, and more tears along with them. In that second, she realised that she had been completely taken in and taken over by her feelings, something she had sworn would never happen to her. She had become one of those girls she had derided in the past, whom she had seen as victims. And that was exactly how she was feeling now, a victim. But try as she might, she just couldn't pull herself together. The pain was just too much to bear.

As her friends followed her out, Anna looked over at Mitch with hatred, but he had not been aware of their presence and he was totally oblivious to the devastating affect he'd had on the girl he'd said he loved. They tried to comfort her, but Melanie stood up unsteadily.

"I need to get away from here and be on my own" she managed to say. She turned her back on them and slowly started to walk away. Sammy, shooing the other two away, followed her and put a comforting arm around her best friend, but this only served to send Melanie into more convulsive fits of sobbing.

"Don't, please, no kind words. I can't bear it," was all she could manage to say as her friend tried to brush away the tears from her face.

"Do you want to go and speak to him? Do you want me to?" asked Sammy. She would have loved to confront Mitch, for she was raging inside at seeing her friend in so much distress.

"No, I just can't face him like this. And what's the point?" Melanie's hands twisted and clenched together.

"Come back to my place and stay the night," replied Sammy. "You can't go home in this state. You'll have plenty of time to get your act together, and when you have you can ring your mum from mine and let her know you are staying over." Melanie began to sob and shake uncontrollably again with the shock and realisation of what she'd witnessed.

Once ensconced in Sammy's bedroom, Melanie crawled onto the bed, curled into a ball, and gave in to her grief. Her chest was so tight she had difficulty in breathing, and she was feeling panicky and light-headed. It was as if something had wound itself around her heart and was squeezing the life out of her.

After a while, Sammy quietly raised the fact that Melanie would have to phone her mother. "Don't worry, I'll dial the number, put you on and then I'll get my mum to OK it," she said. "You won't have to keep it together for long."

Giving Melanie no further time to think, Sammy took her hand and led her back downstairs to the phone, dialled the number and pushed the phone into her friend's trembling hand. Somehow, Melanie held herself together just long enough to blurt out "Hi mum, the dance was rubbish so I've come back to Sammy's." She was fighting to keep the emotion out of her voice. "Can I stay over? Mrs C says it's OK. I don't want to walk home in the rain on my own. Anna went off with some other friends, and I don't want to drag Dad out now."

Seeing that Melanie was about to start sobbing uncontrollably again, Sammy grabbed the phone and handed it to her own mother to confirm the arrangement.

The girls returned to the bedroom and shut the door on the outside world, where Melanie found that Sammy had managed to sneak some much-needed alcohol into her bag. When Melanie tasted it, she spluttered "What the hell is this?"

"It's gin. It's all I could get hold of. Don't be so ungrateful." They laughed briefly before Melanie broke down again. Sammy said gently, "I know it hurts but we need to talk about this. You need to talk about this. You'll feel better if you get it all out."

"There's nothing much to talk about, is there?" said Melanie. "It's happened. You were right. All of you were right, and I've been such an idiot. There's no going back." Yet she wished with every fibre of her being that there was. Her mind raced with countless unanswerable questions. How could this be happening to her? How could he do this to her? How could she have been so wrong about him? Why did it hurt so much?

Try as she might, Sammy could not console Melanie. She knew in her heart it was a waste of time trying to get Melanie to open up and discuss the matter further so, as the gin had the desired effect and calmed the churning of Melanie's stomach, the two girls lay together in silence. Sammy's heart went out to Melanie and instinctively she put her arm round her friend, drew her closer to her and whispered gently in her ear, "I wish I could do or say something to make it better for you Melanie. You're like a sister to me. I love you and I'll always be here for you. You know that. It will get better, believe me, you'll see. Try and get some sleep now."

Melanie's usually clear blue eyes were cloudy and misty with the remnants of tears. Sammy knew it was pointless saying anything more. They lay there and Melanie drifted in and out of sleep, with Mitch's face and voice at the forefront of her mind; his lovely face with its beguiling smile and that voice which could be so tender and say such beautiful things echoed in her head. The thought that this was all to be relegated to just a memory was torture every time she woke.

When she looked in the mirror the following morning in Sammy's bedroom, she saw what looked like a ghost looking back at her. She was pale and her eyes were red and swollen. Her world had crumbled around her and she sincerely believed that nothing would ever be the same again.

Melanie was totally unaware that she had only seen half the picture when she'd spotted Mitch the previous evening. What she wasn't to know was that Mitch hadn't betrayed her, quite the opposite in fact. For in truth he was missing her badly.

Still mixed up, still confused, and intent on drowning his sorrows, he'd ventured into town on his own that night. He'd hit the beer fairly hard in a number of his usual haunts before eventually ending up at the Palace in a somewhat drunken state, still thinking, hoping, he might chance upon Melanie there with her friends. He didn't know what he would say or do if he did bump into her. He just knew he needed to see her and be with her again, whatever it took.

As it happened, by a cruel twist of fate it wasn't to be Melanie that he chanced upon that night. It was Sarah, Angie's friend, the girl he'd walked home from the Villiers. She'd made a beeline for him on seeing him wandering around on his own, and had encouraged him to come and join her and her friends sitting at the side of the dance floor. To all but Mitch it was obvious that she fancied him. Sarah was not shy and blatantly flirted with him, but Mitch's mind was elsewhere and initially he was oblivious to her advances. However, as time passed and she became more direct in her approach it eventually dawned on him where she was coming from.

As he scanned the dance floor hoping to catch sight of Melanie he felt a hand squeezing his knee and turned to see Sarah looking directly into his eyes and smiling as she strained to make herself heard above the sound of the music.

"Mitch, you're not listening to me, are you?" she said.

"Sorry" he replied. "I was just caught up in the music. What were you saying?"

"Oh, nothing important, I don't suppose. Just that I

really fancy you, and wonder if you'd like to go out with me?"

"What? Are you serious, or just larking about?" Mitch responded.

Sarah shook her head and laughed. "I'm deadly serious. Why would I joke about something like that?" she said.

"Oh. Well, erm, I'm flattered Sarah, honestly I am. I'm sorry, but I came here looking for someone who's special to me, but she doesn't seem to be here. I'm not looking to go out with anyone else. I've realised that she's the only one for me" he said.

Mitch couldn't fail to see the look of disappointment and embarrassment on Sarah's face and realised that it must have taken a lot for her to leave herself open to rejection as she had. But it turned out that Sarah wasn't a girl to be deterred that easily.

"Okay Mitch. I understand. At least I think I do. Won't you at least have a dance with me though?" she enquired playfully.

"Why not?" Mitch replied. "What harm can that do?" With that he reluctantly let her pull him up from his seat and lead him by the hand onto the dance floor, little knowing that Melanie was watching, transfixed with horror and disbelief.

But Melanie hadn't witnessed the whole scene. She wasn't to know that as soon as he took to the floor and started dancing, Mitch knew even in his drunken state that this wasn't right. He didn't want this girl. She wasn't Melanie, and it was Melanie he wanted to be with. When the music ended Mitch made a hasty, embarrassed apology to Sarah, turned away and wandered off, forlornly searching the ballroom, seeking out Melanie, the girl he knew he still loved. But his search was doomed to be in vain, for his dream girl had seen enough. She had gone.

CHAPTER 22

Reality dawns

Julia's concerns after the previous night's phone call were justified on seeing her beautiful daughter's face when she returned home that day. She looked drawn and pale and was without her usual lovely smile. Much as she wanted to hug her and help her with whatever was troubling her, she didn't want to intrude. She understood the ways of her daughter and recognized that she wouldn't thank her for it and would want to work through whatever it was in her own time. She had been watching her daughter trying to take on adulthood, but knew she hadn't yet developed the emotional capacity to handle what it was going to throw at her. Her heart ached for her, for she knew there had to be a boy involved. As a child, whenever she had been hurt

Melanie had always withdrawn into her own space, as she was doing now. Julia also knew that whatever pain Melanie was going through she would come out the other side, move on and eventually be happy again. This would serve to make her stronger as she grew emotionally, but it would be pointless and inappropriate to try to tell her that now. She would tell her mother what was troubling her when she was good and ready, and not before.

As soon as she deemed it appropriate Melanie excused herself, went to her room, pretending she didn't feel well, and curled up again, on her own bed this time. Now she was alone, she tried to take in what had happened to her last night. She felt a vacant space inside her that had been filled, although all too briefly, with something so special, that it gave her such a sense of loss; the grief was unbearable, for her heart was broken. She turned the radio on so her parents wouldn't hear her crying to herself, but the music only made everything worse. Every love song reminded her of when she had been in Mitch's arms, kissing his lips and resting her head on his shoulders. He was so gentle and caring with her as he stroked her hair. That gentle touch that roused so much passion inside her was now an agonising thought, raw and stinging. How was she ever going to overcome the intensity of this pain and heartache?

She remembered how, when he had kissed her, a spark had lit up her heart, how she had looked into those mesmerising eyes of his, and believed in him, in everything he'd said. This made her feel angry and stupid. Without any explanation, she had quickly lost the one person she really believed she had truly loved. She couldn't make any sense of any of it, and for her that was the hardest thing of all. Why had she lost him?

On the Sunday morning, soon after Melanie arrived home, Julia was attempting to share her concerns about her daughter with Jim, who, as was his custom, had his head buried in his Sunday paper. "Melanie doesn't look her usual happy self today, to put it mildly" Julia sighed.

"Really? I didn't notice," said Jim, without raising his head from his paper.

"No, you wouldn't" Julia murmured. She knew he thought the world of his daughter but couldn't spot the subtle changes that were happening to her. "I just hope some boy's not broken her heart Jim. You know how sensitive she is."

"You did say it was inevitable in the scheme of life, Julia. In fact, I think those were your very words," he responded, raising his head only briefly from his paper. Julia felt cross and helpless at the same time. That might be true, but it didn't stop her feeling her daughter's pain. She said nothing, realising it was futile continuing her conversation.

Unknown to Julia though, she was indeed being too harsh on Jim. He knew his daughter well, as they had always been very close. He had seen the recent changes in her, but didn't want to acknowledge them, for that would mean him admitting to himself that he was losing his little girl. He understood her need to work things through in her own way, in her own time and on her own. They were very alike in that respect; it was the way Jim approached life as well.

He wouldn't, or maybe couldn't, talk about it to Julia, for somehow that would make it real. He didn't want to lose the father/child bond he had and so, in typical male fashion, he boxed it off in his mind and buried himself further into his newspaper.

The following week, Melanie carried on with her daily tasks, putting one foot in front of the other, even though they felt like lead, and hurting so much deep inside. She tried to put on a brave smile through the tears. She had been so happy and excited by the new feelings that had overwhelmed her, that she had tried to share with her friends, but now there was nothing, just a big, gaping hole. In her mind, she'd gone from that dizzy emotional high to what she considered to be the depths of despair. She wandered between feeling vague and disjointed to panicky and as if under water, unable to think straight. Her mother worried about her moping, but when she knocked on the bedroom door or tried to speak at dinner, Melanie just clammed up. She didn't feel she could talk to anyone about it, not even to her best friends, and least of all her parents. She had no appetite for the gossip and chit chat that surrounded her at home and at work, and she couldn't have dealt with company or advice. There was a bottled-up rage inside her. And it hurt so much knowing that her friends had been right. Her pride was wounded. They had seen what she hadn't, and now she knew that she should have listened to them. They had not just been right about him, but about her too. She had let her guard down completely, become totally immersed in the affections of a boy who had now cut himself out of her life. She realised that she should have known that they only had her best interests at heart and that they could see what she was blind to. She felt a hole where her heart should be, as if someone had ripped it out. But she still didn't feel she could explain this to them, didn't believe that they could possibly understand the way she was feeling.

And she still loved Mitch. That was what really hurt. How could she still love him? How could he be so cruel? In the weeks that followed, she avoided most of the places she knew he frequented, especially the Palace. She could no longer face the beach, now the last place on earth she wanted to be.

One evening the ever-caring Shirley again came to visit her friend, only to be told to go away. Julia asked her, "What's wrong with Melanie, Shirley? Is it a boy that's hurt her, messed with her affections, or is it something else? I've never seen her like this before and I feel so helpless. She won't tell us anything and I so want to help her."

"It is a boy, Mrs Jackson. She fell head over heels in love with him and he's broken her heart. She won't talk about it so I guess its best just not to ask," replied Shirley. "You know her best, what a private person she is, how stubborn and proud she is. I'll see if I can get through to her eventually. We all will, we just need to give her some time. She's been hurt badly, but she's strong, she'll come through it. And when she comes through it we'll all be there for her, won't we?"

"I knew it. I just knew it had to be a boy. You're wise beyond your years, and you're right, she is strong and she will come through it. I just wish she wasn't so damned stubborn, but that's our Melanie, isn't it?" She shook her head.

One afternoon Melanie wrote a poem:

I've loved you since I met you, but there's nothing I can do

You've really hurt my feelings, the pain you've put me through

I know you said you loved me, but how can that be true?

The anguish that you've caused me, I know I deserve better than you.

But she didn't send it. She wrote a letter too, but she didn't send that either, for there was too much anger and pain in it and her pride was such that she didn't want him to see how badly he had affected her. Instead, she resorted to writing her thoughts down in a diary, a habit that would remain with her for the rest of her life, whenever life's inevitable twists and turns arose, confusing and engulfing her brain, for she had a driving need to analyse her thoughts, to find reason when there appeared to be none. When she needed to talk things over, share her deepest thoughts and insecurities, her diary would become her closest friend. Those thoughts were hers alone and her diary would eventually unravel them. It was her coping mechanism. She could not open up and share her most sensitive thoughts and fears with anyone, but she could tell her diary anything. After all, it was never judgemental. She could say things to her diary, have conversations in her mind that she couldn't bring herself to have with others.

And this is where her diary journey first began, as she

had imaginary discussions with her diary that she could not bring herself to have with Mitch.

It was dusk and the street lights were on. You started laughing. I love it so much when you laugh. It makes me so happy.

You stopped and kissed me, I looked up and your face was wet and beautiful.

My heart stood still and I knew at that very moment that whatever happened in my life and wherever it took me, that moment would remain in my memory for ever, to be brought to the forefront of my mind now and again and studied, like a photograph evoking all those feelings in me and bringing them to the surface again.

I knew that this was real. I didn't know what my feelings meant then, my whole body felt hot and confused. I now recognise them as desire and longing. It was where I wanted my life to be, I wanted you to be my life. I thought everything and anything was possible.

But where on earth had my independence gone? What had happened to my belief that I would never succumb to stupid teenage crushes? But surely it was much more than that? All those girls I'd ridiculed for changing from intelligent, clear thinking beings to silly, giggling, blushing wrecks in the presence of boys. I swore that would never happen to me. Is this how they had felt? This wasn't what I'd wanted or expected.

All my certainties in life had suddenly become uncertain. The passion and senses of my childhood were bubbling away inside me and threatening to come to the surface and be all consuming.

I would have done anything, been anybody at that moment, and for what? For a boy?

You made me the happiest girl. I felt like someone really loved me and wanted to be with me.

I will never forget those nights earlier this summer, although it already seems like a dream now.

I don't understand what happened to our love, and sadly those days are gone forever.

You were my summer love. It was just that feeling that you know that you've found the one.

I should just let it go, but...

She wanted to confront him. She needed to know why he'd left without warning, what had gone wrong, what she had done wrong. But she hated conflict and her pride wouldn't let her go looking for him in any case.

Her mother called upstairs one evening to say there was someone called Tom on the phone for her, but she refused to take it. She was too hurt, too proud, too scared, or just too stubborn. She didn't know which, but what did it matter? Deep down she had always loathed confrontation. Secretly, what she really hoped for was a letter from him, a lovely letter like the one she'd had before, in which somehow everything could be explained and forgiven, but none came.

Melanie would sometimes go for long walks, but everywhere she went she saw happy young people, laughing together, and sharing special looks, all the time reminding her that she'd been just like that herself only a few short weeks before. He had come into her world, lifted her up and placed her on the top of it, and now? Now he was gone.

She felt her world was spinning out of control, and she was in danger of falling off it as it whirled faster and faster.

On one of these walks, it started to rain heavily. She was totally unprepared for the rain, dressed only in a flimsy top and shorts, but it felt like a welcome relief and at least made her feel alive again. For the first time since the break-up, she headed for the beach, which was now deserted. She sank onto the cold wet sand, leaning against the sea wall, and taking deep breaths. She remembered those cuddles and kisses she and Mitch had shared in that very place where she now sat cold and soaked through.

As Melanie sat on the wet sand, drenched and lonely, her head drooping listlessly on her chest, her gaze suddenly alighted on a shard of glass shining up at her from amongst the glistening wet pebbles at her feet. She picked it up and, without further thought, drew the sharp glass across her arm. It didn't go deep, but it hurt. As Melanie stared at the cut, a bead of blood appeared, oozing mesmerically from her skin and slowly mingling with the rain trickling down her hand. She immediately felt a release from all her pent-up emotions. She felt her anger drain away and a kind of calmness take its place, for she knew that this was her pain, not pain inflicted by someone else. She was back in control again. She was in charge of her own emotions. She'd made a breakthrough. She could deal with her own pain.

After a moment, realising what she had done, she ran to the water's edge and washed her arm in the water. She was shocked to her core that she could do such a thing to herself, but whereas previously she had not been able to see any further than the day ahead, now something seemed to have snapped inside her. Everything seemed to have fallen into place. It was as if she had been seeing herself through the eyes of a stranger, this pathetic, bedraggled figure sitting alone on a wet, cold beach. For the first time in days the overwhelming self-pity which had engulfed her seemed to melt away. She was suddenly furious that she had been so taken in and that she had let herself down. But this was a new sensation, anger, and it felt good. In that moment, she realised that she had been in danger of losing any pride and independence she had left. She knew that she couldn't, and wouldn't, allow herself to continue behaving in this way.

She dragged herself to her feet and headed home, talking to herself constantly. She would survive without him. She would make her mind go blank, stop thinking, and stop feeling. She would rebuild that wall of hers that he had broken down, put that barrier up. She would be strong again. She would hold her head up high, forget the tears, and say goodbye to her first love.

As she neared home she spotted her friend Mark appearing from the gate to her house. When he saw her and waved, her heart sank. She knew her parents were out and she had been hoping just to take some time out and contemplate it all over a long hot bath.

"There's no one home!" he shouted as he waved and crossed over the street towards her. "Oh Melanie!" he said, as he saw the state of her, the forlorn look on her face, the mascara stains on her cheeks from the rain and her tears, the bedraggled hair stuck to her face. He put his arms round her and pulled her into him. For once she didn't resist. It made her feel warm and wanted again. He looked into her eyes and sighed. "I hate to see you like this Mellie,' he said. Then he slowly leaned in and kissed her.

She did not resist. There was none of the passion and fire she had felt when Mitch had looked so intensely into her eyes, touched her, kissed her, but it did feel good to be loved after feeling so abandoned. She knew Mark loved her, and she wished she could love him back, experience all those tingling sensations and that buzz of excitement, but she couldn't. All he provided her with was an invisible blanket of comfort.

The next morning, although with that nagging pain still deep in her chest, she opened the curtains to a beautiful cloudless sky and decided it was time to join the world, and be happy again. "There is a whole world out there that you, Melanie Jackson, are missing out on" she told herself "I've neglected my friends, the beautiful, wild Sammy, the caring, loving Shirley and the funny and forthright Anna. Oh, how I've missed them" she realised. It was time to put matters right.

The fun-loving Melanie who was always ready for some adventure was resurfacing. She looked in the mirror and smiled for the first time in what seemed like a long time. 'I can do this' she thought 'Get my life back. It's up to me, it's within my power and only I can do it.' Gradually she would rebuild the confidence that had been so seriously and callously knocked by her all-too-short relationship with Mitch. She would build herself up piece by piece and never be hurt like this again, never! On this she was determined.

CHAPTER 23

Mitch's misery

Following the evening of the Palace débâcle, Mitch was still in a dreadfully confused state over his feelings. In typical fashion when it came to his emotions he continued to dither, weighing up what to do, hedging his bets and putting off acting upon his feelings, one way or the other.

Eventually, acting on impulse one evening, he picked up the phone and rang Melanie at home. But it was her mother who picked up the call. He told her he was Tom and waited nervously, trying to compose himself before speaking to her, only to be devastated when her mother returned and told him apologetically, and with some embarrassment in her tone, that Melanie couldn't come to the phone. That was it. She didn't even want to speak to him. It was over.

The next few weeks were hell for Mitch. He kept visiting all Melanie's usual haunts with the boys, desperately hoping to bump into her, but to no avail. It was as if she'd simply disappeared off the face of the earth, and he came to the conclusion that she was avoiding him. He couldn't blame her. She must have wondered what the hell was going on. He was hurting, so he knew she must have been too, and worse still he knew that it was all down to him at the end of the day. He'd done wrong by her, let her down badly, and because of his stupid pride he hadn't had the balls to make things right.

But he was a young boy, with all the urges that boys have, and as time passed the pain and guilt eased, pushed to the back of his mind. After all that had happened with Melanie he was determined that he was staying clear of the love thing in future, but he was still going to have fun. One night he arranged to meet three girls at the Palace on the same night, and alternated between the three throughout the evening. The Palace was big, but not that big, and the night turned into a disaster.

He was damaged by what had happened with Melanie and filled with guilt, though it was no excuse for his actions, he would act thoughtlessly over the next couple of years. He became totally self-centred, arranging dates then not turning up because there was something on with the lads which he thought would be more fun, and vice versa, not turning up to go out with the lads if there was more fun to be had spending an evening with a girl. He would bin girlfriends without warning or explanation, and he never stayed with one girl for any length of time. At one point the girlfriends of one of his victims were so disgusted with his behaviour that they got together to date him and drop him one by one, to teach him a lesson. But he did not want to get close to anyone anyway, so sadly, their treatment had no effect on him.

CHAPTER 24

Melanie goes off the rails

As the winter months approached, Melanie's and Sammy's frustrations with the often predictable and, in their eyes, somewhat tame pastimes enjoyed by their more conservative group of established friends and acquaintances resulted in the pair gradually gravitating more and more towards the more risqué and wilder lifestyle enjoyed by Mark and his group of male friends. The two girls, attracted by the rebellious natures, sense of adventure and fun that the boys possessed, were drawn in by their characters and lifestyle, which seemed so much more adventurous and exciting than the relatively quiet and humdrum existence they both sensed was becoming the norm for them and their established circle of friends.

Mark and his entourage seemed to the casual observer, at least on the surface, to be charming, polite, and well-educated young boys, every teenage girls' mother's dream in fact. However, underneath that deceptive facade, and when left to their own devices, they were wild, uninhibited in their behaviour and seriously bent on testing society in general, authority in any form, and school and family values, in no particular order.

Melanie was at an impressionable stage in her life. The boys appeared to encapsulate the feelings, spirit of adventure and devil-may-care approach to life that she admired so much and was beginning to acknowledge and warm to within herself. At this stage, although she recognised that they were even more rebellious than she'd ever considered being, she was not yet truly aware that hanging around with them would inevitably lead her into dangerous situations, because to her they were simply such fun to be around. They 'borrowed' cars in the middle of the night, drove at high speeds around the Island and had all-night parties fuelled with large amounts of alcohol.

Sammy and Melanie, almost by default, became an integral part of their group, Sammy because of her reckless, carefree attitude and Melanie partly because of her natural rebellious streak, but also as a coping mechanism for the most painful rejection by Mitch.

During the winter months, as the days became shorter and the nights longer, the two girls sought more ways to relieve the boredom and restrictions of their everyday existence. They became more involved in this potentially harmful lifestyle. Shirley and Anna, concerned as they were for their two friends, were unable to bring any of their previous influence to bear upon them and, much to their chagrin, could only remain on the periphery, looking on in horror at what they saw as the girls' downward spiral as they withdrew gradually from their company.

Melanie's and Sammy's wilfulness got worse as the weeks and months went by. They constantly lied to their parents as to their whereabouts, sneaking out in the middle of the night at the weekend, joining in on the high-speed drives and consuming copious quantities of alcohol. They developed contrary and radical views on anything and everything and were taking ever-increasing risks. Melanie's only source of comfort at that time was Mark, to whom she was slowly beginning to open up. He didn't judge, didn't question, just listened patiently and was always there for her. She didn't realise it yet, but these feelings of anger and resentment were helping her on the road to recovery from her heartbreak. At least her passion was back. She would snap at Mark, but he would just take it with good grace, then she would be so sorry. Why couldn't she love him? But it was not to be.

Mark was something of a Jekyll and Hyde character, on the one hand being wild and adventurous, but also possessed of a really sensitive and romantic side when it came to Melanie. He loved everything about her but, as far as she was concerned at least, he held no romantic interest for her; he was never going to be more than a close friend. He was charming and easy-going and got on with everyone, whatever their age. He was happy spending time with Melanie's parents, especially Julia, to whom he often sat and chatted when he visited her home. He even confided in Julia how much he loved and adored Melanie, but that sadly it was unrequited.

He penned love letters to Melanie to explain how he truly felt, and she would look up into those soft blue eyes of his, so often glistening with the threat of a tear, and wish she could love him. "I don't think you can love anyone, Melanie," he said. "Will you ever be ready to love again?" Those words would always be left hanging in the air, unanswered on every occasion.

The protective side of Mark's character ensured that, come what may, he always looked after Melanie on their adventures. He was always by her side when danger was imminent. During one drunken escapade, he even lay across her on the roof of a car to make sure she didn't fall off. He was always there for her when she managed to extricate herself from the many romantic disasters she got herself involved in. Without really meaning to, Melanie took advantage of his love, took him for granted, and treated him like the brother she had never had: sometimes hugging him and kissing him, but other times telling him to leave her alone, that she didn't need a shoulder to cry on, she could look after herself. However, although he was confused and hurt by her actions, his devotion to her never wavered. He was always there for her, steadfast as ever.

By this time, Melanie had been on a few inconsequential dates with Johnnie, mostly at the insistence of her girlfriends as he was very good-looking, clever, and quick-witted. His perseverance was such that she eventually couldn't ignore his approaches. She was flattered by his attention, he was good fun, and she was drawn to him, but for a while she kept him at arm's length, although none of her friends could understand her; they couldn't see her own invisible protection, the barrier she had built inside herself against being hurt again and she never mentioned it, not even to Sammy, for that would have been a sign of weakness, an admission of her own vulnerability.

Eventually Johnnie's perseverance paid dividends for him when he asked her to the college dance that November and they became an item. She gradually began to let her barriers down. If she loved him, it was not with the passion she had felt for Mitch, but there was something between them which couldn't be put into words. She was moving on from her desperate desire to find Mitch again, but he was still never far from her thoughts. There were occasions when she allowed herself to revisit those intense feelings she had experienced when with him though, and it saddened her as she believed she would never feel that way again.

One drunken night Melanie became a blood brother, or sister may have been a more apt description, to one of Mark's best friends, Rob. Being more than slightly inebriated, he wielded the knife more enthusiastically than was strictly necessary, and even Sammy screamed at the sight of the wound opening up before her eyes on Melanie's arm and backed away. But not so Melanie, who was full of bravado and looked on in awe, her glazed eyes staring unblinking as he cut himself and they shared their blood. She embraced the moment, all the while savouring the feelings that swept through her mind and body, the welcome and somehow satisfying release from her intense and difficult emotions and from the build-up of inner pain; for a moment, she felt elated and triumphant, the physical pain seemingly wiping out the mental pain.

But the next morning, upon seeing her bandaged arm, a wave of emotions swept through her: shame, embarrassment, astonishment and confusion. She was shocked and disturbed that she could be so violent to her own self. The scar would remain with her throughout her life, a memory of having gone just too far and at such a young age.

Whereas at around the age of thirteen Melanie had shared her mother's tastes in music and clothes, over the following years her choice of music changed. As her rebellious streak increased, she leaned more towards the protest songs which were popular with older teenagers and young adults at the time. She embraced songs questioning society, and songs with a message, and she developed a taste for the blues. Her fascination with the hippy movement continued, and she was drawn by the almost hypnotising, psychedelic qualities of the music, thoughts and ideas that were gripping the youth of the mid to late 1960s. Her clothes became more outlandish and expressive. She became a typical anti-everything student and, encouraged by Mark and his friends, joined a political underground movement on the Island, their protests directed at authority in general and politicians and educators specifically.

By 16, Shirley and Anna had left school, and the close friendships formed by the group of four had faded. Sammy and Melanie were still close to Mark and his friends. Unfortunately, Mark tended to tell Julia most of what the 'boys' got up to, and although he carefully left out Melanie's participation, Julia realised that her daughter was sneaking out to join them. She would lie awake at night worrying until she heard her daughter sneaking back in again. She realised that Melanie's behaviour amounted to teen rebellion rather than simply the pursuit of greater independence. She hoped it was just a phase that Melanie was going through and that in time she would settle down again, and she was wise enough to know that any intervention by her would only serve to push her lovely daughter further down the rebellious path she was following, with possible damaging results to their relationship. So, more often than not, she kept her counsel, refraining from intervention in the hope that in the fullness of time her daughter would come to her senses.

Melanie was now living a double life. Her relationship with Johnnie could best be described as fractured. The pair split up regularly, and always temporarily, usually caused by Johnnie's resentment of her continued dependency on the thrill of the relationship she continued to maintain with Mark and his friends, a relationship which she steadfastly refused to forego; it was like a drug to her.

In the periods when Johnnie and Melanie were separated she embarked upon a few semi-serious relationships, but in the back-ground there was always the pull and the thrill of the adventures late at night that became known as the 'midnight magicals'. However, although it took a long time, eventually it would dawn on Melanie how damaging these wild escapades and antics were and what a detrimental effect the relationships with these boys were having on her, until it reached the point where even she could see that if she continued along this path then she was doomed to meet disaster.

CHAPTER 25

An unexpected encounter

Shortly before her sixteenth birthday, Melanie began to realise that she had broken her own promise to herself to remain strong and determined, proud and happy. From this point on, she made up her mind that she would never again be so easily led either in romance, wilful destructive behaviour, or anything else. She would remain true to herself and her pride. She mentally made sure that her protective wall was in place, and she vowed that no one would ever get through it and into her heart as Mitch had, the very thought of which, even after the passage of time, was occasionally as painful as ever. She also knew she would never again recapture the joy of overwhelming, starry-eyed young love.

She had now been in an on-off relationship with Johnnie for some time. It had its moments and sometimes she thought she even loved him, but she could never get Mitch completely out of her head. The pain of the breakup had subsided with time, but the love had stayed with her, deep inside.

She had seen no sign of Mitch for a long time, as they had socialised in different circles during the winter. It came as a shock, therefore, when one night at the Palace ballroom she saw him walking towards her. Immediately feelings and emotions that had been quelled over time came rushing back. She instinctively wanted to run away, but somehow she managed to stay fixed to the spot with Sammy and another friend by her side. She took a sidelong glance at Sammy and could tell by the look on her face that it had also registered with her what was about to happen. Would he speak? Would he even recognise her? How would she react? Somehow, she resolutely held both her ground and her nerve. She wasn't going to make this easy for him after the anguish and pain he'd caused her, that much she was sure of.

Mitch spotted her at the same time, and was astonished. The girl he had loved was no longer an innocent young girl. In just a year she had matured into a confident and exceedingly attractive young woman, and the change in her took his breath away. His heart flipped and he was immediately aware of the pounding in his chest. He was overcome with a mixture of joy, embarrassment and excitement. He stopped dead in his tracks, nearly dropping the drinks he was carrying. She was even more beautiful than he remembered.

Should he turn on his heel, or face up to her? But it was too late. She had seen him, and cowardly though he had been, he wasn't prepared to turn his back on her again. Thoughts raced through his brain. Would she speak to him? What could he say? Would she forgive him? Worse still, she might ignore him. And her friends were with her, which only served to make it more embarrassing for him.

The mere sight of her had turned him back into the nervous, timid young lad he had been when they had first met on the dance floor. She still fascinated him, more so now than ever.

Taking a deep breath and trying desperately to maintain some vestige of composure, Mitch walked slowly towards Melanie, a sheepish smile on his face, acutely aware of the withering looks of contempt on the faces of her two friends and wishing like hell she was on her own. Little did he know it at the time, but Melanie was thinking exactly the same thing. But it wasn't to be, for Sammy and the other girl stood their ground defiantly alongside her, ranks closed as if to face the enemy approaching.

As Mitch drew slowly ever nearer, Melanie braced herself, trying desperately to calm her racing mind, the emotions pulsing through her body and those familiar tingling sensations inexplicably cursing through her. Her stomach churned, her brain seemed scrambled, her mouth became dry, her breathing shallow and rapid as the moment of truth approached. She too had suffered sleepless nights, and wasted countless, endless hours contemplating just such a moment, imagining how it would feel if they could only meet again, sometime, somewhere. But in her wildest dreams Melanie had never imagined a situation such as this. It should have been a beautiful moment, a moment to treasure, a coming together of like minds and hearts, not a confrontation in company with her close friends present in such a setting. She simply wasn't prepared for this. It was so sudden, so unexpected. Sheer panic and fear hadn't featured in any of her dreams. This felt so wrong somehow, but she couldn't deny the feelings of love and desire that were overwhelming her at the same time.

Mitch was taller than she remembered. His hair was shorter, and his teenage body had filled out and matured. He was still extremely good looking, and she felt her heart racing. All those feelings of love which she'd somehow managed to suppress swarmed through her again at the very sight of him. She knew that she still loved him.

As they drew closer she was struck by his embarrassment, how uncomfortable he seemed, so like that younger boy who had first approached her in the very same ballroom when she was only fourteen. His normally confident, almost cocky air, had somehow deserted him and been replaced by an air of vulnerability.

He stood in front of her, those intense eyes staring directly into hers, seemingly piercing her very soul. Her heart was racing. Melanie's beauty was the only thought in his head as he stared longingly into those beautiful eyes of hers. His normal patter had deserted him.

"Hi Melanie. Well, er... how are you?" he asked.

Melanie was on the verge of responding but was cut short by Sammy, who could contain her anger no longer "How are you?" she echoed. "Is that the best you can do? You walk out on her nearly a year ago, dump her without so much as a goodbye, no explanation, and the best you can come up with is how the bloody hell are you! You're despicable, just bloody despicable Mitchell. Why don't you just bugger off back to where you came from?"

Melanie was mortified. This wasn't meant to be happening. She hadn't even had a chance to say hello before the moment had been turned on its head. Mitch did not respond to Sammy's rant, other than simply turning to give her a hostile look, and Melanie, wishing to avoid any form of confrontation at all costs, knew she had to defuse the situation.

"I'm fine Mitch thanks. Maybe this isn't the best time to meet. Another time maybe? We're in company, so we have to go. See you around."

With that, she linked arms with Sammy and strode away, flashing a brief backward smile of regret in Mitch's direction as she did so.

Shaking inside and hurt by the suddenness and brevity of what had happened, Melanie made her way back with her friends to where they'd been sitting, her mind in meltdown. Why did it have to be like that? She knew Sammy was talking to her, but she was so preoccupied that nothing registered. Sammy was still animated. She could see her face twisted in anger, see her mouth opening and closing, knew words were coming out but she simply couldn't take them on board. Everything seemed like a bad dream. Was this real, or was she just an outsider looking in, watching a horrible scene take place? If only it was so, but it wasn't. It was real. It was so painful, so disturbing, and it was happening to her, which was so hard to accept. It hurt. It really hurt, and she knew that if she didn't get a grip on herself soon the tears would start to flow, as she could feel the emotions welling up inside her.

Sure enough, as time passed, sitting at the table with her friends and gulping down her vodka and coke as if on auto pilot, she could sense those emotions growing stronger by the minute. Sammy intuitively sensed it too, and knew she had to do something. "Come on Melanie, I need to go to the loo. Are you coming with me?" she asked.

Melanie didn't need a second invitation and jumped at the chance of escaping from the milling crowd around their table. She somehow managed to keep a lid on her emotions and hold herself together until they reached the sanctity of the ladies' room, where the tears did flow. Thankfully, giving in to her emotions was a welcome relief. Her insides had felt like a wound-up spring but the outpouring of her frustration and emotion was akin to the release of a safety valve, relieving a good deal of the tension inside her.

Admittedly, she was still angry inside, frustrated and upset with Sammy, but she couldn't bring herself to blame her or take issue. True, her intervention had ruined everything but, after she'd allowed her emotions to get the better of her, her head began clearing, her senses began recovering. She felt a degree of rationality and control returning to her previously irrational thought processes. Deep down she knew she could no longer be cross with Sammy. She was her best friend. She knew how much Sammy cared for her, and she'd been trying to protect her in the only way she knew how.

"Are you angry with me?" Sammy asked nervously.

"No, I'm not angry Sam. I know you were only trying to

protect me. It's just that, well... there are things I needed to ask him, things I needed answers to. I've had so many questions buzzing around in my head since he walked out on me and I just hoped that one day I'd get the chance to talk to him, really talk to him. It's been nearly a year now, months of not knowing, not understanding. Did he ever really love me? Did he mean those words? Why did he just walk out of my life? I may never have another chance to talk to him. I may never find out now. And that's what hurts, really hurts. It's not your fault. Don't blame yourself. He walked away from me. He never had any intention of explaining why back then. Why should I think anything would be different now? Maybe you did us both a favour. Maybe I'm better off not knowing and just getting on with my life."

Sammy listened to what Melanie had to say, but she could not for the life of her understand why Mitch still meant so much to her closest friend. In her mind, he was a waste of space. All she was concerned about was Melanie's wellbeing, and she couldn't bear the thought of her being hurt again.

"Too right you should just get on with your life. Let's start right now, get back to the table, have a few drinks and forget it ever happened. You're supposed to be meeting Johnnie later, remember?"

Meeting Johnnie, or anybody else, was the last thing Melanie needed. All she wanted to do was to go home, to be on her own with her thoughts. But she nodded in agreement and the pair of them made their way back to their table, with Melanie determined to put a brave face on for her friends and for Johnnie.

As Melanie and her friends moved away, Mitch thought he had glimpsed a brief smile flicker across her face. Had she been about to apologise for her friend? He couldn't be sure; it had all happened so quickly. His head was in too much turmoil to take everything in. He stood rooted to the spot as he watched the girl he adored disappearing. Was he going to lose her again? So many thoughts flashed through his mind as he watched her disappear into the crowd of people on the walkway. His heart sank and his stomach churned. He was confused, angry, and totally devastated all at the same time.

But he wasn't angry with Melanie. He couldn't be. He loved everything about her, the way she walked, the way she talked, her smile, and those eyes, those bewitchingly beautiful eyes of hers. But now she was gone, out of sight. He cursed his luck, cringed with embarrassment at how facile he'd been when they met face to face, how he'd blown everything. He could have kicked himself. Yes, it was wonderful to finally see her again, see how she'd matured. He marvelled at the beautiful creature she'd developed into. She was just so, so desirable, and now? Well now? Now that beautiful creature was lost again.

It wasn't meant to be like that, shouldn't have been like that. Why, oh why, did she have to be with Sammy, of all people? But then, in his heart of hearts he knew he couldn't blame Sammy. Yes, she'd ruined everything for him, but then that was all he deserved really. He knew he'd got his just desserts, his comeuppance. Deep down, he knew that Sammy was right. He'd wronged her best friend. That had been truly despicable. And that's what really hurt. He had never come to terms with that himself. He was still filled with remorse.

Mitch turned away and made his way back to where Tony and Dixie were seated. They knew something was wrong as soon as their pal hove into view, for his shoulders were hunched and the usual bounce in his stride was missing. They waited until he had placed their drinks on the table and slumped into the vacant seat alongside them. Then they sat in silence for a short while, looking at Mitch staring into his pint.

Tony was first to break the ice. "What the hell's up with you then?"

"Nothing. Nothing's up. I'm fine." Mitch's gaze stayed fixed to his beer.

"What a load of bollocks!" Tony retorted. "You've got a face like a slapped arse, for christ's sake."

Mitch glared at Tony. "It's nothing. I'm fine, just drop it. Give me a break, To."

An uncomfortable silence descended. Tony could see it wouldn't be a good move to pursue the matter further so, with a shrug, he took Mitch's advice and concentrated on doing his pint some justice. Mitch, on the other hand, sat in sullen silence, churning the events of the evening over and over in his head, vainly trying to analyse Melanie's attitude. Had she been pleased to see him? Did she bear him any malice? Had she smiled, or had he imagined it? Why on earth had he come out with what he realised now was a stupid greeting? Was Melanie as upset and furious as Sammy clearly was? He cringed with embarrassment as he replayed their meeting over and over in his mind.

Dixie, being of a more sensitive disposition than Tony,

knew that something was seriously amiss. He had never seen his pal so downhearted. It was as if something, or someone, had knocked the stuffing out of him – a girl, probably. He could think of nothing else which would have had such an effect on him, but he also knew that he wouldn't spill the beans with Tony around. Spotting that Tony had nearly finished his pint, Dixie nudged him discreetly under the table and said "Right To, it's your round. Get 'em in mate. And don't rush back. Have one while you're at the bar, why don't you? You're drinking quicker than us anyway."

Tony saw Dixie's glare and realised his presence was not required for the next few minutes. He stood up, turned on his heel and headed off in the direction of the bar.

Dixie watched Tony disappear into the crowd before turning his attention to Mitch. "OK sunshine, I'm not stupid. What's the problem?"

Mitch looked him straight in the eye, intuitively knowing he could talk to Dixie, share things with him.

"Everything's wrong Dix. The arse just fell out of my world," he said.

"Go on then. Tell me about it. Spit it out before that insensitive sod gets back with the ale" Dixie urged gently.

"I bumped into Melanie, Dix. That's what's wrong."

Dixie shook his head in bafflement. "But that's what you wanted isn't it? You never stop banging on about how much you wish you could meet up with her again."

"I know Dix, I know. But it wasn't like I'd imagined it. It all went tits up on me. I blew it, big time. The most amazing girl I've ever met standing right there in front of me. And I blew it. Again."

"It couldn't have been that bad," Dixie responded, trying

to get his pal to open up.

"Oh, it was, Dix. Sammy was with her, wasn't she? I was taken by surprise, her appearing out of the blue like that. I was so embarrassed it was unbelievable, and I just opened up with some stupid comment." Mitch squirmed inside, his voice trailing off despondently as the scene replayed in his head.

"Well, how did Melanie seem? What did she have to say?" Dixie asked.

"She didn't say anything. She didn't get a chance. Well, not initially anyway. Sammy jumped in almost before I'd finished speaking. Tore into me she did. Nothing more than I deserved, I suppose. But her timing sure was shit."

"OK, I get that" Dixie said. "What about Melanie though? How did she react?"

"She hates confrontation and she was just so embarrassed. She just muttered something polite and ushered her friends away before it could turn nasty I think. I really felt for her. She didn't deserve to be caught up in the middle of that. She'll be upset, I know she will. It's a disaster matey, a total cock up. And I'm leaving soon as well."

"Leaving? What are you on about? It's only early. And it's not like you to just give up. Get off that arse of yours and go and look for her, get her on her own, sort things out." Dixie was shocked by his mate's defeatism, which was so out of character.

Mitch gazed at his friend silently for a moment or two, and another rueful smile flickered across his face. "No. You don't understand. When I said, I'm leaving, I meant I'm leaving the Island, in a couple of months. I was going to tell you two tonight anyway as it happens, just waiting for the right time. Don't say anything to Tony when he gets back. I want to tell him myself. He's my mate, I owe him that."

Dixie stared at Mitch, his mouth open, a look of shock and disbelief on his face.

"You're what? Why? Are you serious? Where the hell are you going to, you daft ha'porth?"

"I've never been more serious. I'm heading off to Manchester to live. Got myself a job in a bank there, the offer letter came through a couple of days ago"

"Manchester? Why the hell do you want to live in Manchester?" he queried.

Mitch laughed. "United Dix, I'm going to watch my boys playing at the Theatre of Dreams. Plus, I need to go places, see different things, travel. I've been thinking of it for a while. I've been in touch with Herb, he's got a job there and he's renting a place with a mate of his, says I can shack up with them. The pair of us are going to put some money together over the next six, twelve months, who knows, then we're off on our travels. We're going to bum our way around the world, well Europe initially. I've only ever been to Manchester and Liverpool. I want to travel, have new experiences, live a little. So, there you go matey."

Dixie sat with a bemused look on his face as he took in this bombshell. "Wow" he said, eventually. "You're a dark horse, aren't you?" He shook his head. "Why the hell didn't you say something sooner? I didn't have a clue."

"I didn't want to say anything until I knew for certain Dix, until my mind was made up, that's all, and the job offer clinched it for me buddy. But now I've seen Melanie I'm confused again. She's amazing Dix, so beautiful. Now I know what I'd be leaving behind. I walked away from her once and I don't think I can do it again, not without putting things right with her anyway, explaining everything, telling her what an arse I was. I need to tell her why I just disappeared from her life, tell her it wasn't her fault, how I was scared, did what I thought was best but chickened out of the hard bit, telling her. I need to tell her I'm sorry. I need to tell her how much I still love her. Maybe she'd understand now, who knows? But I've got to try. I need to make things right between us."

Dixie could now see why his friend was so down. He had to say something to try and snap him out his mood. "OK" he said thoughtfully "So what are you going to do about it buddy? It's not like you to sit around moping. She's out there somewhere, so get off your ass and go and find her."

Mitch grinned. "You know what Dix? You might be a dickhead, but occasionally, just occasionally, you do have your uses. Cheers matey." He raised his glass. "A couple more pints and I just may take you up on that."

Right on schedule, Tony reappeared from the bar, complete with a tray full of pints, as instructed. On spotting him approaching, Mitch turned to Dixie. "Don't say anything to Tony about Manchester, Dix. I'll tell him later when I get him on his own."

"OK, sunshine, no problem, but you'd better mention about seeing Melanie. He'll be well pissed off if you don't tell him why you were in a bad mood."

Tony could see the change in Mitch immediately. He was obviously more relaxed, and supping his ale again, which was a big improvement. "Bloody hell, you're not actually smiling are you, you grumpy sod?" he said, clearly relieved.

"Does this mean we can start enjoying ourselves again then?"

Mitch was feeling positive again and made light of his earlier mood to Tony, explaining how seeing Melanie had been a shock, and how the tongue lashing he'd received from Sammy had ruined everything for him. For once, Tony's sensitive side came to the fore as he listened earnestly to Mitch's summary of the encounter. Having got the tricky stuff out of the way, Mitch downed his pint and got to his feet.

"That's it, I'm going to make things right," he announced. His mind was made up. He was going to go in search of Melanie. He turned to Dixie. "Thanks Dix. You're the dog's bollocks mate. Think I might even love you." With that he turned on his heels and headed off, with Dixie's fond "Piss off" response ringing in his ears.

Mitch had no set plan in his head as he searched for her, eyes scanning the room as he went. His head was in the right place though, and he knew that whatever obstacles stood in his path, he'd handle it, smooth things over with her friends and, somehow or another, get to speak to her on her own. He would pour out all the feelings he'd felt over the last year and do his utmost to make things right between the pair of them, in the hope that she would understand, that she still loved him enough to forgive him. He wouldn't screw up this time, he couldn't. He loved her too much to let that happen.

Meanwhile, Melanie too had been drinking. Their meeting had aroused all those latent feelings which had been lying dormant under the surface. She was not drunk, but she had had enough to cloud her thinking to the point where the anger and resentment she had felt when Mitch had abandoned her had resurfaced. After all, she had her pride and her dignity. If Mitch was still there she was going to make damn sure he knew, in no uncertain terms, that she had a life without him. She had moved on, and was having the time of her life.

Mitch made his way slowly along the walkway beside the ballroom floor, his eyes feverishly scanning the heads bobbing up and down to the beat of the music. Suddenly he spotted Sammy and the other girl who had been with Melanie dancing together deep in the crowd. There was no sign of Melanie, but he knew that she wouldn't be far away. His hopes rose again.

And suddenly, there she was. He could see her dancing, her head swaying in time to the music, hair swirling around her face as she moved, just as he remembered. She had such natural grace and movement.

He was just about to step onto the floor to make his way over to her when he stopped in his tracks. Hang on – she wasn't dancing with another one of her friends. She was with a bloke. That wasn't part of the game plan. He hadn't bargained for that.

In fact, Melanie had spotted Mitch from the corner of her eye as he was approaching. She had seen him standing there at the side of the floor, gazing in her direction, and knew that he was looking for her. Somewhat out of character for her, but emboldened by the alcohol she had consumed, and on the spur of the moment, she decided that this was payback time. Without further thought, she drew Johnnie in close to her, slid her arms around him and kissed him passionately, more passionately than Johnnie had ever experienced before. Surprised as he was by this show of passion, he was a typical teenage boy, so he didn't question it; he just took advantage of his luck and savoured it, reciprocating her passion in full.

Mitch could only look on in horror; but then it got worse. As Melanie slowly withdrew from her embrace, she spied through a slightly drunken haze that Mitch was still there, still gazing directly at her and Johnnie, as if transfixed. Revelling in the feeling of euphoria that was sweeping through her in getting her revenge at last, she flicked her head at Johnnie, linked her arm lovingly around him and led him in Mitch's direction, her head resting on his shoulder, gazing lovingly up into his eyes. The pair of them were laughing and joking as they weaved in and out of the other dancers surrounding them on the floor, to all intents and purposes unaware of Mitch's presence.

As they drew closer it dawned on Mitch that the boy she was with was the college guy who'd been sniffing around her, trying to get off with her before Mitch had appeared on the scene. Now he was with her. And they looked as if they were an item, so comfortable in each other's company, so happy. Shit, this wasn't meant to be happening.

Now they'd stopped and she was kissing him again. His Melanie, for that was how he'd come to think of her, wasn't his any more. She was somebody else's Melanie. And that hurt – so much it was unbelievable. He'd never experienced feelings such as this before, never been so committed to a girl before.

Panic crept through him as they drew nearer, so caught up in each other that they were seemingly unaware of his presence, anyone's presence for that matter. He couldn't stand the thought of coming face to face with Melanie now. Not when she was with somebody else.

He turned to make his getaway, sick to the stomach with despair. The dream was gone, faded before his very eyes. He felt empty as he made his retreat. His legs were heavy. The bitter taste of defeat and rejection rose in his throat. He'd never felt like this before, didn't know how to process it in his mind. But he knew he had to be alone. There was no way he could face anyone, not feeling like this. Like a beaten man, he slunk out of the Palace by himself, alone with his thoughts. He needed time to think, time to come to terms with what had happened.

It was a long and lonely walk home along the promenade, but by the time he was home his thoughts were clearer, his resolve stronger. That was it; he had lost her to somebody else. "Look out Manchester, here I come," he muttered to himself.

In the hallway, he was greeted by his father "Are you all right son?" he enquired.

"I sure am Dad. Get the whiskey out though. It's been a shit night. And no, I don't want to talk about it."

CHAPTER 26

Life moves on

The sun came streaming through Melanie's bedroom window the following morning, heralding a bright new day. But Melanie was lost in a dream. Mitch's beautiful face was in front of her, smiling, those eyes looking at her with such love it was like a flash of lightning striking at the centre of her heart. She could feel his presence, so close she could feel his breath like a whisper on the back of her neck. His arms were round her, holding her tight against him, and she never wanted the feeling to end. She willed herself to stay asleep, keeping her eyes closed and her mind switched off, clinging to the dream, until that fleeting moment of not knowing where the dream ends and reality begins had drifted away, and she was awake.

Her head hurt. Her mind was foggy, and for just a moment she still felt that her dream was reality, although her heart felt heavy in her chest. She couldn't initially think why. She knew she had consumed far too much alcohol. But gradually, as the fog cleared, the hangover paled into insignificance as scenes came to her mind, events from the night before, Mitch's face.

'Oh god, Mitch!'

Startled, she sat bolt upright. He was there. She had seen him – she had spoken to him, if briefly.

Her feelings for him had faded with time, but now they had resurfaced and felt as raw and precious as ever. She had always dreamed he would come back into her life. She had missed him so much since he had abandoned her and she had felt so alone for a long time afterwards. All those feelings were swamping her again now.

Melanie buried her face in her pillow, punching it with her fists in her frustration and anger. She couldn't bear thinking about this missed opportunity to put things right, the chance she had been dreaming of for nearly a year.

Then she remembered dancing with Johnnie, so provocatively and seductively, kissing him passionately. She tried to rub the memory out, but it only became more vivid, and she cringed. She would never normally behave in such a shameless manner in public, drunk or sober, it just wasn't in her nature. But in her intoxicated state, feeling hurt, angry, and resentful, she had made a complete exhibition of herself. She had used Johnnie, and she felt mortified. She was going to be really embarrassed when she next saw him, but that wasn't what was at the forefront of her mind. What went so deep was that now she knew in her heart that she had lost Mitch, possibly forever. She'd had a chance to find out the answers to her never-ending questions. She had even thought that if they met again, there might be a chance to put things right between them. And she'd blown it, big time.

She had engaged in behaviour which was alien to the real Melanie, and knew it would have destroyed Mitch's image of her. The repercussions were too much to bear. She knew, without a shadow of a doubt, that her hopes had been dashed by her own stupid behaviour, and he was now lost to her forever. She felt sick with anger and self-revulsion.

After a while, mentally exhausted from the turmoil within her, she turned on her back, lying there motionless, just staring up at the ceiling. The anger and shame she had felt slowly drained away and gave way to a painful acceptance and reluctant admission that maybe Sam was right. Maybe it was time to move on, forget the past, and get on with the rest of her life.

CHAPTER 27

The wisdom of parents

Over the next year or so, Melanie gradually came to realise just how much time and energy she'd wasted through deliberately rebelling against the social norms. Whereas previously she had thought she had just been asserting her independence, now she had the experience and maturity to understand that she had been channelling her frustration and energy in the wrong direction. Being a highly intelligent girl she could see that being headstrong and rebellious was no bad thing in itself, as long as those traits were combined with an awareness of where and when they were needed.

Whilst Melanie was going through her rebellious years, Julia and Jim worried that her behaviour would lead her into harmful situations and she would reject all the guidance, support and structure that had been provided during her childhood. They could feel her pushing them away. They worried about her self-esteem, and saw her wilfulness as self-defeating and self-destructive. Yet Melanie believed she was just building her own identity and, in doing so, tended to cut herself off from her parents. Although she always pretended to respect what they had to say in order not to be antagonistic, for that just wasn't in her nature, they knew it was all an act. They were neither stupid nor naive, and knew that she wasn't really listening to what they had to say. She would patiently wait at the door on her way out until they had finished their lecture before giving her customary nod of acknowledgement and supposed approval of their advice, and then she would be gone.

But gradually, as Melanie matured, her relationship with her parents improved, much to their relief. She still harboured a rebellious streak, but she had learned to use it in a positive way. She slowly learned to appreciate and value her parents more, and realised that their approach to parenting was actually quite free and progressive. She began to realise how they had merely tried to make everything happen for her while trying to keep her safe, when compared with the approach adopted by some of her friends' parents who had imposed rules without clear thought or reasoning.

Melanie began to understand that she was who she was partly because of the role her parents had played in her life. Over time, she also realised that she could retain her new-found identity within the framework of her relationship with her parents instead of outside it, particularly where her mother was concerned. They were not a demonstrative family, but Melanie never had any doubts that she was loved, and subconsciously she always felt safe and protected.

Melanie and her mother gradually became closer, and they started to share conversations, laughing together at situations which they would previously never have seen with the same eyes. Julia and Melanie had never had long, heartfelt conversations. However, as Melanie got older there was a subtle change in their relationship as they developed a deeper understanding and enjoyment of each other's company. Conversations in general were light and impersonal but Melanie started to listen to her mother's stories and appreciate her outlook on life, her relationships with her own friends of her generation, and what they talked and laughed about. She learnt to appreciate that her mother had gone through some, if not all, of the same emotions growing up as she was experiencing herself. Maybe they were from the same planet after all.

Melanie had never been comfortable with the way her friends valued Julia's friendship and always seemed relaxed in her presence. Yet over time it slowly dawned on her from their feedback how progressive she was compared to their own mothers, and how much Julia had actually known about Melanie's dangerous and reckless escapades with the boys through her conversations with them. What Melanie wasn't aware of was how hard it had been for her mother; how her heart would be in her mouth when her lovely daughter disappeared, how she could never be sure where she was, although she did at least know that all Melanie's friends cared about her wellbeing and looked out for her, even though their own behaviour was foolhardy. She had gleaned some comfort from knowing that they would have done their best to make sure she came to no serious harm.

Melanie slowly started to appreciate just how amazing both her parents had actually been. With the benefit of hindsight, she could appreciate that they had been nowhere near as restrictive as they had seemed at the time. They had chosen not to inhibit or restrain her unnecessarily, letting her make her own mistakes, become her own person, express her individuality. They had merely been trying their best to guide her through what was a difficult time for her, but so much harder for them as parents. The emotional changes that had framed Melanie's adolescence had felt like a roller coaster ride for Julia.

Women were said to have everything they could wish for in the sixties, with all the new 'mod cons' that were available to them, but that just left Julia with time on her hands to ask herself who she was, and wonder if life had more to offer than just being a wife and mother. True, she was in a much more equal and loving marriage than many others of her generation, but it did not stop her questioning her life regularly.

All around her, Melanie was beginning to see the rise of feminism. She was aware of strong women speaking out; her own mother even, less vociferous, but with equally valid views, some of her teachers at school, women on the television. She could sense that she was entering a different era as far as women were concerned. She knew that she would become a part of it and would take full advantage of it. She had already experienced great freedom for a young girl. She was off to university in London soon and she felt sure that she could encompass this new quest for female equality in the life that lay ahead of her as a young adult.

At seventeen, Melanie was still a closed book when it came to her personal life, and she wasn't too comfortable when her mother suddenly started a conversation one day about the strength and pain of teenage love. Melanie was at the kitchen table, half-heartedly reading a maths textbook for an imminent A level exam, when Julia casually said, "I do know how hurt you were, by that boy, you know. It seems such a long time ago now. Mark and Shirley both told me all about it. He had a nickname... Mitch, that was it."

Melanie's heart leapt at that name. She still found herself feeling pain and hurt, despite suppressing her feelings for so long. A tear suddenly formed from nowhere, rolled down her cheek and landed on the open book she was staring blindly at.

"I felt for you at the time, I knew how much you were hurt," her mother continued. "There was always going to be that first one you'll never forget, and to say goodbye to that is painfully sad. I just wanted to wrap you up and protect you from the pain. As a child, although you didn't always come to me I could still look after you and protect you from whatever it was that had hurt or upset you. You were growing away from us, which I know is only natural when you're a teenager, but I think that was the first time in your life that I felt unable to help. I felt so protective of you because you didn't protect yourself, but I just knew I couldn't comfort you at the time. I didn't know how, and you wouldn't have thanked me for anything I would have said to try and help you work through it. He's a teenage boy, that's what they're like, you'll get over it. The pain will get less. I don't think any of that would have helped coming from me, do you?" She gave a wry smile. "It seems so long ago now, but to me you have never been quite the same carefree, happy girl. You're a naturally fun-loving person, but from what I can tell, you don't seem to have let yourself move on properly. You've been driving yourself into self-destructive situations where you didn't seem to care what happened to you, and now it's like you protect yourself in relationships.

"Look at Mark. He loves you. He's told me enough times. He's always loved you, but you never seem to see the emotions in him, let him in. You just take him for granted. And what about Johnnie? He adores you, but you keep him at arm's length. The pair of you are always splitting up. You jump headlong into a relationship with someone else for a while, but it always ends in disaster and you get back with Johnnie. I've seen the affectionate way he looks at you when you are together, and you seem to be happy enough to be with him, but you seem to hold back, almost as if you have built a wall to shield yourself from hurt. You try to hide your feelings behind that wall. Maybe you need to learn to let your guard down again, be yourself, let yourself get hurt if necessary. It's all part of growing up and learning what real love is all about. Maybe you need to let that heart of yours properly feel again."

"Mum, please, I'd rather not be having this conversation" Melanie replied, feeling very uncomfortable. She was about to leave, but Julia had not finished.

"Did you know I fell in love when I was nearly sixteen?"

"Really?" Melanie looked up at her mother to try and gauge her expression.

"Yes, really. He was seventeen at the time. We were very

much in love, but then war broke out just as he turned eighteen. We had a wonderful six months, but then he was called up. As I had turned sixteen by then we got engaged. My father wasn't exactly happy about it, but he went along with it. That's what people did during the war, they lived for and appreciated every moment, and didn't look too much to the future. He joined the Air Force as a pilot, completed his training and was sent directly abroad straight into the thick of it without even the briefest visit home.

"When he went away I was so upset, but at the same time I was sure we would be reunited one day. The war couldn't last forever, or so they said. During the following weeks, the feelings of anticipation of that special moment, the day when he came home to me and we'd be together again were what gave me strength. I just needed to get to that day, but sadly I never did. I wrote letters every week, but I never received a reply, and then one day there was a knock at the door. It was his father to say he'd had a telegram informing him that he had been killed.

I was devastated. It took a long time for me to believe that he was never coming back to me. Gradually, though, we all move on, and experiences like that only serve to make a person stronger.

And don't misunderstand me. I love your father very much. It was over eight years later when I met him. I was much more mature and level-headed by then, and I knew straight away he was the one, the person I wanted to spend the rest of my life with, have a family with. You will know too when the time comes."

Melanie sat there in silence, spellbound. Wasn't the war ancient history, something that had happened so long ago?

And here was her mother recounting a love story, one with her as the central character. Unbelievable. She had only ever thought of her parents as having always been together. She had never even considered that they might have had a life before they met.

Melanie was stunned and saddened by her mothers' story, and the knowledge that she had experienced so much pain when she was young. As she gazed up at her mother, she couldn't help but notice that she was still young and pretty and so gentle in her ways, something which she'd never totally absorbed previously. No wonder her friends had always found it easy to talk to her and enjoy her company.

It dawned on her that her mother's experiences as a teenager explained how much she cared about her daughter, her depth of feeling, her free-thinking attitude, how she had tried to support her rather than chastise her. She was beginning to feel pangs of guilt that she had never really let her mother into her life. She thought back on how her and her dad had ganged up on her when she had been trying to make a serious point, giving each other knowing looks, even though it had always been meant in a light-hearted way. She began to see her mother and their relationship in a whole new light.

Their shared intimacy was broken by the sound of the front door opening. They looked at each other and smiled as they heard the familiar greeting from her father coming home from work.

Melanie had always felt more of a natural closeness to her father, probably because they were so similar in nature. They were both intelligent, but also shy and sensitive, although like many men, Jim tried his best to cover those traits up.

As Melanie realised that her rebellious streak could be used in a more constructive way, she began to develop a social conscience, and during the summer before she left for university she started to have conversations late in the evening with her father, sitting on the floor at his feet sharing a drink and a cigarette. Julia was dismissed with good nature on these occasions for being too frivolous in her way of thinking. These were serious issues that they were talking about and they saw her participation as humorous but superficial. Jim always said she wasn't equipped to express views at this level, although views she certainly had, but that his daughter was different. She had inherited his serious, deep side and constantly analysed and questioned, whereas Julia simply accepted the world as it was.

Melanie's beliefs were much more one-sided, radical, more political than Jim's, which was only to be expected; she wanted to save the world, while her father, having served in the war and lived through the subsequent peace and prosperity, had a much more realistic view. Their discussions were free-ranging. They shared their differences in opinions on politics, news events of the day, the meaning of life, mathematical theories. Although their views were quite often opposite, they were very much alike in their approach, and their understanding of each other grew and developed. Their love and respect for each other was as strong as ever. He had his daughter back and she had a father she respected, loved, and valued, a father who she knew she would always be able to rely on in the future.

Melanie learnt a great deal from these debates, which would stand her in good stead in her future academic years. Jim taught his daughter that you can stay connected with a person, appreciating their views, whilst still being true to yourself. He showed her how she could retain her position on any issue and hold her own without becoming defensive or angry, as she had done all too readily in the past.

This sat comfortably alongside Julia's encouragement and hopes for her daughter's future. She encouraged her to lead her own life, take risks and learn from her mistakes, not to settle down too early, gain a good education, experience life at university to the full, and seek a role in life that would make her happy and fulfilled. She instilled in her the value of having strong views and not being afraid to express them, the value of her own self-worth, a heady combination indeed of values that would help shape her into a confident young woman ready to experience life away from her island home.

Melanie came to understand that being true to yourself means to believe in who you are. She knew the value of allowing your individuality and uniqueness to develop. Before leaving the Island, she would at times experience feelings of euphoria and at others, periods of quiet reflection. She was aware now that she had outgrown Island life and was ready for bigger and better things, new experiences. She would be starting a new life, but she was excited rather than scared by the prospect. She would be leaving her parents behind, but they had prepared her well for this. She knew she had treated them badly at times, knew that they hadn't deserved it, but she resolved that from now on she would make them proud of her.

She would also be leaving behind some very close friends and losing some of them for good, but she would make new ones, have new relationships. She would revel in meeting different people, in throwing herself into relationships to experience intensity, sensuality, and desire, embracing all those feelings and more to the full, brimming with passion for life and love. She no longer felt innocent. She knew what loving and passion were all about. She was more mature, more level-headed and she knew she would cope on her own.

She recognised that some of the people she would meet might well be more sophisticated, worldly-wise, talented and trendy than her, but she was ready to learn, absorb the environment and the diversity and become a part of it all.

The day came when Melanie boarded the boat bound for Liverpool and she stood at the back of the ship, waving goodbye to her parents and watching the Island as it disappeared from her sight. Without any warning, Melanie's thoughts drifted back to Mitch. It had been over two years since their disastrous brief encounter at the Palace, and she wondered where he was, what he was doing. Was he even still there or had he too left his island home to experience something new? She had no means of knowing, as she'd lost all contact with him. The thought had never occurred to her before, but maybe he had left and she'd never see him again. That thought shocked her, and she shivered even in the warm sunshine. Why hadn't she thought of it before? That could so easily explain why she had never set eyes on him again. Whatever life held in store for her though, she knew she would never forget the memories, those nights, that summer with Mitch, when she believed she had found true love.

Even though it mostly seemed like a dream to her now, she would never forget the heights of excitement and intensity of young love that she'd experienced and, although it had proved destructive, her resolve had been strengthened through the experience rather than destroyed.

CHAPTER 28

The flame that never dies

Although Mitch enjoyed his junior high school years and flourished there initially, he slowly grew to resent his mother's attitude to his progress and educational achievements. Her attitude was relentless. There were no words of encouragement, simply constant demands to work harder. She had taken great personal pride in basking in his reflected glory and would never miss an opportunity to sing his praises to others, but all he got in return was her constant refrain "You can't afford to relax, Tom. Remember, it's hard to get to the top but it's a damn sight harder to stay there. Don't even think of relaxing for a minute if you want to get on in life."

His mother's attitude gradually eroded any natural enthusiasm he had and hardened his resolve to rail against her approach, with the result that by the time he entered his teenage years, the rebel in him was already emerging, to defy not only his mother but authority of any kind.

Nothing his mother tried could dampen or restrain Mitch's wilder instincts and bring him back into line. Eventually, the relationship between Mitch and his mother deteriorated to the extent where they would hardly communicate and Mitch would go out of his way to avoid her. Although he knew his mother loved him in her own way and only wanted the best for him, he often wished she had had the capacity to be more relaxed and affectionate. She did, however, possess huge determination, which was instilled in Mitch from a very early age, and was probably the quality he admired most in her.

He knew his mother would never understand him. He knew that she would continue to try to impose her own hopes and expectations and to try to live her life through him, so her actions only succeeded in alienating him and pushing him away from her, creating a divide between them which would never truly be overcome. She had never really grasped that her desire to impose her wishes on her son was self-defeating.

Ironically, his father, who Mitch remained close to, understood this, and the bond between him and his son grew stronger. He was astute enough to recognise the problem, and his role became that of peacemaker or go-between, restoring family harmony and a more peaceful existence between the two strong-willed and stubborn people he loved.

Gradually Mitch became more disillusioned and dissatisfied with his lifestyle, and craved nothing more than to leave the nest. By the age of seventeen, a once highly-promising student with designs on university had become totally disenfranchised. All he wanted to do was leave school, break away from the restrictions it imposed on him and forge a new life where he was in control of his destiny.

Once he'd left school and had a taste of the outside world, in the environment which he now considered to be somewhat restricted, Mitch lusted for more. He wanted to break free from the confines of Island life and, more importantly, from his mother's continuing restraints and constant nagging. He made the decision to head for the mainland and go to Manchester, where some friends had already moved to and where he could experience the real world and freedom. He had already secured a job just before what turned out to be his calamitous final meeting with Melanie, and that was, for him, the catalyst to leave his Island home behind.

He did get to see his boys play at the Theatre of Dreams, but not to see the world. He met beautiful, gentle, easy-going Kate, and the relationship between them grew and proved stronger than any he had experienced since Melanie. He sensed love growing inside him again and, at the age of twenty-one, upon discovering Kate was pregnant, in typical Mitch fashion he fully embraced the next chapter of his life, that of being a father and family man, and they were married.

As Mitch settled down into married life, Melanie too was embarking on a whole new chapter of her life, as a student in the decade that was to become famous for its women's movement, fully embracing its hippy peace and love philosophy and its freedom of thought.

Mitch and Melanie had shared fun, laughter, hopes and dreams, and a love of the intoxicating music in that summer of '67. But they were both vulnerable, impressionable and immature teenagers. Sadly, peer pressure on both sides had ultimately conspired to force them apart. Melanie had gone against the advice of her closest friends, who had kept telling her that he wasn't right for her. She had hidden her deep young love from her parents. She had refused to listen to others. She had been addicted to Mitch and his love, a feeling she couldn't have explained to anyone, and it had ended in disaster. Her love for him had been so deep that his unexplained rejection of her was to shape her life and behaviour for a long time to come. He had callously walked away from her, a painful and unexpected experience for a beautiful young girl who was so innocent and sensitive, and still in the first flush of true love. Mitch had given no words, no explanation, to the girl he'd loved and adored. She was so beautiful, so utterly desirable in his young eyes, yet so much younger than himself.

Full of the uncertainties of youth, he had been emotionally ill-equipped at the time to deal with life's complexities, and had been torn apart both by conflicting emotions, the ridicule and jibes of his boyhood friends on the one hand and his feelings for his first true love on the other. He'd been confused and bewildered. His heart had been bursting with passion, his brain teeming with mixed feelings but, sadly lacking the wisdom and clarity of thought that life would eventually bestow upon him, he'd chosen the easy option; the coward's way out.

He would always remain full of remorse for not facing her, for not explaining, and Melanie always remained deep in his heart. It's said that some men carry a torch for a woman. A few of those men cling to that torch throughout their lives, never allowing the flame to be extinguished. Mitch was one of those men, forever holding a torch for Melanie.

The hurt and pain of a love lost can often fade quickly in young lives, as exciting new loves come and go. Somehow love's mysteries deemed that the memories of their first true love were destined never to fade from those two teenage hearts, memories so strong they would remain lodged firmly in some small pocket of their minds for years to come. And Mitch was nothing if not determined. Failure was not in his makeup. Losing Melanie forever was never going to be an option in his mind.